·THE·DEDALUS·BOOK·
of
Decadence
(Moral Ruins)

Edited, compiled and with an introductory essay
by Brian Stableford

DEDALUS

with the support of the Eastern Arts Association

For Jane

Published in the UK by Dedalus Ltd
Langford Lodge, St Judith's Lane, Sawtry, Cambs, PE17 5XE

ISBN 1 873982 01 1

Published in the US by Hippocrene Books Inc,
171, Madison Avenue, New York, NY10016
Distributed in Canada by Marginal Distribution,
Unit 103, 277 George Street North, Peterborough, Ontario, KJ9 3G9
Distributed in Australia by Peribo Pty Ltd,
26 Tepko Road, Terrey Hills, N.S.W.2084

Publishing History
First published in December 1990
Second edition (with minor corrections) in May 1993
Compilation, essay and French translations (unless otherwise
stated) copyright © Brian Stableford 1990
La Panthère, Les Vendanges de Sodome
© Mercure de France 1900

Printed in England by Loader Jackson, Arlesey, Beds.

A C.I.P. listing for this title is available on request.

Dedalus would like to express its gratitude to David Blow for his
help in originating the Decadence from Dedalus series and for
suggesting the title for this volume.

CONTENTS

INTRODUCTION

1.

MAD EMPERORS:
THE EVOLUTION OF AN IDEA

The English word "decadence", and its French counterpart *décadence*, derive from the Latin *cadere*, to fall. But the kind of fall indicated thereby is a special one, as signified by the verbs to which the nouns are parent: the obsolete *decair* in Old French and "decay" in English. To decay is to rot, to fall away from a state of health into a gradual ruination which is punctuated, but not begun or ended, by death.

A complete account of the evolution of the concept of decadence is unnecessary for the purposes of this introduction; there is a single crucial moment which can be appropriated as a starting point. In 1734 Charles-Louis le Secondat, Baron de La Brède et de Montesquieu, published his *Considérations sur les causes de la grandeur des Romains et de leur décadence*. The essay was marred by a certain disregard for the full extent and exact implication of the factual evidence, but it was nevertheless an important work in that it sought to discover some kind of theoretical basis for historical explanation. For Montesquieu, the slow disintegration of the Roman Empire was not to be seen as a series of unhappy accidents, but as the inevitable unfolding of a pattern governed by a quasi-scientific law.

Whatever its faults as proto-social science, Montesquieu's work was rightly acclaimed as a bold

1

adventure of the intellect, and the case which he put forward was instantly enshrined as a modern myth. Rome, it was henceforth accepted, had fallen because all empires must fall, and the map of that fall - which was also to serve as an explanation - was to be found in its *décadence*: in the simultaneous rotting of its cultural life and its military might.

The chief anti-hero of this new myth was Nero, who allowed the political fabric of the empire to become corrupt while he entertained his court with extended examples of his (imagined) literary genius. Nero - according to legend, at least - was prepared to fiddle while the city burned; and the decadence of his morals was readily revealed by the fact that his mimicry of the affectations of the Greeks extended as far as marriage to a castrated male slave.

Montesquieu, in claiming that there was an underlying logic to the fate of Rome, implied that some such pattern would be repeated in other empires. Civilization, in his view, carried the seeds of its own inevitable destruction, because a secure, rich and comfortable aristocracy was bound to be slowly enervated by addiction to luxury, until the time finally arrived when the barbarians without could no longer be kept at bay.

****

The first translator of Montesquieu's work into English did not retain the word "decadence" in its title, choosing to render *décadence* as "declension", but the term had its effect nevertheless. The British were passionately interested in Rome, on the grounds that they were by far the most successful of modern Imperialists, and it is hardly surprising that it was an

Englishman, Edward Gibbon, who undertook to repair the factual inadequacies of Montesquieu's work and to offer a far more minute and scrupulous analysis of *The Decline and Fall of the Roman Empire*.

The first volume of Gibbon's work, published in 1776, quickly achieved notoriety because of the uncharitable treatment afforded to the birth and early evolution of Christianity by its concluding chapters; he saw the conversion of the crumbling empire to the new religion simply as one more stage of its declension. For Gibbon, Rome had briefly achieved an altogether admirable ideal, and his account of its decline is redolent with a special sense of tragedy; for all its cynicism his was essentially a Jeremiad: a Book of Lamentations. Thus was the myth of Rome's decadence amplified and set in stone.

The British, of course refused to believe the lesson which Montesquieu's science of history was trying to teach them, and would not accept that just as the Roman Empire had fallen, so in its time would theirs. The French, by contrast were much more ready to believe in the inevitability of their own decline. *"Après nous, le déluge!"* as Louis XV was widely misreported to have said, became and remained a popular catch-phrase.

Gibbon died in 1794, four weeks after Napoleon Bonaparte took Toulon for the Revolutionary forces and set himself on the road which would lead to a fabulous (and doomed) adventure in European Imperialism. For ten years, between his promotion to the rank of Emperor in 1804 and his exile to Elba in 1814 Napoleon was the modern Julius Caesar and Paris the new Rome; hope was briefly renewed again in 1815 but quickly foundered at Waterloo. The *ancien régime*, whose corruption had been a favourite topic of the Revolutionists, was restored - decadence and all.

Europe's year of revolutions, 1848, brought another Napoleon, but he too met his Waterloo at Sedan in 1870; in the following year Paris fell briefly under the control of the Commune, which revisited the city with a second dose of post-Revolutionary Terror. In the aftermath of all this it became very easy to believe that the nation and all it had once represented was half-way down a slippery slope. The time was ripe for a cultural movement which not only recognised and owned up to the decadence of the times, but accepted its inevitability and was unashamed.

****

A certain dissatisfaction with the forms and mores of contemporary civilization had long been manifest in the world of French letters, most extravagantly exemplified and encouraged by the mid-eighteenth century writings of Jean-Jaques Rousseau.

Rousseau argued that men were naturally good, but that their goodness had been warped and corrupted by civilized life. He became a fervent champion of Nature and the Noble Savage; he advised his fellows to beware of sophistication and put their trust instead in the moral influence of nature and the spontaneity of natural feeling. He was not a particularly good advertisement for his own ideas, abandoning all his children to die in the foundling home, but he became the guru of the cult of *sensibilité* and an early hero of the Romantic movement in the arts.

The Romantics may have considered the crass civilization which has spawned them to be decadent, but they were careful to exclude themselves from their indictments. The Romantics and their heroes were rebels against decadence who were perfectly certain that there was a better way. By means of their reverence for Nature and their carefully nurtured "sensibility" they sought to discover a new Utopia instead of a Dark Age; they could not believe that modern men were doomed to repeat the worst errors of their Roman forbears.

Though Romanticism set itself against the kind of conservative resistance to decadence which led to Victorianism in Britain, it shared some of the same nightmares. Such deserters as there were from the common ground where Romanticism and Classicism overlapped seemed, initially, to be every bit as mad and monstrous as Nero; prominent among them was the infamous Marquis de Sade. The Divine Marquis, ever generous with his hatreds, was no less contemptuous of Rousseau and his admirers than he was of the champions of official morality who comprised the twin hierarchies of Church and State.

Sade argued that just as the protestations of the godly were false and stupid, so too were Rousseauesque pleas on behalf of Natural Virtue; it was plain to anyone who cared to inspect the evidence that Nature had not an atom of inbuilt virtue, and must sensibly be reckoned the enemy of mankind, more unreasonably oppressive than any mere political tyranny. The only man who might be reckoned truly human, according to Sade, was a man bold enough to outrage Nature and Morality alike, who would dare to cultivate perversity and learn to love that which other men consider horrible. How seriously one can take the constructive part of Sade's argument is highly debatable, but the force of its destructive edge is undeniable. Rousseau was indeed quite wrong; the Utopian hopes of the cult of sensibility were always fatuous.

It is entirely reasonable, therefore, that there should have grown up in opposition to the cult of the natural a cult of the artificial, which set out to denigrate everything which Rousseau's followers revered. The adherents of that cult of artificiality were prepared to accept that the luxuries of civilization were indeed enervating, but argued that such luxuries were nevertheless very succulent, and must be savoured rather than denied. In that proposition can be found the underlying philosophy of literary Decadence.

****

In spite of the poverty of some of its philosophical pretensions, Romanticism flourished in the early part of the nineteenth century. It had the good fortune to take up arms against an established order whose flaws were easily seen, while never having to make any practical demonstration of its own potential as a promoter of the common weal. It offered an attractive cocktail of righteous wrath and numinous hope, whose power as a secular substitute for religious faith was quite sufficient to sustain itself against ordinary scepticism.

Inevitably, though, there were among those who embraced Romantic Ideals most ardently a few who found that those Ideals were impotent to deliver the goods. These dissenters were in an awkward position, confounded by a double negation which had first accepted the corruption and decadence of civilization and had then acknowledged the failure of Romantic rebellion against that corruption. The cult of artificiality offered an exit route from the double bind.

As second-rate comedians are fond of pointing out, no one was ever hurt by a fall, however steep; the abrupt halt at the end does all the damage. Since the invention of the parachute, in fact , it has been possible for the adventurously-inclined to make a sport out of free-falling, to savour the aesthetics of descent. This, in metaphorical terms, was the strategy of those writers we now call

Decadent; they accepted that their Imperially-ambitious societies were in a state of irrevocable decline, but they sought no scope for or virtue in Romantic rebellion, electing instead to explore and advertise the aesthetics of cultural free-fall. But this intellectual move was not without its costs.

****

The true Decadent believes that faith in any kind of progress is misplaced; there is no better world to come, which is still to be made by yet another revolution. He accepts also that salvation is highly unlikely to be found at the personal level; the quest for ideal love cannot succeed because people are not naturally loving and monogamous at all, but fundamentally duplicitous, ever ready to betray those whom they claim to love. Thus, the wholehearted Decadent renounces eutopia, euchronia and euspychia alike, and contents himself with making what adjustment he can to their irrevocable loss.

Decadence is not a happy state, and the Decadent does not bother to seek the trivial goal of contentment, whose price is wilful blindness to the true state of the world. Instead, he must become a connoisseur of his own psychic malaise (which mirrors, of course, the malaise of his society). He is the victim of various ills, whose labels become the key terms of Decadent rhetoric: *ennui* (world-weariness); *spleen* (an angry subspecies of melancholy); *impuissance* (powerlessness).

Gripped by these disorders, the Decadent is thoroughly apathetic, but his apathy is not so much a failing as a kind of curse visited upon him by the times in which he must live. If it is to be reckoned as a king of sin - and we must remember that what we would nowadays call "clinical depression" was once reckoned by the

7

Catholic Church to be the sin of accidie - then it is a sin from which conventional morality offers no hope of redemption. If the flame of his ashen spirit is to be reignited he must have recourse to new and more dangerous sensations: the essentially *artificial* paradises of the imagination. He is likely to seek such artificial paradises by means of drugs - particularly opium and hashish, but also absinthe and ether - but he remains well aware that the greatest artifice of all is, of course, Art itself.

The Decadent is a pessimist, in both historical and personal terms, but he acknowledges that in the comfortable and luxurious artifices of civilization, no matter how hollow they may be, a good deal of pleasure is to be found. He is therefore an unrepentant sensualist, albeit of a peculiarly cynical kind. Such meagre rewards as life has to offer the honest and sensitive man, he thinks, are to be sought by means of a languid hedonism which is contemptuous of arbitrary and tyrannical rules of conduct and scornful of all higher aspirations.

Not all the writers called Decadent conform to this ideal type in every particular, of course, but the extent to which they resemble it - in the advocacy of their work and in the examples set by their private lives - is the extent to which they are worthy of the title.

****

When one attempts to record the literary history of Decadence one inevitably runs into acute problems of delineation. There was a definite self-defined Decadent Movement in France in the 1880s and a short-lived echo of it in England in the 1890s. An analogous phenomenon can be observed in Russia shortly after the turn of the century, and there were writers in one or two other nations who were happy enough to be labelled Decadent (at least for a while). In addition to the handful of writers who were proud to accept the label, however, there were dozens of others identified by critics and historians whose inclusion must depend on externally- imposed rules of definition.

Critics, as is their wont, have conspicuously failed to agree on these difficult matters of definition. According to some, French Decadence flourished for a few years, but then it was displaced and overtaken by a distinct and separate Symbolist Movement; but according to others the terms Decadent and Symbolist are very nearly synonymous. In England, the concept of Decadence was considerably diluted and swiftly discredited, encouraging critics and historians to dissolve the short-lived English Decadent Movement into the Aesthetic Movement which preceded it and the Symbolist Movement which replaced it. In most other nations, which had the English example before them, "decadent" was used entirely as a term of abuse and never accepted by any of the writers threatened by the label, who frequently named themselves Symbolists in self-defence.

It is certainly true that Decadent literature overlaps several other genres and movements, and that many of its key works can equally well be discussed under other labels. At least some of the Decadents were interested in Symbolism and helped to develop its techniques; others were on the fringes of Naturalism, espousing a cynical and somewhat grotesque version of seedy realism. It is also the case that the great majority of writers who produced Decadent works also produced work of very different kinds, many temporarily adopting a Decadent sensibility by way of experiment only.

The situation is further complicated by the fact that there are some interesting literary accounts of the

Decadent personality which were set down, with horrified disapproval, by writers who were anything but Decadent in their own outlook. There were also writers for whom Decadence itself was a matter of pure artifice, who championed all manner of lurid perversion in their work while living entirely respectable private lives. The most wholehearted Decadents were, of course, those whose lifestyles were as Decadent as their works, but they constitute the nucleus of a much larger phenomenon whose edges are very blurred indeed.

The ideal type of the Decadent personality is an artist who rejoices in his power to analyse and display his own curious situation; life itself must become for him a kind of art-work - an exercise in style - because there is nothing else it can be. This ideal type is rare enough, however, that one might easily make a case for its non-existence in the purest possible form. This is not entirely surprising, given the inherent self-destructiveness of the philosophy.

There is a sharply ironic paradox in the fact that a creed which puts such a heavy emphasis on the comforts of artificiality proved to be desperately uncomfortable for all of its most fervent adherents. Many of them did indeed destroy themselves, aided by the scorn of their enemies; others set out more-or-less hastily on various roads to Damascus in search of magical renewals of faith which would restore the layers of spiritual insulation they had earlier discarded. While braver Decadents perished the more cowardly relented, but either way a Decadent Movement could not help but be a short-lived affair.

History cannot offer us a single example of a thoroughly successful Decadent career, but this is hardly surprising, given that the philosophy of Decadence has so little room in it for success. It was almost *de rigeur* for

conscientious Decadent in his earlier days similarly enhanced the value of Huysmans' conversion in the eyes of those who received him into the bosom of the Roman Church. Perhaps one should also recall, however, that Gibbon's overview of the Decline and Fall of Rome saw the ancient empire's conversion to Christianity merely as one more stage in its long decay. If we are to accept (on the evidence of its dubious pseudo-psychological underpinning) the conclusion that Decadence was really a species of silliness, we can hardly make out any better case for Catholicism. What Huysmans and Durtal - and all those who followed their example - mapped out was not really a road to salvation, but merely a path from frying pan to fire. On the other hand, it must remain a matter of opinion as to whether any of the other escapes from Decadent consciousness measured out by other writers were, in the end, any more satisfactory.

****

It was not religious faith but the attractions of a Symbolist movement shorn of Decadent pessimism and *impuissance* which were to provide a refuge for the majority of fair-weather Decadents who found the going too tough. Some critics have, indeed, suggested that there was little more involved in the displacement of Decadence by Symbolism than a change of name.

Evidence to support this case includes the facts that Mallarmé's reputation was substantially boosted by the revelation in *À rebours* that he was Des Esseintes' favourite writer, and that Verlaine's "Art poétique" (written in 1874 but not published until 1882) was adopted by the Symbolists as a key point of inspiration. Further evidence was supplied by the short-lived English Decadent Movement, whose promulgator Arthur Symons

41

was quickly moved to protest, after the trial of Oscar Wilde, that it had really been a Symbolist Movement all along. In actuality, though, the two terms should by no means be regarded as synonyms; what the Symbolists inherited (or took) from the Decadents was style without substance. They were sympathetic to the Rimbaudian rational disordering of the senses and its careful avoidance of mundane description, but they were mostly uninterested in the anguish of the Decadents and its supportive apparatus of ideas.

Mallarmé's achievement in producing Symbolism to eclipse Decadence was in contriving, after some initial dithering, to discover that which the Decadents thought impossible: a new poetic Ideal and a new quasi-religious poetic mission. Though Mallarmé never actually produced the *Grand Oeuvre* about which he was always talking, it nevertheless sufficed as a hypothetical goal towards which all his work could be orientated. He lay down for his followers a manifesto for life and art which was less uncomfortable to follow and more attractive as an item of commitment. Mallarmé was, of course, a much happier man than Baudelaire, Rimbaud or Verlaine: he was more successful in love, and eventually succeded - as none of them had done - in providing himself with a good living and a sound reputation.

As the protopsychological theories which had briefly dignified their excesses fell into decline, it is hardly surprising that all but the hardiest of the Decadents deflected their careers into more promising literary territory, accepting Mallarmé's offer of renewed hope and revitalised significance. Nevertheless, the legacy of Decadence lingered at least until the end of the century, and its impact was not insignificant even upon the work of those writers who must be considered to have been on its periphery.

5.

FIN DE SIÈCLE:
THE DECADENCE OF DECADENCE

Barbey d'Aurevilly was wrong, of course, to argue that the only possible escape routes for the earnest Decadent were Catholicism and suicide. Religious faith is not the only ideal to which a man might commit himself in order to recover the sense of being and doing something worthwhile. Aesthetic and political creeds could both offer convenient exits for Decadents disenchanted with disenchantment, and did so; others could simply learn to look at themselves and their work more ironically, becoming self-mocking satirists.

In exactly the same way, there were many writers contemporary with the Decadent Movement whose unwillingness to give up some such commitment, or whose inability to become entirely earnest about Decadent themes, kept them on the periphery despite the influence of the same ideas and preoccupations which attracted the Decadents to Decadence. Some of these writers warrant discussion in the context of Decadence if only to assist in the marking out of its blurred boundaries, and one or two of them produced important Decadent texts among works of other kinds.

The Comte de Villiers d'Isle Adam, whose *Contes cruels* (1883) were praised by Des Esseintes in *À rebours* would certainly be included with the Decadents were it not for an urgent Idealism in his work which kept *ennui* and *impuissance* from his literary agenda. The *conte cruel* sub-genre which he pioneered, and which was subsequently taken up by writers like Maurice Level,

43

certainly contains some Decadent items, but it is also possessed by a strong sense of irony which is much less narrowly-focused than the irony of Mendès' work. The Decadent aristocrat Lord Ewald in Villiers' misogynistic fantasy *L'Eve Future* (1886) finds an extraordinary way to transcend his predicament, when the inventor Edison builds him a perfect woman, thus taking the cult of the artificial to a new extreme. In his own art-work, Villiers could never be content for long with apathetic accidie; some of his "cruel tales" exhibit an uneasy callousness which is perfectly Decadent, but they are not typical of his outlook; he went on to develop a conscientiously neo-Romantic extravagance in such visionary dramas as the posthumously-published *Axel* (1890).

Insofar as Villiers de l'Isle Adam was a Decadent at all one could argue that a Decadent consciousness which he would dearly have wished to avoid was briefly thrust upon him by circumstance. He came from an aristocratic family in dire decline and failed utterly to redeem his position by making a useful marriage; small wonder, therefore, that he was occasionally possessed by splenetic hopelessness. He was not the only writer to be thus seized against his will; Gérard de Nerval was to prove an unfortunate prototype for a group of writers who were gradually toppled into the abyss of mental disorder - usually by the ravages of syphillis. Guy de Maupassant, who was a thoroughgoing realist in the greater part of his work, became increasingly fascinated by the effects of morbid hallucination as the spirochaete disordered his senses, and some of his work of the late eighties has a paranoid intensity. The fact that he was never able to accept the literal existence of ghosts did not stop him from exploring the psychology of fear in a scrupulous and intense fashion, and his work in this vein is sometimes very close in spirit to the supernatural stories of Jean Lorrain.

Visionary drama of the kind developed by Villiers de L'Isle Adam was also the preferred medium of the Belgian writer Maurice Maeterlinck, whose early work is very closely associated with the Decadent Movement, displaying passive characters helpless to defy the frankly mysterious forces which impel them towards their various dooms. From *La Princesse Maleine* (1889) to *La mort de Tintagiles* (1894) his work is thoroughly pessimistic, but his most famous work, *L'oiseau bleu* (1909; tr, as *The Blue Bird*) is a much more hopeful allegory in which the power of the dreamer becomes sufficiently assertive to control and defy the threat of nightmare.

The theatre is not, in any case, a suitable medium for the Decadent consciousness, which requires more interiorization than drama can usually sustain, and more freedom from censorship than the stage usually allows. The dilution and divergence of the Decadent consciousness after 1890 is much better exemplified by a handful of poets and novelists who, although preoccupied with certain characteristic Decadent themes, avoided any wholehearted immersion in the Movement. All of them existed on the margins of Decadence, and were selective in those aspects of it which they elected to extrapolate.

****

All of Jules Laforgue's work was published during the heyday of the Decadent Movement, and he was readily associated with it by contemporary critics, but his poetry and short fiction are saved from authentic Decadent consciousness by the fact that his sense of irony was far too powerful. Laforgue, like the poet Tristan Corbière before him, contrived to transform a fundamentally gloomy outlook by the power of ironic wit. He quickly developed a penchant for sparkling word-play and pyrotechnic sarcasm, shown to best effect in his collection of six *Moralités légendaires* (1887), in which the pretensions of heroes like Perseus, Lohengrin and Hamlet are mercilessly deflated. There is a full enough measure of *ennui* and *spleen* in Laforgue's work, and he certainly exhibited the customary Decadent traits in his private life - even to the extent of dying young of tuberculosis in 1887 - but the work which he completed in his final years gives every evidence of the fact that he had turned satirically against the Movement which had briefly involved him.

Pierre Louÿs, by contrast, is not generally included in lists of Decadent writers, and understandably so - his use of Classical themes takes no account of Montesquieu's theory of Roman decadence, being far more interested in the aesthetic glories of Greece than the tarnished grandeur of Rome. But he did translate Lucian's teasing series of dialogues concerning the pragmatic ideology of the courtesan, and he devoted much effort to a quasi-Decadent celebration of Lesbianism in *Les Chansons de Bilitis* (1894). The glorification of Sapphic love is also a significant sub-text of his exotic historical novel *Aphrodite* (1896), which is set in Alexandria during the reign of Cleopatra's elder sister Berenike. There is nothing particularly neurasthenic about the characters who figure in this tale of fatal infatuation, but it stands in a direct line of descent from Gautier and makes rather less concession than Gautier did to the saving grace of grand passion.

Louÿs followed *Aphrodite* with *Les Aventures de roi Pausole* (1901), a Rabelaisian fantasy set in the imaginary realm of Tryphême - which, the author is careful to state, should not be mistaken for Utopia. Here the tone is deft and amusing; the eroticism is light-hearted, and literally pleads not to be taken seriously. In more earnest work Louÿs retained a deep suspicion of the redeeming quality of love, as evidenced by the quasi-masochistic tale of disappointments *La Femme et le pantin* (1898; tr. as *The Woman and the Puppet*) and the book which he could never bring himself to finish for publication, *Psyche* (issued posthumously, and incomplete, in 1925), and he spent the latter part of his life as a virtual recluse, but his incipient Decadence was compromised by a sentimentality which made him excessively regretful about the failure of sexual passion to live up to human hopes.

Louÿs' protegé Charles Bargone, who wrote under the pseudonym Claude Farrère, might have been a much more enthusiastic Decadent than his mentor, but he was far too late coming upon the scene to get involved in the Movement itself and his Decadent affectations were soon nipped in the bud. He has the distinction, however, of having belatedly produced what probably deserves to be considered the ultimate study of the Decadent use and abuse of drugs, in his remarkable story-cycle *Fumée d'Opium* (1904; tr. as *Black Opium*). There had been many previous accounts of the careers of drug-users - notably Marcel Mallat's *La Comtesse Morphine* (1885) - but most had followed Baudelaire's example in being both *recherché* and censorious. Farrère's story-cycle follows the example of Jules Boissière's *Les Fumeurs d'opium* (1896) in paying much more attention to the exoticism of the lands from which opium comes, where its use confuses and blends exotic dream-experiences with exotic landscapes. It is, however, a more ornate and multi-faceted work than its predecessor, beginning with a group of "legends" and passing through "annals", "ecstasies", "doubts" and "phantoms" to a concluding

47

"nightmare".

Farrère was to go on to produce many more works of an entirely un-Decadent stripe, most of which recall the upbeat exoticism of the sailor "Loti" (Julien Viaud). His reinvestment in optimism was aided by political commitment, but it is perhaps significant that his vivid futuristic fantasy *Les condamnés a mort* (1920; tr. as *Useless Hands*) features a hopeless revolution against technologically-sophisticated Capitalists whose comforts have robbed them of all moral sensibility.

Political commitment of one kind or another kept many of the leading French writers of the 1880s away from Decadence altogether. When Anatole France abandoned the aristocratic values which he had inherited and turned against Catholicism he never paused to dally with Decadence but kept his hopes firmly invested in alternative visions of a better future. The same was very nearly true of Octave Mirbeau, but the anarchism to which Mirbeau was attracted was a less dogmatic creed than France's communism, and his novels are correspondingly unfocused.

Mirbeau's work is too full of righteous wrath against the evils of the day to be reckoned properly neurasthenic (despite his use of the word in the title of one of his later books), but he was to produce in *Le jardin des supplices* (1899) a key work of quasi-Decadent fantasy. The character of Clara, who entrances the hero and deflects him from his semi-purposeful journey to the East, is both a descendant and marvellously grotesque exaggeration of Gautier's Cleopatra or Rachilde's Marquise de Sade. The allegorical tour of the garden of tortures which she takes in the company of the intimidated anti-hero is a portrait of the Decadent in search of distraction to end all such portraits, and represents the true culmination of that particular aspect of the Decadent adventure.

Afterwards, there really was nowhere else to go in search of intensity-through-sin.

****

It is not easy to register a death-date for French Decadence as certain in its propriety as the birth-date which was registered by the publication of *Les Fleurs du Mal*. The notable works by Mirbeau and Farrère cited above are really distanced studies of the Decadent outlook, arguably more comparable with Sainte-Beuve's *Volupté* than with the novels cited in the previous section, and it would be a distortion to select one of them as a kind of tombstone.

Decadent style, in being superseded by Symbolism, was transformed rather than destroyed, and the same might be said of certain Decadent themes which were taken up in a flirtatious fashion by the first surrealists. Alfred Jarry and Guillaume Apollinaire both deployed in their prose works ideas which had formerly preoccupied the Decadents, but they made a macabre comedy out of them. Jarry, in particular, occasionally came close to the Decadent spirit in *Les jours et les nuits* (1897), in which an unfit soldier seeks release from his predicament in hallucinations, and in his vivid historical melodrama *Messaline* (1900), set in decadent Rome.

One can find such echoes wherever one cares to look; however quickly Decadence may have passed from fashion it had made an indelible impression on the heritage of French literature. The Decadent Movement was virtually extinct in France by 1900 (though some other nations had yet to produce their own quasi-Decadent literature at that time) but it left descendants to carry forward certain of its traits, and occasional throwbacks would be produced by those descendants for many years.

There is, in any case, a certain ironic futility about any attempt to register a time of death in respect of Decadent literature; the very essence of the idea of decadence is that death is merely a passing moment within a continuing process of decay, and it is entirely appropriate that echoes of the Decadent consciousness should continue to crop up long into the Twentieth Century, sometimes at long distances from the point of origin in Paris. Baudelaire's work, after all, remains very much alive, and though his celebrations of *spleen* and *ennui* have to be understood - if they are to be understood properly - in their proper historical context, they have nevertheless become immortal in the crystallizations of Decadent sensibility which are provided by *Les Fleurs du Mal*. The flowers of evil were not hardy perennials, but because they are poems and not real flowers they cannot entirely wither into dust.

****

6.

THE YELLOW NINETIES: DECADENCE IN ENGLAND

What passed for Decadence in England was but a pale shadow of French Decadence. In the eyes of upright Victorians *all* French literature seemed dreadfully decadent, and "decadent" was freely bandied about as a term of abuse which carried a distinctly xenophobic implication. The idea of historical and cultural decadence never acquired, in England, the same specific connotations which it had in France; despite Gibbon's amplification of Montesquieu' arguments the term was not tied to the idea of failing and falling empires; rather it was used - promiscuously, one might say - to refer to moral licence and moral laxness.

Such was the English attitude to Paris that "French" and "decadent" were virtually synonymous in certain realms of discourse. The Rev. W. F. Barry contributed two articles to the *Quarterly Review* in 1890 and 1892 entitled "Realism and Decadence in French Literature" and "The French Decadence", under which titles he subsumed discussion of writers as varied as Balzac, Zola, Maupassant and Daudet, all of whom he found morally suspect by the standards of British neo-Puritanism. The customary subject-matter of run-of-the-mill Decadent novels would have been considered so indecent by an British publisher as to be ruled out of the question. Poetry was granted more latitude, but an English writer who wrote in the manner of Baudelaire would have been regarded as hopelessly corrupt. Nevertheless, there were English poets whose attitude to Paris was different - who saw in the salons and Bohemian circles of Paris an enviable enthusiasm, freedom of expression and stylishness. They saw the importation of a modest measure of French Decadence as a desirable thing, but in order to keep the measure modest they were forced to import the style without the substance.

The would-be champion of English Decadence was Arthur Symons, who was willing enough to wear the label until it became too great an embarrassment, and urged others to wear it too. His essay on "The Decadent Movement in Literature", published in *Harper's New Monthly Magazine* in 1893, begins by regretting the confusion of terms currently being deployed in the hope of capturing the essence of the major currents in European art, and admits that Decadence overlaps somewhat with Symbolism and Impressionism. Symons asserts, however, that the notion of Decadence best captures the temper of the work, which he is happy to accept as "a new and beautiful and interesting disease". The character of the new art, he argues, echoes the character of the art produced by the Greek and Latin cultures in their senescence; his description of it includes: "intense self-consciousness...restless curiosity...an over subtilizing refinement upon refinement, a spiritual and moral perversity."

All of this Symons was initially enthusiastic to take aboard. The writers he offers as the most meritorious contemporary examplars of the Movement are Verlaine, Huysmans and Maeterlinck. In the first version of the essay Symons names Walter Pater and W. E. Henley as significant English proto-Decadents, but he removed the references for diplomatic reasons when the essay was reprinted in book form.

Symons was a member of the Rhymers' Club,

which met at an eating house in Fleet Street; his fellow members included Ernest Dowson, Lionel Johnson, John Davidson, Richard le Gallienne and William Butler Yeats. Some of these agreed with Symons sufficiently to allow a measure of Decadent influence into their work, and none of them entirely escaped guilt by association, but if it is to be reckoned as the spearhead of an English Decadent Movement their work is distinctly half-hearted. Fugitive Decadent elements are easy enough to find in the work of Johnson and Yeats but only Dowson, apart from Symons himself, was really significantly affected by the Decadent attitude. In Dowson's case this influence was greatly assisted by his infection with the tuberculosis which drove both his parents to suicide, but the morbidity of his supposedly Decadent work is straightforwardly melancholy; the paradoxical thrill of perversity which so entranced the French Decadents is simply not there.

None of the Rhymers ever lost sight, even temporarily, of aesthetic ideals which might give their work some kind of uplifting quality, and most retained religious faith as well. In addition, they exhibited a tendency, even when they took Decadence seriously, not to take it too seriously. Lionel Johnson's essay on "The Cultured Faun" in the *Anti-Jacobin* (1891) offers a portrait of the contentedly neurasthenic artist which is nine parts parody, and the only English writer of the first rank who took care to flaunt his Decadent life-style, Oscar Wilde, relied constantly upon his elegant wit to excuse and explain himself.

In the main, though, English Decadent poetry is simply listless, its *impuissance* unredeemed by any semblance of calculated intention. If one compares such poems by Symons as "The Opium-Smoker" (in *Days and Nights*, 1889) and "The Absinthe-Drinker" (in *Silhouettes*, 1892) with the rhapsodies of Gautier,

53

Baudelaire and Farrère they seem dreadfully anemic. Although Symons did a considerable service in translating a good deal of French Decadent poetry into English, his translations of Baudelaire seem prettified to the modern reader.

****

Just as the French Decadents had inherited a doctrine of art for art's sake from Gautier, so the Rhymers and their contemporaries inherited one from Walter Pater and Swinburne (whose masochistic streak moved some of his poems as close to the spirit of Decadence as any existing English material). But Pater's exemplary Epicurean Marius is a man of far greater austerity, decorum and moral rectitude than the pagans of French fiction, and the English art which was done for English art's sake was similarly constrained; the lush and gaudy extravagance of much French art was absent. Swinburne often achieved a fevered intensity, reflected in the rhythm as well as the imagery of his poems, but his work lacks a cutting edge.

Like the most nearly-Decadent of the pre-Raphaelites, Dante Gabriel Rossetti, Swinburne was looked after by Theodore Watts-Dunton when his life-style made him ill, and similar benevolence may have softened the splenetic tendencies of other beleaguered British poets. Eugene Lee-Hamilton, who certainly warrants inclusion among British proto-Decadents, spent twenty years as a chronic (possibly psychosomatic) invalid, but was apparently saved from undue bitterness by a thoroughly British expectation that it was simply not done to be too self-indulgent in one's misery. From *The New Medusa* (1882) to *Sonnets of the Wingless Hours* (1895) his work toyed incessantly with Decadent images, but retained a measure of reserve which was echoed in real life when, after publication of the latter collection, he made a complete recovery from his illness. Lee-Hamilton went on to write a phantasmagorical historical novel, *The Lord of the Dark Red Star* (1903), whose vivid imagery recalls the French historical fantasies peripheral to the Decadent Movement; his half-sister Violet Paget, who signed herself Vernon Lee, incorporated similar elements into some of her own historical fantasies.

Those Rhymers most closely associated with Symons' Decadent Crusade could lay claim to equally adequate neurotic symptoms, and they mostly contrived to die young as a result. Dowson died at 33, having spent his last years as an exile in France. Lionel Johnson was an alcoholic who eventually became a recluse and died at 35. Even Symons contrived to have a nervous breakdown in 1908 (when he was 43), was certified insane and was diagnosed as suffering from "general paralysis" (a term usually employed as a euphemism for syphillis); but he defied fate and his doctors by recovering and surviving to the ripe old age of 80.

Others whose fates might be added to this catalogue of misfortunes include John Davidson, who hurled himself from a cliff at 52, having been deeply affected by Nietzschean ideas of the redundancy of contemporary man, and a writer very heavily influenced by Davidson, James Elroy Flecker, who died of tuberculosis at 31. Flecker was born too late to be labelled a Decadent - his first volume of poems was published in 1907 - but his career followed a course mapped out by countless French writers, including a voyage to the Orient whose legacy had a powerful effect on his later work, and his novelette *The Last Generation* (1908) is a thoroughly Decadent piece of work in the futuristic mode into which British ideas of Decadence were mostly transplanted.

Despite all these stigmata the English Decadents never subscribed to a medicated theory of artistic creativity in the way that so many of the French Decadents came to do. They did have medical men associated with the movement - most notably Havelock Ellis, whose pre-Freudian investigations of the psychology of sex were a significant, if soon out-dated, contribution to the development of human science - but Ellis's proto-psychology could not find room for the follies of Moreau de Tours and Lombroso, and his literary criticism was in any case much more closely associated with his philosophical interests; like Davidson, Ellis was fascinated by Nietzsche, who was too positive a thinker to licence any kind of languorous self-indulgence. When writing as a literary critic, Ellis was also enthusiastic to use the cautionary argument with which British Decadents habitually defended themselves against the pejorative implications of the word; his notable essay on Huysmans in *Affirmations* (1898) takes care to emphasize that Decadence ought to be viewed entirely as an aesthetic concept and not a moral one.

****

This insistence that English literary Decadence did not intend to be subversive of moral standards, and had nothing to do with morality at all, was so frequently reiterated by its supporters as to constitute an Ophelian excess of protestation. One of the epigrammatic remarks prefacing Oscar Wilde's *Picture of Dorian Gray* (1891) takes care to allege that there is no such thing as a moral or an immoral book - but Wilde was persuaded to admit privately that of course the novel was (and unashamedly set out to be) a powerful moral allegory.

Wilde visited Paris regularly in the early 1880s; he

was acquainted with Decadent writers like Lorrain and theorists of Decadence like Paul Bourget and was a great admirer of the literary work then being done in France, but he knew well enough that its methods and concerns could not be imported into English literature without great difficulty. His most calculatedly Decadent work, the play *Salomé*, was written in French, and subsequently banned from the London stage by the Lord Chamberlain.

Despite that he was the target of the crusade which effectively assassinated the English Decadent Movement, Wilde wrote relatively little Decadent material, and all of it is much more moralistic than it could possibly have been if he really had been the narcissistic and quasi-demonic character he appeared to his enemies to be. A close inspection of Wilde's work reveals that his philosophical affiliation to Decadence was much more apparent than real. Dorian Gray, having taken a full measure of inspiration from *À rebours*, reaches a far more frustrating impasse than des Esseintes, and must ultimately pay a dire price for the privilege of having lived the life of a work of art while his portrait accepted the burdens and penalties of actual Decadence.

It is significant that the most contemplative and rhetorically effective works which Wilde ever produced are not his fervent essay on "The Soul of Man Under Socialism" and his bitter letter "De Profundis", and certainly not his plays; they are in fact the four stories, ostensibly written for children, which make up *The House of Pomegranates* (1891), which are somewhat Gautieresque in style but much bleaker and more thoughtful in outlook. These heartfelt and rather harrowing tales, especially "The Fisherman and his Soul" and "The Star Child", express a resistance to Decadent self-indulgence which makes a complete nonsense of the notion that Wilde had much in common intellectually with Johnson's Cultured Fauns. His public poses continually flirted with the outrage of his enemies, but his own defence of unconventional moral values - unlike Sir Henry Wootton's in *The Picture of Dorian Gray* - is not founded in any celebration of their defiance of Nature, but rather in deep complaints against the standards of natural and social justice alike.

****

In going beyond Decadence to search for new and better ideals Wilde was certainly not alone. Even for French writers Decadence was mostly a phase through which they passed - for English ones it tended rather to be a matter which they contemplated, and then side-stepped or reinterpreted to their own convenience. It is hardly surprising that when it ceased to be convenient the English writers who had been called Decadent wasted no time in renouncing the label altogether.

To the extent that Decadence caught on among the poets of England it caught on as a fairly restrained and entirely superficial stylistic affectation. There is more genuine Decadence to be found in the work of Russian writers who would mostly have preferred to be known as Symbolists. When Wilde's trial sent Symons and the rest scurrying in search of a less embarrassing label they were quick to argue that no Englishman had *ever* meant anything by the word except a kind of style, and although that claim is not really supportable by Symons' essay, it is borne out by the literary material.

For a brief period before Wilde's trial the idea of Decadence did become fashionable enough in London to generate its own periodical press, whose flagship was John Lane's quarterly *Yellow Book*, launched in 1894. By far the most famous (or notorious) contributor to the

Yellow Book, however, was not a writer but an illustrator - the art editor Aubrey Beardsley, who had also designed the cover which united the works in Lane's "Keynotes" series, in which several notable Decadent works were featured. It is Beardsley's illustrative work rather than any production in poetry or prose which provided English Decadence with a memorable image. His astonishing decorations for Lord Alfred Douglas's English translation of Wilde's *Salomé* (1894) were far more original, exotic and daring than any other products of the Movement. The evidence of his incomplete baroque romance *Under the Hill* (1897), suggests that Beardsley might have become a genuine Decadent writer too, but he was given no opportunity to do so, dying of tuberculosis in 1898.

The early issues of the *Yellow Book* did endeavour to provide Beardsley's art-work with some appropriate textual support, but the poetry was essentially staid and the most interesting item - Max Beerbohm's ironically flippant commentary on the cult of artificiality, "A Defence of Cosmetics" - only proved controversial because some readers did not realise that it was a joke. A similar flippancy was exhibited by a series of "Stories Toto Told Me" which was contributed by the colourful con-man "Baron Corvo" (Frederick W. Rolfe).

Any pretensions to authentic Decadence which the *Yellow Book* may have had were instantly jettisoned in the wake of the Wilde trial, though Wilde had never actually been a contributor to it. Beardsley was sacked for having (innocently) kept such bad company, and though he was promptly hired by Arthur Symons to work on *The Savoy*, a new periodical which was supposed to take up where the *Yellow Book* left off, the hastily-dropped torch of English Decadence proved too hot to handle. *The Savoy* lasted only eight issues, closing with a December 1896 issue in which all the text was supplied by Symons and all the illustrations by an ailing Beardsley; when it died, the English Decadent Movement, such as it had been, died too. A book by Symons which had already been advertised under the title *The Decadent Movement in Literature* was ultimately to appear in 1899 under the more diplomatic title of *The Symbolist Movement in Literature*.

****

The body of English work which was produced with the Decadent label actually in mind is understandably thin, given that the term was in vogue for little more than three years, and the work to which the label can be attached at second hand is not much larger. The most intensely lurid products of English Decadence can be found in a small group of short story collections issued between 1893 and 1896: Count Eric Stenbock's *Studies of Death* (1893); R. Murray Gilchrist's *The Stone Dragon and Other Tragic Romances* (1894); and three "Keynotes" volumes: Arthur Machen's *The Great God Pan and the Inmost Light* (1894); and M. P. Shiel's *Prince Zaleski* (1895) and *Shapes in the Fire* (1896).

Stenbock, who was by far the most enthusiastic Decadent in London, was not an Englishman by birth, though he had studied at Oxford and wrote in English; because he was a foreigner his conspicuous indulgence of the Decadent life-style was deemed understandable, if not forgivable. He lived amid absurd decorations, addicted to drink and drugs, and was more flamboyantly homosexual than Oscar Wilde. His mostly self-published poems had long been ignored, and he must have greeted the advent of an English Decadent Movement gladly, hopeful that he might now be discovered. Alas, though

Symons did condescend to notice Stenbock, he did not shirk from describing him as "inhuman". As it turned out, *Studies of Death* was his last work, though he probably would have soldiered on unrepentantly had he not died (his end hurried by contributory negligence) in 1895.

Gilchrist, Machen and Shiel, by contrast, were all writers at the beginning of their careers. Although, as in Stenbock's case, the collections named above are remembered today mainly because the supernatural stories in them are sometimes reprinted in collections of horror stories, all three went on to produce an abundance of work in a less Decadent vein. Two of the three, though, had been marked deeply enough by their flirtation with Decadence that they never quite shook off its legacy. Gilchrist, the odd one out, died in 1917, but Machen and Shiel both survived until 1947, when they were both in their eighties. Though neither of them was subsequently to write anything quite as over-wrought as "The Great God Pan" or the stories in *Shapes in the Fire* they retained certain Decadent motifs and stylistic sympathies well into the twentieth century.

Machen's best novel, *The Hill of Dreams* (written 1897; published 1907), is a story of escape into the past more extreme and more determined than Huysmans' *Là-Bas*, and presents a memorable account of splenetic civilization-phobia. Shiel's best novel, *The Purple Cloud* (1901), has the last man alive in the world giving extravagant vent to his anguish amist the ruins. Machen and Shiel both sought philosophical foundations for their sustained Decadent consciousness, Machen in mysticism and Shiel in a quasi-Nietzschean conviction that the coming of the *übermensch* was vital to a renewal of the cause of progress.

It is no coincidence that all four of these short story

writers made extravagant use of the supernatural, nor that they did so in a more straightforwardly horrific way than either Gautier or Farrère. The English attitude to Decadence, even among its practitioners, was always spiced with a revulsion which lent itself readily to the construction of stories which are both macabre and morbid. "The Great God Pan", one of the most nasty-minded stories ever written, extrapolates and displays this element of revulsion very cleverly. Machen, like Yeats, was very interested in contemporary occultism, and not merely as source material (which is how Rimbaud and Huysmans treated their readings in alchemy and satanism). Both were briefly associated with the Order of the Golden Dawn, which supported life-style fantasies combining Decadent elements with pretentions to esoteric Enlightenment, and it might be argued that the most wholehearted of all English Decadents was the one-time star of the Order, Aleister Crowley.

Like his Decadent countrymen Crowley selected out that part of the Decadent apparatus which suited him (drugs, sexual perversion and charismatic wickedness) and left behind that which did not (neurasthenia and pessimism) but he proved less repentant in the face of popular scandal than any of those who needed a broader audience for their work - though he was ultimately forced into exile as a result. His poetry and his prose fiction are of some relevance but slight merit.

There were other, much better, English writers whose life-styles tended towards what was popularly regarded as Decadent, and whose lives - for that reason - were spent mostly in exile. One was the lesbian Vernon Lee whose excellent supernatural short fiction plays lovingly with some Decadent motifs; another was Norman Douglas, whose novel *They Went* (1920) is an interesting late addition to the ironic tradition of English Decadence. Baron Corvo, who died in Venice, might also be added to the list, though the fact that he was *persona non grata* almost everywhere had as much to do with his sponging as any marginally-Decadent affectations he had once harboured. And, of course, Wilde too died in exile - in Paris, the one and only true home of all true Decadents.

****

Supernatural fiction was not the only genre into which the Decadent elements of English fiction could be safely transplanted. Shiel has the distinction of having penned the only collection of Decadent detective stories in his Keynotes series volume *Prince Zaleski* (1895) but he made more extravagant use of futuristic settings, as in *The Purple Cloud*. The idea of futuristic decadence as a probable - perhaps inevitable - fate for the human species is very noticeable in British fiction, and recurs obsessively in the work which H. G. Wells did during the brief period when the idea was fashionable in Britain, as in his evocation of "The Man of the Year Million" (1893) and the image of the decadent Eloi besieged by brutal Morlocks is the central motif of *The Time Machine* (1895). Future decadence came to be seen as a particularly horrible threat by the writers of scientific romance, who devoted much imaginative effort to the quest for a happier fate without ever quite putting the nightmare behind them.

The manner in which the future decadence of mankind became a favourite bugbear of writers of imaginative fiction is, of course, symptomatic of a hostility deeply embedded in English culture - a hostility which is peculiarly revealing. Its force was given to it by Victorian moralism but its fury testifies to the essential corruption of that very moralism. From a modern standpoint we cannot help but take the side of Oscar Wilde against the Marquess of Queensbery, not simply because Wilde was a great writer while Queensbery was an intellectual nonentity, but also because we can now appreciate that the Marquess's stern repression of his own homoerotic tendencies into a fondness for watching semi-naked men beat one another half to death was no more laudable than Wilde's addiction to the services of rent boys.

On the day after the abandonment of the libel action which Wilde unwisely launched against Queensbery the *National Observer* published a leading article which asserted that : "There is not a man or woman in the English-speaking world possessed of the treasure of a wholesome mind who is not under a deep debt of gratitude to the Marquess of Queensbery for destroying the High Priest of the Decadents. The obscene imposter, whose prominence has been a social outrage ever since he transferred from Trinity Dublin to Oxford his vices, his follies and his vanities, has been exposed, and that thoroughly at last. But to the exposure there must be legal and social sequels...and of the Decadents, of their hideous conceptions of the meaning of Art, of their worse than Eleusinian mysteries, there must be an absolute end." Given such strength of feeling it is hardly surprising that the label was instantly abandoned by those who had briefly adopted it, and ardently denied in retrospect by all those who had never made the mistake of admitting to it. Art, whether wrought for art's sake or not, was compelled to make its obeisance before the altar of morality like a reluctant heretic in the shadow of the Inquisition.

Such an acute sense of danger speaks of a more than ordinary fear. It speaks, in fact, of an acute awareness of crisis. The English writers of Decadent poetry and fiction refrained from calling the British Empire decadent, and refused to think of the future as a hopeless condition - but their enemies, reacting as if they had, gave the game away. The Empire was in a state of irreversible decline, and what the future held was not a war to end war which would secure Anglo-Saxon hegemony for all time but a great orgy of stupid butchery which would test almost to destruction every optimistic philosophy of progress which could be rallied against its apocalyptic implications, whether religious, political or technophilic. The crucifixion of Oscar Wilde by the rampant spirit of imperial vanity proved to be the prelude to the crucifixion of an entire generation, sent to die in the muddied fields of northern France.

We do not think of the English poets of World War I as Decadents, nor do we attach any such label to the futuristic writers of the period between the wars who foresaw another war which would put an end to civilization, and of course they had none of the affectations of the aesthetic Decadent - no impuissant neurasthenia, no splenetic interest in opium or perversity - but such writers certainly had what the French Decadents had initially failed to export to England: a sense of hopelessness; a haunting suspicion that all that was left for men to do was fiddle while Rome burned.

And then, of course, came a new wave of mad emperors....

The only possible conclusion which the modern commentator can come to, in looking back at the English Decadents, is that they were not nearly Decadent enough. Though they wrote horror stories and stories fearful of a far future decline into comfortable *impuissance*, modesty forbade them seeing anything horrible enough to awaken them or their readers to the historical peril in which they actually stood.

7.

INFLUENCES:
DECADENCE IN OTHER NATIONS

No other nation except for France and England had a recognisable and self-declared Decadent Movement; there were, nevertheless, many individual writers in various other countries who came under the influence of the French Decadents and echoed the themes and methods of Decadent writing in their own work. However one cares to construct a definition of Decadence one will inevitably discover that some of the most interesting examples can be found in languages other than French or English.

The nation which came closest to producing a Movement akin to those of France and England was Russia, which had more than its fair share of neurotic writers. Indeed, some of the main themes of French Decadent fiction had already been anticipated in Russia in the work of Dostoyevsky and Turgenev. While the novelists of Decadence were first becoming busy in France the Russian writer Vsevolod Garshin, while going mad himself, was producing, "The Red Flower" (1883), in which a patient in a lunatic asylum "discovers" that all the world's evil is contained in three poppies growing in a garden and must lay an elaborate plan for their destruction. A similar interest in morbid states of mind can be found in the work of writers heavily influenced by Dostoyevsky, including M. N. Albov and Prince Golitzyn Muravlin, the latter of whom took as his project the identification of the principal pathological types of the decaying aristocracy.

Many of the younger Russian writers of the *fin de siècle* period found themselves gathered together by the anchorage of Maxim Gorky's publishing house, Znanie. Most of these writers were politically radical champions of realism, but there nevertheless grew up in their midst a Symbolist Movement which took its inspiration from France and - like the English Movement - took aboard a selective measure of Decadence as well. They came to prominence somewhat later than the equivalent English writers but enjoyed a similarly brief vogue after the demoralizing Russo-Japanese War and the consequent Revolution of 1905.

The most successful writer of this period in Russia was Leonid Andreyev, who did not belong to the Symbolist group but who influenced and shared certain concerns with them. Like Baudelaire, Andreyev was a great admirer of Edgar Allan Poe, and was inordinately impressed by the power of Poe's studies of abnormal states of mind; he also followed Poe in becoming intensely interested in metaphysical matters. In many of his later stories Andreyev is concerned to draw links between the encroachments of madness and discovery of the meaninglessness and hopelessness of the human condition; such stories as "Thought" (1902), *The Red Laugh* (1904), "Eleazer" (1907) and "Darkness" (1908) all present harsh statements of the emptiness of existence which begin the stretching of Decadent sensibility in the direction of the bleaker extremes of existentialist *angst*. Very similar themes are extensively developed in the work of Sergey Sergeyev-Tsensky, whose most notable story in terms of its relationship to Decadence is "Babayev", which deals with a neurasthenic officer's obsessive desire to commit a crime. Alexander Kuprin, though primarily a realist, also produced some short stories in this morbid vein.

67

The Russian Symbolists were far more interested in matters metaphysical than their French and English counterparts, becoming very preoccupied with the idea of the world as a vast network of symbols. The Movement's most notable prose writers - although all three wrote poetry as well - were Valery Bryusov, Andrey Bely and Fedor Sologub. Bryusov, who had collaborated on a book on *Russian Symbolists* as early as 1894 took charge of a publishing house in 1900 which then became the focal point of the Movement, issuing a journal called *Vesy* ("The Scales") from 1904-09. His most famous short story is a remarkable futuristic fantasy about an epidemic of madness in a Utopian state, "The Republic of the Southern Cross".

Although the word "decadent" was not bandied about as freely in Russia as it had been in Britain by those intending denigration, Bryusov was so charged and so was Bely. The latter was condemned partly for his ironic sensibility - though he could not really be accused of not taking the metaphysical matters which fascinated him seriously. The prolific Sologub did not suffer from any lack of seriousness, despite casting many of his short tales in a fairy-tale mode, and took great pains to extrapolate his sense of disappointment with the universe. Some of his phantasmagoric allegories are very striking, and such tales as "The Lady in Fetters" are very close indeed to the spirit of French Decadent prose. Sologub's most successful novel was *Mekli Bes* (1907; tr. as *The Little Demon*). The other important members of the Symbolist school were the poets Vyacheslav Ivanov and Alexander Blok; the latter took his place alongside Bryusov as an important promoter of the movement and eventually became its most prestigious member - such poems as "Danse Macabre" encapsulate Decadent consciousness neatly and wholeheartedly.

The history of Russian Symbolism - and of its Decadent inclusions - might have extended over a longer period had it not been for the intervention of the Revolutions of 1917, which ushered in a new era of heavily politicized art. It was not enough for Symbolists and others to convert to Communism; they had also to adjust their philosophies of art. It was not merely Decadence which had become decadent in the eyes of the State, but everything which was not Socialist Realism.

****

Because it had the city of Rome within its bound Italy might, in principle, have been reasonably fertile ground for the philosophy of decadence and a consequent literary movement, but the historical moment was not ideal. The Kingdom of Italy had been proclaimed as recently as ₁861, following Garibaldi's unification, and the newness of the city's role as the capital of a modern nation state was an inhibition to the notion that it was decadent, despite the antiquity and continuing decline of the Roman Church. Nevertheless, Italy did produce one writer of considerable note - indeed, the foremost Italian writer of his day - who was entirely happy to dabble in the Decadent style as soon as it became fashionable in France; this was Gabriele D'Annunzio.

D'Annunzio was by no means possessed of a Decadent personality, though the prolific turnover of his mistresses called his morality into question and eventually landed him with syphilis. He was a man of great energy, ambition and patriotism who looked constantly towards the future; he fought duels over his women, distinguished himself in the Great War, and took a Vernian delight in the technology of transportation. His work was equally wide-ranging, but it is the early poetry and novels, which most clearly show the influence of contemporary French writing, which are today best remembered.

D'Annunzio's first venture in the Decadent style was the poetry collection *Intermezzo di rime* (1883), which declared its intentions with a motto taken from the passage in the Apocalypse which refers to the Harlot of Babylon and was printed on pink paper. It includes, among other items, twelve sonnets celebrating the exploits of famous adulterers, four "nude studies" and various poems of a vaguely sacrilegious character. Two more collections in the same vein followed but D'Annunzio then seemed to tire of being an *enfant terrible* (as he tired of most things) and moved back in the direction of realism. Decadent elements were combined with this new thrust, however, in his two most important novels: *Il piacere* (1889; tr. as *The Child of Pleasure*) and *Il trionfo della morte* (1894; tr. as *The Triumph of Death*). Both drew heavily on his own experiences and his own obsessions with beautiful women, and his vivid depiction of the city of Rome reflects the wide-eyed view of an upwardly mobile country-boy with a hunger for luxury, in much the same way that Rachilde's novels express her similar attitude to Paris. *Il trionfo della morte* is particularly extravagant in deploying Decadent imagery, possessed by a fascination with depravity which converts the central love story into a danse macabre haunted by spectres of the past.

Like some of the English Decadents, D'Annunzio became fascinated with the works of Nietzsche, whose influence combined with that of the Symbolists in *Le vergini delle rocce* (1895; tr. as *The Virgins of the Rocks*), which he wrote for *Il Convito*, a periodical of his own in which he intended to emulate such foreign productions as the *Yellow Book*. Concentrating as it does on the grotesque life of an aristocratic family which has withdrawn from the world, it comes as close as any other novel of the period to producing an image of social decadence in the Decadent style. D'Annunzio's subsequent involvement with the famous actress Eleanor Duse, who built a great reputation for herself as a Decadent performer, inspired further works in celebration of erotic freedom, but after the turn of the century Decadence gradually drained out of his work just as it dwindled away in France.

Almost all of D'Annunzio's Italian contemporaries leaned more towards the realism of Giovanni Verga rather than his own heated example. Federico de Roberto's novel of an aristocratic Sicilian family in decline, *I vicerè* (1894; tr. as *The Viceroys*), scrupulously avoids the Decadent style, having none of the baroque decoration of *Le vergini delle rocce*. Luigi Pirandello, on the other hand, was taken beyond his early realism by the repercussions of a personal tragedy - the insanity of his wife. He developed a fiercely ironic view of life and a preoccupation with the fallibility of understanding and communication which sometimes encourages critics to find Decadent elements in his work, but his more obvious affinities are with the French Theatre of the Absurd. Critics have also found Decadent tendencies in the introspective and *impuissant* work of Italo Svevo, who published his early novels at the same time as D'Annunzio but had to wait thirty years to be "discovered". The Decadent Movement itself probably had more influence, albeit of a negative kind, on Filippo Marinetti's short-lived Futurist Movement, which sought to integrate the Decadent's suspicion of tradition into a far more revolutionary and forward-looking manifesto. If D'Annunzio was not the only Italian Decadent, therefore, he certainly deserves to be considered as the only important one.

****

Despite being the home of Nietzsche, who was an important influence on several notable Decadent writers, Germany produced no Decadent Movement of its own in the nineteenth century, and such traces of Decadent attitude and style which can be found in German writers before the Great War are few and fugitive. As in Italy, the German nation-state was of recent provenance - it was not finally clarified until 1866 - and no German city could begin to compare with Paris and Rome. German censorship was more rigid even than English censorship where matters of moral indecency were concerned, and this too was a strong deterrent to authors tempted by the charm of the Decadent style; Otto Bierbaum's *avant garde* literary journal *Pan* (founded 1894) was, in consequence, rather less ambitious than the *Yellow Book*. In addition, the temper of German Romanticism and the subsequent reaction against it had been markedly different from that of French Romanticism. The influence which Nietzsche had on writers who were already familiar with Rousseau was not the same as the influence which he had on those reared on Hegel or Schopenhauer.

Although Nietzsche had certain ideas which appealed strongly to the Decadent consciousness - including the idea that the modern world had been made rotten by the dominance of a cowardly "ethic of the herd" - he was by no means a Decadent himself. His notion of when and where the rot of historical decadence had first set in was radically different from Montesquieu's, pointing the accusing finger not at the mad emperors of Rome but at Euripides and Socrates, who had previously been thought of as the great heroes of Greek cultural magnificence and Enlightenment. There was nothing at all in Nietzsche to give an atom of encouragement to a cult of artificiality (which accounts for his greater influence on the English Decadents, who could not take such a cult seriously) and he had not time at all for *impuissance*, dedicating his later work to a lyrical celebration of the "will to power" which must convert man into *übermensch*. Even those German writers who could not contrive a similar hopefulness - Thomas Mann remained a doubter whose work is haunted by the idea of society possessed by an incurable sickness - were nevertheless deflected away from French Decadent consciousness.

It is not surprising, in view of this, to find German studies of decadent aristocracy presented in a style more reminiscent of de Roberto than D'Annunzio. Ricarda Huth's *Erinnerungen von Ludolf Ursleu dem Jungeren* (1893; tr. as *Unconquered Love*) is one example. The period produced some exotic and impressionistic poetry, notably that of Max Dauthenday, but Symbolism made less impact than a belated renewal of native *sturm und drang*. The nearest thing to *spleen* and *impuissance* which German writing produced was Jakob Wassermann's *trägheit* (sloth), which was extensively discussed in *Caspar Hauser* (1908).

The most significant work of the *fin de siècle* period in Germany which invites discussion on account of its Decadent elements is Frank Wedekind's play *Lulu*. Evidence of the strength of German taboos is provided by the fact that the work was not published in its proper from until 1962, but it was known in bowdlerized and divided form as *Der Erdgeist* (1895; tr. as *Earth Spirit*) and *Die Büchse der Pandora* (1902; tr. as *Pandora's Box*). The play is an elaborate account of the destructiveness which can overcome the sexual impulse in a society where it is rigidly repressed, dressed up with various baroque elements in order to mask and excuse its underlying ferocity.

Mention must also be made, however, of the slightly later writings of Hans Heinz Ewers, who wrote poetry, short stories and novels in a determinedly Decadent vein. Two of his novels featuring the Decadent anti-hero Frank Braun enjoyed considerable commercial success; the better of them is *Die Zauberlehrling* (1907; tr. as *The Sorceror's Apprentice*), in which Braun seeks relief from boredom in persuading a peasant girl that she is a saint, and then must watch as she pursues her career to the bitter end of martyrdom; this was followed by the stylistically-exotic *Alraune* (1911), which inverts the theme by producing a female incarnation of evil. Ewers later added a third novel to the series, *Vampir* (1922; tr. as *Vampire* and *Vampire's Prey*) in which Braun is infected with vampiric compulsions.

Wedekind became an important precursor of German Expressionism and his work came to seem much more important and prophetic when, in the years following Germany's humiliation in the Great War, Berlin suffered a dramatic inversion of former intolerance and experienced a virtual epidemic of calculated Decadence. Ewers, having been an ardent German patriot campaigning for his country in America during World War I, was converted to Nazism but could not adapt to the pressures of that creed as well as D'Annunzio adapted to Mussolini's Fascism, and seems to have ended his life as an official non-person.

Ewers was not the only German writer to go to America; most of the others, for obvious reasons, never came back. It is probably worth noting as an afterword to the story of absent German Decadence that one of the most interesting works of American Decadent fiction was written (in English) by an emigré who, like Ewers, subsequently became a Nazi. George Sylvester Viereck's *The House of the Vampire* (1907) is a homoerotic fantasy of enervation by psychic theft which has strong echoes of Wilde's *Picture of Dorian Gray*. Viereck's poetry is also in a distinctly Decadent vein, and he went on to write with Paul Eldridge a series of popular novels featuring the erotically-inclined adventures of the Wandering Jew and other immortals.

****

It is hardly surprising that the search for American Decadents should first stumble across a European emigré; America is the last place on Earth which one would expect to provide fertile soil for literary Decadence. It was the nation most thoroughly infected with the mythology of progress and the home of the frontier spirit; in the eyes of every right-thinking American, decadence was a purely European problem - even though America had in Edgar Allan Poe the writer who had inspired Baudelaire more than any other.

Poe had no followers in his own country as enthusiastic as Baudelaire and Andreyev. Such accounts of hereditary decadence leading to exotic perversion as "Berenice" and "Morella" had far greater influence in France than in Poe's native land. The Poesque elements in Nathaniel Hawthorne's work are strictly subdued by moralism, although the curious fantasy "Rappaccini's Daughter" may have given Baudelaire the cue which led him to call his seminal work *Les Fleurs du Mal*. Later generations tended to regard Poe as an un-American wimp, and this, combined with a rigid puritanism which considered almost all French fiction indecent and all pretensions to literary style effete, was even more powerful as a disincentive to would-be Decadents than the intellectual climate in turn-of-the-century Germany. It was an attitude which infuriated some of the more cultured immigrants, for its absurd self-righteousness as well as its idiocy, and it may be credited with having eventually produced, by way of angry reaction, one of the most determinedly and extravagantly Decadent of all literary productions: the novella *Fantazius Mallare* (1922) by the Russian-born Ben Hecht. Like most suspect literary productions of its day this was issued in a limited edition for "private circulation" to "subscribers" because it could not be openly sold - a fate which overcame almost all French fiction, Decadent or not.

Despite its lack of promise as host to a Decadent Movement, however, some American writing was marginally infected by the spirit of Decadence. Gautier was first translated in the U.S.A. in 1882 by Lafcadio Hearn, a writer of similar stylistic ambition and morbid interest. He was, however, too much of an outsider to survive happily in America and in 1890 he went to Japan, where he spent the remainder of his life writing essays and stories based in Japanese mythology, in languidly lapidary prose. Another writer briefly infected with Francophilic enthusiasms was Robert W. Chambers, who was an art student in Paris in the late 1880s. The influence of his Parisian experiences is elaborately displayed in his first two books, *In the Quarter* (1894) and *The King in Yellow* (1895). It is revealing that the stories are feeble except for a group in which the corollary influence of Poe is displayed in no uncertain terms - the first four items in the second book are a group of powerful baroque horror stories, among the best of their kind; while the fifth, "The Demoiselle D'Ys" is a heavily sentimentalized Gautieresque timeslip romance. The same impetus, slightly weakened, can be seen in one subsequent collection, the *Mystery of Choice* (1897), but

Chambers was then thoroughly reinfected with the attitude of his native culture and his work became carefully commercial and utterly trivial.

Part of the background to the *King in Yellow* stories was borrowed from the work of Ambrose Bierce, the most notable writer of horror stories to be found among Chambers' contemporaries. Despite his intense interest in the literary representation of abnormal mental states Bierce does not really warrant consideration as a Decadent; like Poe's work, his is the kind of thing which French Decadents would have loved to read for its eccentricity, but its aesthetic ambitions are not flaunted, its erotic elements are carefully understated, and it is devoid of any preoccupation with *spleen* or *impuissance*. But Bierce was to influence, directly and indirectly, several other writers who lived, as he did, on the Western seaboard of the U.S.A., among them Edward Markham and George Sterling.

Sterling, in particular, was Bierce's protegé and found in Bierce one of the few men able to provide an understanding and sympathetic audience for his morbid and highly-decorated work. He was doomed to be esoteric and largely unread while he lived (and to remain so) but he enjoyed a brief moment of celebrity - or notoriety - when Bierce persuaded *Cosmopolitan* to publish his bizarre poetic masterpiece "A Wine of Wizardry" (1907). Like Hecht's *Fantazius Mallare* this piece reacts against an arid aesthetic climate by going to extremes, but in a different direction; it is a hymn to escapism far bolder than Chambers' "Demoiselle D'Ys" or Arthur Machen's *Hill of Dreams*.

Sterling not only wrote Decadent verse but tried to live a Decadent life-style, from which he eventually perished - but not before he had attracted a handful of protegés of his own, among them Clark Ashton Smith,

77

who took over where Sterling left off as the poet of American Decadence, translating a good deal of Baudelaire and writing his own imitations thereof before outdoing "A Wine of Wizardry" in his own escapist epic "The Hashish-Eater" (1922). Like Sterling, though, Smith had no hope of finding a wide audience for his work, and he was able to carry his enthusiasm into prose fiction only because of a brief period of fluky fashionability which he enjoyed in the pulp magazines *Weird Tales* and *Wonder Stories*, for which he produced some of the most lushly exotic fantasies ever written.

With Smith, the outsidest of all outsiders, the hardly-started story of American Decadence effectively came to an end, its marvellous visions cast out to the furthest reaches of time and space in search of the ultimate extremes. It was, in its fashion, an end which one cannot deem entirely inappropriate, for Smith's was excellent work despite its absurd *milieu*, and may serve as a sharp reminder that Decadence never really did get the audience it needed - and perhaps deserved - even in the gloriously decadent city which gave it birth, let alone in any of the world's other great cities.

****

8.

ECHOES IN TIME:
THE ACHIEVEMENTS OF DECADENCE

Obsolete literary fads never really die, nor do they entirely fade away. They merely dissolve into the organized chaos of potential influences, preserved in memory as treasures to be looted, follies to be satirized, and bad examples to be avoided.

Any account of the achievements of Decadence must begin by admitting that the foundations of the movement were built on sand. Its central myths were quite false, and its shocking innovations have lost their shock-value in becoming familiar. A sensitive study of history provides little evidence to support the notion that all great civilizations must crumble because the comforts consequent upon success are fatally corrosive of further ambition or effective self-defense, and modern psychology has quite outgrown the idea that genius is a species of madness. There is nothing particularly startling to the modern mind in the notion of art for art's sake, and there is no longer the least air of mystery surrounding hashish or opium derivatives. Nobody these days talks about a cult of artificiality, but the merest glance at the contemporary genre of "shopping and fucking" best-sellers testifies to the fact that its modern equivalent is more of a religion. A contemporary essay on the defence of cosmetics, however broadly the term might be construed, could only be a conservative reaction against the shocking radicalism of greens and feminists.

One could, of course, make out an apologetic case for Decadent Movements on the grounds that they helped lay the groundwork for subsequent movements like Surrealism and Modernism, and offered useful exemplars to writers as varied as Gide, Cocteau, Céline and Genet, but that would be rather weak-kneed. The Decadents themselves certainly did not intend to be a passing phase on the way to something more worthwhile; they thought they were harbingers of the apocalypse, and they wanted to reach an extreme which could not be surpassed. Had they been able to anticipate the extent of their failure to achieve those extremes which were realized within forty or fifty years of their passing they would probably have been depressed - but because they were Decadents, they were no strangers to depression, and one more *impuissant* shrug of the shoulders would have been no big deal.

Let us, then, in remembering the celebrants of Decadence, try to discover something more appropriate to say than they they added a few extra drops to the great stream of literary history. Let us try to find something which they say directly to modern readers, which modern readers need to hear.

If we do this, we will find that there are two elements of the Decadents' gospel which have neither been falsified nor over-familiarized. Both, as might be expected, are denials of things which the people of the 1880s would very much like to have believed, and which the people of the 1990s are *still* trying to believe. The Decadents were right, and are right, about two matters - one important and one admittedly trivial - which have not yet been universally conceded, but ought to be.

The important matter about which the Decadents were right is their opinion of the veneration of Nature. They thought that it was stupid; it was; and it is. Where they had to live with the legacy of Rousseau we have to live with a growing Ecological Mysticism which is a lethal pollutant of green politics and the parent of an indiscriminate hostility to exactly those aspects of technological progress which might yet save us from the filthy mess which we are making of the world. There is a widespread popular misconception to the effect that turning forests into deserts and rivers into sewers is the perogative of modern men armed with sophisticated technologies, and that if only technological progress could be reversed all would be well. In the ears of people who believe such nonsense there is no more euphonious word than "natural", which has come to be a synonym for "good".

The Decadents treated such ideas with a scorn which they thoroughly deserve. They recognised that all the triumphs of mankind are based in artifice, and that the principal condition of the success of human life is a secure and complete control of nature. The Decadents would have condemned as shallow fools those critics who find something perverse and unnatural in the notion of taking control of genetic processes so that we may become true governors of creation, and they would have been right to do so. The Decadents might have remained pessimistic about the actual project of deploying sophisticated techniques of genetic engineering in time to save the world from ruin, but they would have had no doubts about its propriety. If one can speak at all about a Decadent Ideal World (and one has to admit that there is a certain paradox in the notion) then that Ideal World would be a world in which people had total control over all matters of biology, including their own anatomy, physiology and physical desires; it is an Ideal which we can and ought to share, though far too few of us actually do.

The trivial matter about which the Decadents were right, although this point might arguably be reckoned as a mere corollary of the first, concerns their cynical attitude to matters of sexual morality - and, indeed, their dismissal of the ambitions of all prescriptive systems of morality. They were right - but not particularly original - when they argued that no set of rules could ever succeed in dampening the perverse curiosity of the human mind; they were right, too, to be severely sceptical as to whether that acknowledged impossibility is altogether to be regretted. The mythology of ideal romantic love which is peddled in today's world is not much different from that which was peddled in the 1880s, and there are probably no more people who think that actual contemporary relationships are accurately reflected in that mythology than there were then; that is not surprising. What is surprising is there are probably as many people, or more, who think that the world would be a far better place if the real world were more like the mythological world of romantic fiction. A healthy dose of Decadent fiction may still be capable of curing victims of that particular delusion, and ought at least to be tried.

Even the Decadents, it must be confessed, did have a tendency to regret the non- existence of Ideal Love, but their sense of tragedy was outside the common rut. They shed their fair share of tears over the fact that real people have to make do with lesser affections, which must of necessity be granted to relatively undeserving recipients. But they were also prepared to take an experimental attitude to the problem by suggesting that if the mythology turned out to be an abject failure (as it inevitably would) perhaps it might be stretched and twisted into a better shape by trial and error.

The quest for new sensations - which, inevitably, can also be seen as a search for new sins - is sometimes seen even by the Decadents themselves as little more than an elaborate process of self-destruction, but its underlying attitude of combative derision towards received mythology is perfectly healthy. We live, alas, in a world which is still obsessed with the project of finding and maintaining the perfect relationship, and where a substantial fraction of the periodical press, ads and all, is devoted to an extraordinary elaboration of the typical concerns of "agony columns". The Decadents can tell us, as they told their own contemporaries, that all the advice about how to build the ideal relationship is not only bullshit but *unnecessary* bullshit, and that the only sensible reaction to the discovery that it never really works is to say "What the hell!" and try something else instead. Decadents admit that the way the cards are stacked, everyone's life is likely to be a long catalogue of mistakes - but they point out that one doesn't actually have to keep making the *same* mistake over and over and over again.

It is mainly because the Decadents say these things, which still need to be said, that there is still some point in reading them. Their stylistic coquetry is not empty even when its illusions have been stripped away; their calculated indecency still poses a real challenge. They can still be alarming and surprising, and even their constant flirtation with certain ideas fit only for the dustbin (which they were unfortunate enough to inherit from incompetent intellectuals) still has a certain redeeming quaintness. Stricken they might have been by *ennui, spleen*, and *impuissance*, but when the time came for a Big Push they were never afraid - in spite of their debilitating neurasthenia, cynical wit and calculated charm - to go over the top and charge headlong into the barbed wire.

****

A SAMPLER OF FRENCH DECADENT TEXTS

1.

TO THE READER
by Charles Baudelaire

Stupidity, soul-sickness, and errant sin,
Possess our hearts and work within our flesh,
Our fond remorse is nursed within the crèche,
As beggars take their lice to be their kin.

Our sins are stubborn, our penitence is mean;
We fatten the confessions that we make,
We revel in the laxness of the path we take,
As though our paltry tears could wash us clean.

Cushioned by evil, Satan Trismegistus rests,
Ministering to our souls entranced,
Melting the metal of desire enhanced
By the vain sublimation of the alchemists.

The Devil pulls the strings which make us dance,
We find delight in the most loathsome things;
Some furtherance of hell each new day brings,
And yet we feel no horror in that rank advance.

Like some impoverished debauchee greedily teasing
The martyred breast of some ancient whore,
We steal what joy we can as we go before,
Though the fruit has shrivelled with the squeezing.

A great demonic host, a million parasites,
Swarms and seethes within our drunken brains,
With every breath we take, the mortifying pains
Descend invisibly to spread their fatal blights.

If rape and poison, cutting blade and fire,
Have not inscribed their tale upon our souls,
To display the banality of our appointed roles,
They fail because we find the thought too dire.

But among the jackals and the carrion-birds
The monkeys, the scorpions and the serpentine,
And the monsters which screech and howl and whine,
In the infamous chaos of our vicious words,

There is one more stained with evil than the rest.
Although it makes no signs or savage cries,
It cannot rest content until the whole world lies
In desolate ruins, and sorely distressed;

It is that tedious malaise of the tired mind
Which sheds a tear while lost in opium dreams.
You know him, reader, and all his stupid schemes,
For we, my brother hypocrite, are of the same sad kind.

****

2.

THE GLASS OF BLOOD
by Jean Lorrain

She stands at a window beside a lilac curtain patterned with silver thistle. She is supporting herself upon the sill while looking out over the courtyard of the hotel, at the avenue lined with chestnut-trees, resplendent in their green autumn foliage. Her pose is business-like, but just a little theatrical: her face uplifted, her right arm carelessly dangling.

Behind her, the high wall of the vast hallway curves away into the distance; beneath her feet the polished parquet floor carries the reflected gleam of the early morning sun. On the opposite wall is a mirror which reflects the sumptuous and glacially pure interior, which is devoid of furniture and ornament save for a large wooden table with curved legs. On top of the table is an immense vase of Venetian glass, moulded in the shape of a conch-shell lightly patterned with flecks of gold; and in the vase is a sheaf of delicate flowers.

All the flowers are white: white irises, white tulips, white narcissi. Only the textures are different, some as glossy as pearls, others sparkling like frost, others as smooth as drifting snow; the petals seem as delicate as translucent porcelain, glazed with a chimerical beauty. The only hint of colour is the pale gold at the heart of each narcissus. The scent which the flowers exude is strangely ambivalent: ethereal, but with a certain sharpness somehow suggestive of cruelty, whose hardness threatens to transform the irises into iron pikes, the tulips into jagged-edged cups, the narcissi into shooting-stars fallen

86

from the winter sky.

And the woman, whose shadow extends from where she stands at the window to the foot of the table - she too has something of that same ambivalent coldness and apparent cruelty. She is dressed as if to resemble the floral spray, in a long dress of white velvet trimmed with fine-spun lace; her gold-filligreed belt has slipped down to rest upon her hips. Her pale-skinned arms protrude from loose satin sleeves and the white nape of her neck is visible beneath her ash-blonde hair. Her profile is clean-cut; her eyes are steel-grey; her pallid face seems bloodless save for the faint pinkness of her thin, half-smiling lips. The overall effect is that the woman fits her surroundings perfectly; she is clearly from the north - a typical woman of the fair-skinned kind, cold and refined but possessed of a controlled and meditative passion.

She is slightly nervous, occasionally glancing away from the window into the room; when she does so her eyes cannot help but encounter her image reflected in the mirror on the opposite wall. When that happens, she laughs; the sight reminds her of Juliet awaiting Romeo - the costume is almost right, and the pose is perfect.

Come, night! come Romeo! come, thou day in night!
For thou wilt lie upon the wings of night
Whiter than new snow upon a raven's back.

As she looks into the mirror she sees herself once again in the long white robe of the daughter of the Capulets; she strikes the remembered pose, and stands no longer in the plush corridor of the hotel but upon a balcony mounted above the wings of the stage in a great theatre, beneath the dazzling glare of the electric lights, before a Verona of painted cloth, tormenting herself with whispered words of love.

Wilt thou be gone? it is not yet near day:
It was the nightingale, and not the lark,

That pierced the fearful hollow of thine ear.
Nightly she sings on yon pomegranate-tree:
Believe me, love, it was the nightingale.

And afterwards, how fervently she and her Romeo would be applauded, as they took their bows before the house!

After the triumph of Juliet, there had been the triumph of Marguerite, then the triumph of Ophelia - the Ophelia which she had recreated for herself, her unforgettable performance now enshrined in legend: *That's rosemary, that's for remembrance; pray you, love, remember!* All dressed in white, garlanded with flowers in the birch-wood! Then she had played the Queen of the Night in *The Magic Flute*; and Flotow's *Martha*; the fiancée of *Tannhaüser*; Elsa in *Lohengrin.* She had played the parts of all the great heroines, personifying them as blondes, bringing them to life with the crystal clarity of her soprano voice and the perfection of her virginal profile, haloed by her golden hair.

She had made Juliet blonde, and Rosalind, and Desdemona, so that Paris, St. Petersburg, Vienna and London had not only accepted blondes in those roles but had applauded blondes - and had come, in the end, to expect and demand blondes. That was all her doing: the triumph of La Barnarina, who, as a little girl, had run bare-legged across the steppe, asking no more and no less than any other girl of her age, lying in wait for the sleighs and the troikas which passed through the tiny village - a poor hamlet of less than a hundred souls, with thirty muzhik peasants and a priest.

She was the daughter of peasants, but today she is a marquise - an authentic marquise, a millionaire four times over, the wedded wife of an ambassador whose name is inscribed in the *livre d'or* of the Venetian nobles, and entered upon the fortieth page of the Almanack of

Gotha.

But this is still the same girl who once lived in the steppes, wild and indomitable. Even when she ceased to play in the falling snow, the snow continued to fall within her soul. She never sought lovers among the wealthy men and the crowned princes who prostrated themselves before her; her heart, like her voice, remained faultless. The reputation, temperament and talent of the woman partook of exactly the same crystalline transparency and icy clarity.

She is married now, though it is a marriage which was not contracted out of love, nor in the cause of ambition. She has enriched her husband more than he has enriched her, and she cares nothing for the fact that he was once a celebrity of the Tuileries in the days of the Empire, or that he became a star of the season at Biarritz as soon as he returned to Paris from the Italian court, following the disaster of Sedan.

Why, then, did she marry that one rather than another?

In fact, it was because she fell in love with his daughter.

The man was a widower, a widower with a very charming child, just fourteen years old. The daughter, Rosaria, was an Italian from Madrid - her mother had been Spanish - with a face like a Murillo archangel: huge dark eyes, moist and radiant, and a wide, laughing mouth. She had all the childish, yet instinctively amorous, gaiety of the most favoured children of the sunny Mediterranean.

Badly brought up by the widower whom she adored, and spoiled by that overgenerous treatment which is reserved for the daughters of the nobility, this child had been seized by an adoring passion for the diva whom she had so often applauded in the theatre. Because she was endowed with a tolerably pleasant voice the child had come to cherish the dream of taking lessons from La Barnarina. That dream, as soon as it was once denied, had quickly become an overpowering desire: an obsession, an *idée fixe*; and the marquis had been forced to give way. One day he had brought his daughter to the singer's home, secure in the knowledge that she would be politely received - La Barnarina was accepted as an equal by members of the finest aristocracies in Europe - but fully expecting her request to be refused. But the child, with all the gentleness of a little girl, with the half-grandiose manners of the young aristocrat, with the innocent warmth of the novice in matters of love, had amused, seduced and conquered the diva.

Rosaria had become her pupil.

In time, she had come to regard her almost as a daughter.

Ten months after that first presentation, however, the marquis had been recalled by his government to Milan, where he expected to be asked to accept a position as envoy to some remote region - either Smyrna or Constantinople. He intended, of course, to take his daughter with him.

La Barnarina had not anticipated any such event, and had been unable to foresee what effect it would have on her.

When the time for the little girl's departure came, La Barnarina had felt a sudden coldness possessing her heart, and suddenly knew that the separation would be intolerable: this child had become part of her, her own soul and her own flesh. La Barnarina, the cold and the dispassionate, had found the rock upon which her wave must break; the claims of love which she had kept at bay for so long now exerted themselves with a vengeance.

La Barnarina was a mother who had never given

birth, as immaculate as the divine mothers of the Eastern religions. In the flesh which had never yearned to produce fruit of its own there had been lit a very ardent passion for the child of another's loins.

Rosaria had also been reduced to tears by the thought of the parting; and the marquis soon became annoyed by the way the two women persistently sobbed in one another's arms. He quickly lost patience with the business of trying to patch up the situation, but hesitated to suggest the only possible solution.

"Oh papa, what are we to do?" pleaded Rosaria, in a choked whisper.

"Yes, marquis, tell us what to do," added the singer, as she stood before him embracing the young girl.

So the marquis, spreading his arms wide with the palms open, smiling as sadly as Cassandra, was left to point the way to the obvious conclusion.

"I believe, my dear children, there is one way..."

And with a grand salute, a truly courtly gesture, to the unhappy actress, he said:

"You must leave the stage and become my wife, so that you may take charge of the child!"

And so she married him, leaving behind the former life which she had loved so ardently and which had made her so rich. At the height of her career, and with her talent still in full bloom, she had left behind the Opera, her public, and all her triumphs. The star became a marquise - all for the love of Rosaria.

It is that same Rosaria for whom she is waiting at this very moment, slightly ruffled by impatience, as she stands before the high window in her white lace and her soft white velvet, in her pose which is just a little theatrical because she cannot help remembering Juliet awaiting the arrival of Romeo!

Romeo! As she silently stammers the name of

Romeo, La Barnarina becomes even paler.

In Shakespeare's play, as she knows only too well, Romeo dies and Juliet cannot survive without his love; the two of them yield up their souls together, the one upon the corpse of the other - a dark wedding amid the shadows of the tomb. La Barnarina - who is, after all, the daughter of Russian peasants - is superstitious, and cannot help but regret her involuntary reverie.

Here, of all places, and now, of all times, she has dreamed of Romeo!

The reason for her distress is that Rosaria, alas, has come to know suffering. Since the departure of her father she has changed, and changed considerably. The poor darling's features have been transfigured: the lips which were so red are now tinged with violet; dark shadowy circles like blurred splashes of kohl are visible beneath her eyes and they continue to deepen; she has lost that faint ambience, reminiscent of fresh raspberries, which testifies to the health of adolescents. She has never complained, never having been one to seek sympathy, but it did not take long for La Barnarina to become alarmed once she saw that the girl's complexion had taken on the pallor of wax, save for feverish periods when it would be inflamed by the colour of little red apples.

"It is nothing, my dear!" the child said, so lovingly - but La Barnarina hurried to seek advice.

The results of her consultations had been quite explicit, and La Barnarina felt that she had been touched by Death's cold hand. "You love that girl too much, madame," they had said, "and the child in her turn has learned to love you too much; you are killing her with your caresses."

Rosaria did not understand, but her mother understood only too well; from that day on she had begun to cut the child off from her kisses and embraces; desperately, she had gone from doctor to doctor - seeking out the celebrated and the obscure, the empirically-inclined and the homeopathic - but at every turn she had been met with a sad shake of the head. Only one of them had taken it upon himself to indicate a possible remedy: Rosaria must join the ranks of the consumptives who go at dawn to the abattoirs to drink lukewarm blood freshly taken from the calves which are bled to make veal.

On the first few occasions, the marquise had taken it upon herself to lead the child down into the abattoirs; but the horrid odour of the blood, the warm carcasses, the bellowing of the beasts as they came to be slaughtered, the carnage of the butchering...all that had caused her terrible anguish, and had sickened her heart. She could not stand it.

Rosaria had been less intimidated. She had bravely swallowed the lukewarm blood, saying only: "This red milk is a little thick for my taste."

Now, it is a governess who has the task of conducting the girl into the depths; every morning they go down, at five or six o'clock, to that devils' kitchen beneath the rue de Flandre, to an enclosure where the blood is drained from the living calves, to make the white and tender meat.

And while the young girl makes her descent into that place, where bright-burning fires warm the water in porcelain bathtubs to scald the flesh of the slaughtered beasts, La Barnarina stays here, by the window in the great hallway, perfectly tragic in her velvet and her lace, mirroring in her mode of dress the snow-whiteness of the narcissi, the frost-whiteness of the tulips, and the nacreous whiteness of the irises; here, striking a pose with just a hint of theatricality, she watches.

She keeps watch upon the courtyard of the hotel,

and the empty avenue beyond the gate, and her anguish reaches into the uttermost depths of her soul while she anticipates the first kiss which the child will place upon her lips, as soon as she returns: a kiss which always carries an insipid trace of the taste of blood and a faint hint of that odour which perpetually defiles the rue de Flandre, but which, strangely enough, she does not detest at all - quite the contrary - when it is upon the warm lips of her beloved Rosaria.

****

3.

LANGUOR
by Paul Verlaine

I am the Empire at the end of its decline,
Which awaits the Barbarians fair and tall
While composing acrostics in an idle scrawl
To which sad sunlight lends its golden shine.

The lonely soul is tediously sick at heart.
Down there, they say, the bloody combat wanes.
So faint are the desires, so slow the pains,
No need can ever flourish, nor existence start.

No need, nor facile taste of death at last!
Alas, all gone! Is the laughter of Bathyllus done?
All supped, all eaten, the cause of silence won!

Alone, a newborn poem into the fire to cast,
Alone, to be neglected by dishonest slaves,
Alone, not knowing what the sick heart craves!

****

4.

THE GRAPE-GATHERERS OF SODOM
by Rachilde

When the day dawned, the land was fuming like a
fermenter filled with the grapes of wrath. The vineyard
surrounded by the vast and troubled plain shone redly in
the fierce light of the sun - a sun as bright as the hot fires
which were used to start the grapes fermenting, and
which made the huge pips burst out of them like black
eyes popping out of their sockets. The vineyard seemed,
for a while, to be set at the bottom of a pit of seething
bitumen. While it displayed its own red-and-gold foliage
to the sky, a seeming abundance of monstrous riches, the
ground all around it gave vent to writhing plumes of grey
smoke, which glittered in the sunlight like molten metal.

As the luscious fruits of the vineyard were ripening,
so the softened red clay of the carnal earth was yielding
its own produce of poisonous volcanic gas. Like an over-
fecund beast released from its tethers in order to drop its
litter, the land threw out her vaporous garlands: imploring
arms held out towards the newly-risen sun, delirious
with sinfully ecstatic joy. As the sun-baked surface
cracked here and there, hot liquids oozed out of her like
thick tears. These irruptions gradually condensed into
lustrous brown masses: prodigious fruits of the earth's
womb, distilled by volcanic fire, their dark hue suggestive
of satanic sugar. And from some of these clustered and
half-rotted fruits there continued to ooze a gentle and
abominable liquor whose gaseous exhalation intoxicated

the bees which swarmed about the vineyard, tempting them to their deaths.

Between the clouds, so red that one would have thought them all afire, and the plain, so yellow that one might have believed it powdered with saffron, no creature stirred nor bird sang. Only the vineyard was alive, possessed by a dull humming of busy insects like the gentle vibration of a simmering kettle.

In the midst of that forest of golden boughs, on the rim of the primitive fermenting vat - a huge trough of raw granite, crudely hollowed-out, like an altar of human sacrifice - there sat a fabulous lizard clad in sparkling viridian scales, with darting eyes the colour of hyacinths; it stretched itself out enigmatically, occasionally raising its silvery belly as it took a deep breath. It, too, was intoxicated by the drifting vapours, almost to the point of death.

****

Little by little, as the day progressed, the incendiary glow reflected in the clouds became fainter; they gradually paled, became opalescent, and slowly dissipated. The sky's hot light was gradually concentrated into that solitary blaze which was the sun; the clear sky took on the appearance of the blue sheen which metal has when it has been seared by a fierce torch.

The land of the tribes of Israel extended as far as the eye could see, faintly dappled by the shadows of slender fig-trees. Every one of those puny trees trailed its palmate leaves as though dissatisfied with its lot, and their lighter branches, all entwined, were ringed by unnatural excrescences of sap like amber bracelets. Their trunks had been deformed by the unfortunate combination of the fire above and the fire below, their pliant contours twisted and warped.

Far away, beyond the most distant of these clumps of trees, there stood the protective wall of a town. Behind the wall loomed a tall tower made of stone as white as ivory or bleached bone, whose spire stood out sharply against the vivid colour of the sky, like a road into the infinite or a spiralling flock of great white birds in search of a place to roost.

There emerged from the walled town a party of Sodomites, heading for the vineyard.

The party was headed by a gloomy old man, perhaps a centenarian twice over, whose bony and tremulous head was devoid of hair and who had long since lost all his teeth. He was dressed in a linen tunic which was loosely gathered about his rickety limbs, hanging upon him like a shroud. He was the father, chief and patriarch of the party which he led, and as he marched before them his stern forehead shone with reflected sunlight like a rectangular star as bright as the moon. He directed his charges by signalling to them with his staff, having long since given up speech.

On either side of the patriarch marched his eldest sons: huge and robustly healthy men with luxuriant black beards. One of them, whose name was Horeb, carried suspended from his leathern belt several shining metal cups, which struck one another melodiously as he strode along.

Behind this leading group there came a group of younger sons, headed by one Phaleg, a nearly-naked giant whose smooth flesh was like veined marble, whose beard was rust-red, and who carried on his head a stack of wicker baskets, some of which contained wheat-cakes.

Further behind, keeping a respectable distance, came playful adolescents who were clad in short robes girdled with ornately-embroidered sashes; their fair girlish tresses streamed behind them as they capered about. The most handsome of these was a child with lips the colour of ripe plums or the blurred violet of the distant horizon; his name was Sinéus, and he had innocently dressed his half-open goatskin tunic with plucked flowers. When Sinéus entered the graveyard, the bees swarmed about him, taking him for some mysterious honey-bearer because of his golden appearance, but they did him no harm.

After singing a celebratory hymn the grape-gatherers began to work, using baskets to carry the grapes from the vines to the fermenting-vat. The older ones, as measured and efficient in their movements as they always were, reached up to take the best grapes; the younger ones hurriedly grabbed those which came most easily to hand, crying out with excitement all the while. After a time the old man, who had set himself down on the rim of the stone trough, stood up and raised his staff to signal that everyone should gather round to admire the full baskets; then he sat down again and the work of emptying the baskets into the stone vat began.

As they worked, some of them were accidentally splashed about the legs by the ruddy juice, others smeared it haphazardly upon their clothing. Sinéus fervently set about treading the grape-harvest, occasionally mixing in with it a handful of wild roses. Beneath the hot sun their labour was very tiring, and when they had filled the stone trough they lay down around it to sleep. The old patriarch remained on the rim of the vat, still sitting up but quite immobile, looming over the liquefied mass of the trampled grapes like an image of some long-dead king preserved in stone.

****

After a while, there emerged furtively from the shade of the nearest clump of fig-trees a very strange creature: a girl.

She was thin and wan, and naked - but she was burnished by the sun, and covered with a light down of fair hair, so that it seemed as if she were clothed in linen embroidered with filamentous threads of gold. Her forehead struck such a contrast with the blue of the sky that it gleamed like a polished spear-head. Her long yellow hair was gathered up into a sheaf; her heels were as round as peaches, bouncing off the ground as she danced forward like a delighted animal; but the two nipples upon her breasts were very dark, almost black - as if they had been badly burned.

The girl approached the sleeping Sinéus, who slept very soundly, having eaten abundantly of those grapes which he had gathered and trodden. She too ate greedily, and having done so she lay down beside the boy, entwining herself about him in a serpentine fashion. It was not long before her writhing caused the boy to wake, and he awoke groaning lamentably because he felt that some impure sensation was working within his flesh. He got up expeditiously, crying out to wake his brothers; they responded with roars of their own.

The old man awoke too, stretching forth his staff against the intruder with a deathly gleam in his eye. The girl was quickly surrounded by the entire company.

The girl was one of many who had been condemned as temptresses, and driven out of Sodom at the behest of the priests. In a mad fit of righteous wrath, the assembly of the men of God had decreed that the town must be relieved of the evil passions which haunted it from twilight until dawn. The girls of Sodom, they had decided, had been so badly guided by their lax mothers that they had become voluptuous vessels of iniquity which sapped the strength of the men of the town - strength which would be needed for the harvest, and must be conserved by rigid chastity.

In the grip of this madness, the men of Sodom had repudiated their wives and cast out their sisters; these women had been thrown into the streets, beaten and bruised, their clothes torn from their bodies, and chased by dogs into the wilderness without the walls. Driven into the desert, the women had been forced to cross the burning sands to seek refuge in Gomorrah. Many had died in the furnace of the noonday heat; a few had kept themselves alive by plundering the vineyards. But none of these accursed creatures had been brought to repentance, for their flesh was still inflamed by insensate desires, which took nourishment from the fiery heat of the sun and lusted also after those secret fires which were hidden beneath the surface of the plain.

Now, here was one of these bitches, driven by her appetite for the flesh of men to inflict her attentions upon a child no older than herself.

"Who are you?" Horeb demanded of her.

"I am Sarai!"

Sinéus buried his face in the crook of his elbow, hiding his eyes.

"What do you want?" said Phaleg.

"I am thirsty!"

Oh yes! It was evident to them all that she had a thirst in her!

The sons looked at one another, uncertain what to do, but their grim-faced father raised his staff to issue a command, and each one bowed down obediently to take hold of a stone.

The woman, her golden skin glistening in the sunlight, extended her arms like two beams of light.

She cried out, in a voice so strident that they

recoiled:

"A curse upon you all!"

"Oh yes," said Horeb then, "I recognise you. One night you came to steal the very best of my metal cups."

"I know you too," said Phaleg. "You have tempted me to sin on the Sabbath."

"As for me," cried Sinéus, with tears glimmering beneath his eyelids, "I do not know you at all, nor have I the slightest wish to know you!"

The old man brought down his staff.

"She must be stoned!" they roared in unison.

The woman had no opportunity to escape. Thirty stones were hurled at her all at once.

Her breasts were lacerated and splashed with red; her forehead was wreathed with bands of vermilion. She fell back, writhing desperately, her long hair was loosed, but it clung to her like binding ropes; she tried to make herself very small, and tried to crawl away after she fell, squirming like a snake; but she slipped and tumbled into the great vat where the grape-juice was fermenting. She groped feebly at the crushed clusters, but soon became inert, augmenting the blood of the grapes with the exquisite wine of her own veins. The brief convulsion of her death pulled her down into the depths of the trough, among the burst and trodden grapes which spurted out their black pips - but reflected in her rolling eyes, there was an expression of supreme malediction.

****

That evening, having completed their task in the saintly fashion required of them, the grape-gatherers distributed the wheat-cakes which they had brought with them, and filled their cups. They had not taken the trouble to remove the cadaver from the trough, and they were already drunk - more intoxicated by the killing than by the vintage which they had prepared. They continued to utter blasphemies against the luckless girl while they drank more of the horrible liquor they had made, saturated with poisonous love.

That same night - while unknown beasts howled in the distance all around them, and the atmosphere they breathed was heavy with the odour of sulphur, and the giant tower in the city took on a skeletal pallor beneath the dismal light of the moon - those men of Sodom committed for the first time their sin against nature, in the arms of their young brother Sinéus, whose soft shoulders somehow seemed to be flavoured with honey.

****

5.

AFTER THE DELUGE
by Arthur Rimbaud

As soon as the Flood of the imagination had subsided, a hare paused among the trefoils and the swaying bellflowers, and offered up his prayer to the rainbow through the strands of a spiderweb.

Oh, the precious stones that were in hiding! - the flowers which had begun to look about them!

In the filthy high street the tradesmen set out their stalls, and boats were dragged down to the sea, where the waves rolled in as they always seemed to do in ancient prints.

Blood was flowing - in Bluebeard's house, in the abattoirs, in the circuses where God had set his seal to whiten the windows. Blood and milk flowed together.

Beavers built dams. "Mazagrans" fumed in the taverns.

In the great glasshouses streaming with condensation, the children in mourning-dress beheld marvels.

A door slammed, and on the village green a child waved his arms; and all the cocks and weathervanes on all the church-steeples understood him as the shower burst over them.

Madame X set up a piano in the Alps. Church services and first communions were celebrated at the hundred thousand altars of the cathedral.

Caravans departed. And the Hotel Splendide was built out of the chaos of ice and polar darkness.

Forever more, the Moon heard jackals whining in

the deserts of thyme - and wooden-shoed peasants grunting in the orchards. Then in the midst of the violet forest all in bloom, Eucharis said to me that spring had come.

Surge forth, pond! foam upon the bridge and through the woods - black sheets and organs - lightning-streaks and thunder - climb and roll; waters and sorrows, arise and unleash the flood once more!

For since the waters have departed - oh, the precious stones concealing themselves, and the wide-open flowers! - what tedium there has been! And the Queen, the Sorceress who lights her fire in an earthenware pot, will never condescend to tell us what she knows, and what we need to know.

****

6.

DANAETTE
by Remy de Gourmont

While Danaette dressed herself after dinner, making her special and secret preparations, the snow began to fall.

Through the tiny holes in the lace curtains she watched it falling : the beautiful snow, falling, ever falling. It seemed so solemn and so sad, seemingly ignorant of the occult and ironic power which it had to fascinate the human eye. It seemed to be unaware of its own divine provenance, forgetful of those cold, bleak regions on high where its light crystals were born, disdainful of that human foolishness which analyses everything and comprehends nothing.

"There is a great battle going on in the sky," her old Breton maid said to her. "The angels are plucking out the plumes of their wings - and that is why it snows. As Madame knows very well."

The statement was peremptory. Madame did not dare to utter any contradiction. Every year, often several times during each winter, the old woman would impart that same confidence, always terminated by: "As Madame knows very well." It was irrefutable, and somehow rather menacing. The old servant had similar charming explanations for all kinds of events, always brief and neat, always stated as if they were manifestly obvious.

Madame, in consequence, ventured no reply at all; but as soon as her hair was done she dismissed the old woman.

She wanted to be alone - with the snow.

Her preparations were not yet half-complete, but she could no longer concentrate upon her toilette. She sat down on the divan near the fire, and watched with patient fascination the incessant and luminous flight of the downy feathers plucked from the wings of the angels.

What a bore it had become, dressing herself up like this! Adultery was always agreeable at first, in the early days when everything was still to be discovered - when one offered oneself up to the impatient and imperious kisses of one's lover; when one was driven on by curiosity; when one could think of nothing but the delights of a new and more complete initiation. Then, it was like a beautiful baptism in the delights of sin. But when the intensity of that brief phase began to weaken, it could never be renewed, no matter how one sought to deceive oneself; there always followed a detestable decline into ennui.

How tedious it all was! There were so many things to think of, so many excuses, so many suggestions to be made and precautions to be taken; it was all so discouraging, and - at the end of the day - so humiliating.

"It is always the same," she mused, without taking her eyes from the falling snow. "In spite of the cold, I had better take shoes instead of boots. He made the suggestion himself! The first time, he buttoned me up again so carefully, almost devoutly, balancing my leg upon his knee; the second time, he pulled a buttonhook out of his pocket and put it in my hand; the third time, he had not even thought of bringing one; and I was in sore distress.

"It is the same with the corset and the dress. He is impatient: he snatches at the hooks and gets the laces tangled up. I owe it to him, I suppose, to make up a special outfit which comes undone at a single stroke - in a twinkling of the eye I must stand naked, or very nearly. Yes, actually naked, for he wants me to wear chemises like cassocks, which open like curtains as soon as one has unsprung the tiny catches which hold them - this is the costume which supposedly suits my personality!

"But I must press on, regardless! I must put on my brassière and do up my corset, so that the old Breton will not say to me, in front of my husband, in such a scandalized fashion, when I come back by and by:

'Madame has gone out without her corset! As Madame knows very well!'

"Ah! how beautiful the snow is...!"

They are still falling, always falling, those soft and silky white feathers from the angels' wings.

She who had been a rebellious adulteress mere moments before became chaste and innocent again as that subtle and monotonous snow, perpetually falling past her window, exerted its hypnotic effect upon her sensibilities. The peremptory foolishness of the old maid was recalled to her mind, prompting a strange pang of sympathy for all the angels who had lost their feathers.

That would be a singular sight, would it not? An angel with plucked wings, like one of those geese one sometimes glimpsed in the farmyards of Normandy, which had yielded up its vestments in order to make soft pillows and eiderdowns for the convenience of adulterers!

It was a ridiculous, childish image - and anyhow, the plucked angels would still be angels, and angels were unconquerably beautiful creatures.

The snow fell on and on; it was so dense now that the air itself seemed to have condensed into a polar ocean of white stars, or a flight of immaculate seagulls. Now and then, a breath of wind would send the startled flakes hurrying across the window-pane, futilely trying to cling and settle before sliding down to pile up on the sill.

Forgetting the adulterous rendezvous which she had planned, Danaette became inordinately interested in these unexpected turbulences which dressed the window with clustered flakes. She found a peculiar pleasure in her observation of the way these cloudy constellations would form and crumble away again, slowly and majestically, with the absolute calm of obedience to their destiny. Her eyes began to close, tiredly, but she forced them to remain open, determined that she would not give in to her lassitude, resolved to stay as she was, watching the falling snow, for as long as it might condescend to fall.

She was defeated in this intention, though; her eyes closed again, drowsily, and she slowly drifted off until she was half asleep. But in the sight of her closed eyes, the snow continued to fall....

Now, the window no longer interrupted the flight of the guileless flakes. It was snowing inside the room: on the furniture, on the carpet, everywhere; it snowed on the divan where she was lying, prostrate with fatigue. One of the fresh flakes fell upon her hand; another on her cheek; another on her uncovered throat; and these touches - especially the last - excited in her a sensation of receiving unprecedented and exquisite caresses.

Still the flakes fell: her pale green robe was illuminated by them now, as if it were a meadow spangled with fresh daisies; before long her hands and her neck were completely covered, and her hair and her breasts too. This unreal snow was not melted by the warmth of her body, nor by the heat of the hearth; it dwelt upon her body, dressing her form in sparkling attire.

Deliciously icy, the kisses of the snow cut through her vestments - going, in spite of her defensive armour, in search of her skin and all the folds and creases of her curled-up body. It was marvellously gentle, and it had a uniquely voluptuous quality which she had most certainly never known before!

In truth, the Spirit of the Snow ravished and

possessed her - and Danaette allowed it to do so, curious to savour this new kind of adultery, delivering herself up to ineffable and almost frightful pleasure. She allowed herself to become the amorous prey of a Divine Caprice: a human lover unexpectedly elevated towards the unimaginable realm of the angels of perversity.

Ever and anon the snow fell, penetrating so profoundly into the depths of her enraptured being that she had no room in her for any other sensation than that of dying of cold, and being buried beneath the adorable kisses of the snow, and being embalmed by the snow - and, at the last, of being taken up and away by the snow, carried aloft by a wayward breath of turbulent wind, into some distant region of eternal snows, over infinite ranges of fabulous mountains...where all the dear little adulteresses, eternally beloved, were endlessly enraptured by the impatient and imperious caresses of the angels of perversity.

****

7.

LITANY TO SATAN
by Charles Baudelaire

(translated by James Elroy Flecker)

O grandest of the Angels, and most wise,
O fallen God, fate-driven from the skies,
Satan, at last take pity on our pain.

O first of exiles who endurest wrong,
Yet growest, in thy hatred, still more strong,
Satan, at last take pity on our pain!

O subterranean King, omniscient,
Healer of man's immortal discontent,
Satan, at last take pity on our pain.

To lepers and to outcasts thou dost show
That Passion is the Paradise below.
Satan, at last take pity on our pain.

Thou by thy mistress Death hast given to man
Hope, the imperishable courtesan.
Satan, at last take pity on our pain.

Thou givest to the Guilty their calm mien
Which damns the crowd around the guillotine
Satan, at last take pity on our pain.

Thou knowest the corners of the jealous Earth
Where God has hidden jewels of great worth.
Satan, at last take pity on our pain.

Thou dost discover by mysterious signs
Where sleep the buried people of the mines.
Satan, at last take pity on our pain.

Thou stretchest forth a saving hand to keep
Such men as roam upon the roofs in sleep.
Satan, at last take pity on our pain.

Thy power can make the halting Drunkard's feet
Avoid the peril of the surging street.
Satan, at last take pity on our pain.

Thou, to console our helplessness, didst plot
The cunning use of powder and of shot.
Satan, at last take pity on our pain.

Thy awful name is written as with pitch
On the unrelenting foreheads of the rich.
Satan, at last take pity on our pain.

In strange and hidden places thou dost move
Where women cry for torture in their love.
Satan, at last take pity on our pain.

Father of those whom God's tempestuous ire
Has flung from Paradise with sword and fire,
Satan, at last take pity on our pain.

Prayer

Satan, to thee be praise upon the Height
Where thou wast king of old, and in the night
Of Hell, where thou dost dream on silently.
Grant that one day beneath the Knowledge-tree
When it shoots forth to grace thy royal brow,
My soul may sit, that cries upon thee now.

****

8.

THE BLACK NIGHTGOWN
by Catulle Mendès

Fabrice was waiting for Geneviève. He was entirely at home, clad in a morning-coat, with Turkish slippers upon his stockingless feet, stretched out on the chaise longue beside the fireplace where the coals glowed redly. While he awaited the return of his dear and beautiful beloved he smoked a leisurely cigarette.

She should not be away for long - she had only gone out to do a little shopping. She did not like to be away too long from the love-nest which they had shared for six months, with its characteristic odour of rosewater and tobacco, mingled together because the room must serve as bedroom and smoking-room alike. Soon she would reappear, a little out of breath from having climbed the staircase, her cheeks quite rosy, and she would fall upon the chaise beside him, with that pretty little "ouf!" which no one else could say in quite that way; and they would slowly bring their lips together for another hectic and breathless round of kisses taken and kisses given.

There was a knock at the door.

Already?

No, she would not bother to knock.

"Come in," called Fabrice.

A young girl came in. She was slim, with unruly hair - evidently a servant. She was carrying a huge basket.

"Oh!" she said. "Pardon monsieur, I have made a mistake. I have come from the laundry with Madame's clothes, but this is not her dressing-room - I have made a mistake! The chambermaid told me that it was the second door in the corridor. If Monsieur would kindly show me..."

Fabrice, who had risen to his feet, shrugged his shoulders impatiently.

"Go ask Rosette!" he said.

"She has gone out, monsieur."

"Then put it down on the table or the armchair - it's not important - wherever you wish."

"Yes, monsieur," said the laundry-maid.

She carefully took the clothes out of the basket, some folded and others not, taking care to place them on the table in good order; then, when the basket was quite empty, she gave a little childlike bow, which unsettled her hair even more, and hurried out.

Instead of lying down again Fabrice came over to the table. He looked down at the pile of clothes - at the delicate fabrics, the whites and pale blues, the pinks and the flesh-colours - and he smiled at the memories which they called to mind.

Yes, most certainly, he remembered them all!

That nightgown of Indian muslin, so nearly transparent, with the short sleeves and the trimmings of Valencienne lace - wasn't that the one which he had seen sliding down from her lovely shoulders to reveal the length of her perfectly svelte and perfectly smooth young body, on that evening when, for the first time, Geneviève had surrendered her maidenly virtue? He remembered the rapt feeling inspired in him by the sight of her rounded, rose-tipped breasts, and the way he had hesitated before enfolding her in his arms, fearful of sacrificing to the intimacy of their kisses the delightful sight of her. How cruel it was that one must nearly lose sight of the person whose lips were pressed to one's own!

The other nightgowns recalled other nights to

mind - wonderful nights! And the stockings, too: woollen stockings, chequered stockings, everyday stockings, and stockings of raw silk with gold trimming. They made him think of her neat and slender feet, which he often held in his hands, where they would tremble like turtle-doves nestling together against the cold. And there was a pair of tights, too, which reminded him of a fancy which Geneviève had had, at the end of the carnival, to wear the costume of a page-boy beneath her discreet black domino.

And the light pantalettes of twilled silk! They too made him smile, for those pantalettes had caused a good deal of dissent between the two of them. She insisted on wearing them at all times, being too modest or too fearful of the wind which might lift her skirt to do otherwise, arguing in support of her insistence that she was afraid of having to descend a staircase at the same time that a man might be coming up, and observing that in winter it was so easy to catch rheumatism. He, in his turn, poured scorn upon the idea of hiding such a manly accoutrement beneath a petticoat, where it did not belong, and would not admit that any consideration of modesty, safety or health could possibly justify the inconvenience to which he was put in removing them. Oh, what merry squabbles they were! And yet, in spite of everything, how enchanted he was - how excited! - when Geneviève put on her pantalettes.

As he looked down at all these pretty garments which his beloved had worn next to her skin, Fabrice was overcome, little by little, by a boundless feeling of tenderness. His mistress was not only the prettiest of women, she was the most perfect; a paragon of all the virtues. She was so graceful - in her movements, her choice of perfumes, her smiles - and she was so extraordinarily open and honest! Yes, she was utterly virtuous, utterly faithful; he would not hear anything

115

that might be said to the contrary!

Fabrice, let it be said, was not one of those benighted men who was easily abused; no one could make a fool of him, thank God! He was not one of those imbeciles who were ever ready to believe tales of visits to an aunt's house in the Batignolles or the necessity of accompanying unhappily married friends to the solicitors in order to lend support to their pleas for separation. Oh no, *he* was a man who saw things clearly!

In all the time he had known her, Geneviève had never given him the slightest cause for alarm or suspicion. In her heart she had, undoubtedly, all the ingenuousness of a little girl; it was impossible for her to tell a lie - that was obvious in the innocence of her features, of her expressions, of her whole attitude. She, betray him! - the most hardened of sceptics could not conceive of such a possibility. The fidelity of Geneviève was so incontestable, so utterly beyond doubt, that Fabrice had never suffered a single pang of anxiety on those occasions when he was obliged, two or three times per month, to quit their love-nest and go to Paris to take care of his business affairs, leaving her all alone.

But even as he lost himself in this pleasant reverie - even as his heart slowly melted - he suddenly started with surprise. What was this that he had found? There, underneath the nightgown of Indian muslin, lurking among the woollen stockings and the chequered stockings, the everyday stockings and the raw silk stockings, and the light pantalettes, there was a black nightgown: a twilled silk nightgown which he did not recognise, which he had never seen before - no, never! - but which, in view of the fact that it had just come back from the laundry, must at some time have been worn....which must have been put on - and taken off!

Carried away by awful conviction and intoxicated

with fury, Fabrice would have reduced the tell-tale nightgown to rags, if Geneviève had not reappeared at precisely that moment, a little out of breath from having climbed the staircase, her cheeks quite rosy with the effort.

She cast herself down upon the chaise longue, with that pretty little "ouf" sound which no one else ever made in quite such a charming way.

At that moment, however, Fabrice could not care less whether she said "ouf!" well or badly!

"Madame," he cried, "you have deceived me! Oh, your ruses have been so cleverly contrived that you were doubtless led to think that you could not possibly be found out, and that you acted with impunity. But you reckoned without the vicissitudes of chance - that great enemy of all betrayal! Chance has delivered into my hands the proof of your guilt.

"Look here! Is this a nightgown or is it not? Is it black, this nightgown? Is it silk? You can hardly hope to persuade me that it is white and that it is cotton! It is silk, and it is black! And it is a garment which I have never seen you put on or take off in my presence. It is a nightgown, which I have never seen you wear in our bed - and yet it has been put on, and it has been taken off!

"I must congratulate you on your exquisite taste, Madame: what a fine contrast the blackness of the material must make with the delicate whiteness of your sinful flesh! Clad in silk so dark, you must seem to be a flake of snow which falls in the dark night, or the feather of a turtle-dove between a raven's wings. Miserable wretch! I wish I could put a bullet or a swordpoint into each of your white-rimmed eyes! Let us have it, if you please - your explanation! Tell me everything, without any reticence or subterfuge; and when I have heard it, we shall see whether my anger causes me to hurl you through the window, or whether my contempt will force me to show you the door!"

And while Fabrice - who, as one can easily judge, was not so very well brought up - was launched upon this tirade, what did Geneviève do?

She remained silent.

Advisedly so? Was she silent because she had nothing to say in her defence? Was she silent because, knowing as she did that the chemise was marked with her initials, it was impossible for her to pretend that there had been an error at the laundry? Or was it, perhaps, that she was completely innocent, and remained silent in the face of these calumnies because she would not lower herself to produce the explanation which would exonerate her?

When Fabrice had finished, the young girl got up.

"Adieu, monsieur," she said, turning towards the door.

She seemed so deeply offended, and displayed so dignified an appearance, that Fabrice felt suddenly and singularly troubled. There was in that attitude of injured innocence an inimitable *something* which made him pause, and which caused him to reconsider the awful suspicions which had been raised in him.

"Geneviève," he cried to her, "have you nothing to say in order to justify yourself?"

"No," she said.

"The nightgown does not belong to you, perhaps?"

"It is mine, monsieur."

"Perhaps it was formerly pink or blue, but you have had it dyed at the laundry?"

"It has always been black."

"Tell me, then, that you have not yet worn it - that you have neither put it on nor taken it off, because it is new, and that you sent it to the cleaners for some other reason."

"It is *not* new; I have worn it. Once again, adieu."

And she opened the door, evidently determined to leave. But then it seemed that her resolve faltered and that she was betrayed by her emotions. It seemed that she had not the heart to leave her beloved, no matter how jealous he was, no matter what insults he heaped upon her in his rage. The poor creature burst into a flood of tears.

"Oh, the ingrate!" she wailed. "He does not understand! He does not understand at all!"

Then, her stammering punctuated by the prettiest sobs in all the world, she said:

"You do not remember, of course, that you frequently leave me all alone, for days and nights at a time? Because of your business affairs, you say. And am I, desolate and abandoned, to put on one of the nightgowns - white, blue, or pink - that your impatient desire has so often slipped from my shoulders? How cruel you are to think so! No - for my nights of solitude, for my nights of widowhood, I have black nightgowns: mourning clothes, for the nights when I must go to sleep weeping for the lack of your caresses!"

He looked at her, hesitantly.

"Ah!" she continued. "How many times have I lain in my bed, full of bitterness and jealousy! How often, in the bitterness of my isolation have I wrenched and torn these dark nightgowns, while racked by memories of happier hours! Unless it has been mended, the very one you hold is torn - in more than one place, I think."

Fabrice bent down, and quickly unfolded the nightgown of black twilled silk. Indeed it was torn, here and here. Torn, as she had said it was! With such proof as this before him, he would surely be a very great fool to retain the slightest doubt!

Fabrice threw himself at the feet of his mistress, profusely begging her pardon.

It was, of course, the wisest course which he could possibly have taken; for how could anyone possibly believe that Geneviève - who had such very beautiful eyes, more beautiful still when her eyelashes were prettily moistened with tears - could ever soil her rosy lips with a lie?

****

9.

THE DOUBLE ROOM
by Charles Baudelaire

There is a room which resembles a daydream, a truly *spiritual* room, whose still, stale air is tinted with pink and blue.

Here the soul bathes in idleness, amid the aromas of regret and desire. There is something of the twilight here, in its blueness and its rosiness; it is as though one dreams sensuously during an eclipse.

The furniture extends itself, languidly prostrate. The furniture too seems to be dreaming, as if it existed in a state of permanent sleep, as all things vegetable and mineral do. The fabrics speak a language of silence, as flowers and daylight skies do, and sunsets.

These walls are undefiled by ugly paintings. Relative to the pure dream or the unanalysed impression, specific and assertive art is blasphemous. Here the light is perfectly sufficient in itself, harmonising with the delicacy of the shadows.

An infinitesimal hint of fragrance, chosen with exquisite taste, which carries with it a faint vaporous humidity, floats upon the air, lulling the drowsy mind as if it were a hothouse.

Hectic showers of muslin fall across the window and from the canopy of the bed, displayed like cascades of snow. Here upon this bed lies the Goddess, sovereign of dreams. Why is she here? Who brought her? What magical power installed her on this throne of dreaming and delight? What does it matter; she is here! I know who she is.

Those are the eyes which burn bright in the twilight; subtle and terrifying mirrors of the soul whose fearful malice I know so well! They draw, conquer and devour the unwary gaze of any who looks into them. I have made a study of them, those dark stars which command such curiosity and admiration.

What benevolent demon must I thank for thus surrounding me with mystery, silence, peace and perfumes? O bliss! That which we ordinarily call life, even when it can encompass happiness, has nothing to compare with this life beyond life which I have come to understand, and which I savour minute by minute, second by second.

No! There are no more minutes, there are no more seconds! Time is banished; it is Eternity which rules this place: an Eternity of delights!

****

But a heavy and terrible crash has thundered upon the door, and in nightmarish fashion I feel that I have been struck in the stomach by a pick-axe.

A Spectre has rudely intruded upon the feast. It is some bailiff come to taunt me in the name of the law; or some shameless courtesan come to tell a tale of woe and add the trivia of her existence to the sorrows of my own; or perhaps some editor's errand-boy come to demand a manuscript.

The heavenly room, the sovereign Goddess of Dreams - the Sylphide, as she was called by the great René - all their magic is dispelled by the crude hammering of the Spectre.

O horror! I remember! I remember! Yes, this tawdry place of infinite tedium is indeed where I live. There are the ridiculous furnishings, dusty and bumped; the hearth devoid of flames and glowing embers; the sad windows where the raindrops have made patterns in the grime; the manuscripts scribbed-over or incomplete; the calendar marked with crayon to show the inauspicious passing of the days.

And that otherworldly perfume which exalted me with heightened sensibility is replaced, alas, by the stale odour of old tobacco, mingled with a sickening dampness. The rankness of desolation lies upon everything here.

In this narrow world, full to the brim with disgust, only one familiar object makes me smile: the vial of laudanum; an old and terrible mistress. Like all mistresses, alas, she gives too freely of her caresses and her treacheries.

Oh yes, Time has resumed control! The sovereignty of that hideous ancient Time is now restored, and with him has come his demonic train of memories and regrets, fits and fears, anguishes and nightmares, angers and neuroses.

I can assure you that every passing second now carries a strong and solemn stress, and that each one, leaping from the clock, says: "I am Life: unbearable, implacable Life!"

There is but a single second in a man's life whose mission is to bring good news - *the* good news, which strikes such inexplicable terror into everyone.

Yes, Time rules again; he has resumed his brutal tyranny. And he drives me on, as if I were an ox, with his duplicate threat: "Get on with it, churl! Sweat, slave! Live, and be damned!"

****

10.

THE POSSESSED
by Jean Lorrain

"Yes," Serge told me, "I must be ill. I can no longer live here - and it isn't because I'm still feverish in spite of all the blood which the doctors have given me. My chest is much better, thank God!, and I can keep the bronchitis at bay if I'm careful - but I can't spend the winter here, because as soon as the November weather sets in I begin to hallucinate and I become prey to a truly frightening obsession. To put it bluntly, I'm too terrified to stay."

He read the thought in my eyes, and was quick to contradict me.

"Oh, don't blame it on the ether! I'm cured of that habit - completely cured. Besides which, it's poisonous. For two painful years it spread its poison through my being and filled me with I don't know what delicious sensations, but we know nowadays what it can do to one's arms and legs, and I began to notice an actual deformation in my limbs. It's been a year now since I last took ether.

"Anyway, why should I want to take it? I don't suffer from insomnia any more and my heart's okay. All that trouble with my lungs, and the atrocious pains which used to strike so suddenly in my left side while I lay in bed, making my flesh creep - all that is no more to me now than some far-off nightmare, like a vague memory of the Edgar Allan Poe stories which were read to me when I was a child. Honestly, when I think about that awful period of my life it seems more as if I dreamed it than actually lived through it.

"Nevertheless, I do have to go away. I'd be sure to

fall ill again as soon as November arrives, when Paris becomes fantastically haunted. You see, the strangeness of my case is that now I no longer fear the invisible, I'm terrified by reality."

"Reality?" I was a little disconcerted by what he had said, and could not help but repeat that last word questioningly.

"Reality," repeated Serge, stressing every syllable. "It's reality that haunts me now. It's the creatures of flesh and blood which I encounter every day in the street - the men and women who pass me by, all the anonymous faces in the hurrying crowds - which seem to me to be horrid apparitions. It is the sheer ugliness and banality of everyday life which turns my blood to ice and makes me cringe in terror."

He perched himself on the corner of the table.

"You know, don't you, how I used to be afflicted with visions? When I was a miserable wretch addicted to ether, I changed my apartment three times in two years, trying to escape the persecution of my dreams. I would literally fill my rooms with the phantoms of my mind; as soon as I found myself alone, behind closed doors, the air would be filled with the gibbering of ghosts. It was as though I were looking down a microscope to see a drop of water seething with microbes and infusoria; I would see right through the curtains of shadow to behold the frightful faces of the invisible beings within. That was the time when I couldn't look around my study without seeing strange pale hands parting the curtains or hearing the patter of strange bare feet behind the door. I was slowly being destroyed by my incessant struggle with things unknown: half-mad with anguish, dreadfully pale, cringing away from shadows and nervous of the slightest touch.

"But all that was long ago! I'm cured, thank God!

125

I've recovered my appetite and I sleep as well as I did when I was twenty. I sleep like a log and I eat like a horse, and I can run up hills with all the enthusiasm of a schoolboy - and yet, despite that I feel so healthy, I must be ill - the victim of some vile neurosis which watches over and lies in wait for me. I know only too well that the fear is still lurking inside me - and I am afraid of that fear!"

Serge stood up again; he began to pace back and forth across the room, taking great strides, with his hands crossed behind his back, his brow obstinately furrowed and his eyes fixed on the deep pile of the carpet. Then, suddenly, he stopped.

"You've noticed, I suppose, the remarkable ugliness of the people one encounters in the street? All the little people, openly going about their business: the petty clerks and their managers; the domestic servants. You must have observed how absurdly exaggerated their mannerisms are, and how oddly fantastic they look, whenever they ride on a tram! When the first chill of winter descends upon the city they become quite terrible. Is it their everyday cares that make them so? Is it the depressing weight of their tawdry preoccupations, or the anxiety they feel at the end of every month, when they cannot pay the debts which fall due, or the apathy of the penniless who feel trapped by a life which is stale and devoid of surprises? Is it that they live with such troubles, without their minds being able to entertain a slightly more elevated thought or their hearts a slightly broader desire? It always seems to me that I have never seen such wretched caricatures of the human features! What gives them their hallucinatory quality, I wonder? Does the sensation arise because one is brought abruptly face to face with their ugliness? Is it because of some relaxation brought about in them by the warmness of the benches or the deleterious influence of the stale air? Whatever causes it, there's a sudden increase in their evident bestiality: all the people huddled together on the seats; all those struggling against one another in the gangway; the fat women collapsed in the four corners; the old ones with pinched and green-tinged faces, and knotted fingers whose knuckles are turning white with the cold, and thinning hair, always looking meanly sideways at one another from beneath their flabby eyelids; the dubious characters with their coats buttoned up to the neck whose shirts one never sees...

"I ask you, could there possibly exist beneath the grey November sky any more dismal and repugnant spectacle than the passengers on board a tram? When the cold outside has stiffened all their features, solidified all their characteristics, hardened their eyes and narrowed their brows beneath their caps, their glazed, empty expressions are those of lunatics or sleepwalkers. If they are thinking anything at all, that only makes it all the worse, because their thoughts are always low and sordid and their sideways glances always thievish; if they dream at all they only dream of self-enrichment, and that by venal means - by cheating and stealing from their fellows.

"Modern life, whether lived in luxury or in hardship, has imbued men and women alike with the souls of bandits and blackguards. Envy, hatred and the hopelessness of being poor are remaking people in new images, flattened about the head and sharpened about the features, like crocodiles or vipers; avarice and selfishness give others the snouts of old pigs or the jaws of sharks. Whenever one boards a tram one steps into a bestiary where every base impulse has imprinted its brutal stigmata on the surrounding faces; it is as though one enters a cage where frogs and snakes and all manner of repulsive creatures are together entrapped, grotesquely dressed up as if by some clever caricaturist, in trousers and coats....and since the beginning of the month I have been forced to make such journeys daily!

"My salary, you see, is a mere twenty-five thousand francs, and I must take the tram just as my doorkeeper does. Every day I must share the vehicle with the men who have pigs' heads and the women with birdlike profiles, the lawyer's clerks like black crows with a wolfish hunger in their eyes, and milliners' errand-boys with the flat features of lizards. I'm forced to mingle promiscuously with the ignoble and the unspeakable, unexpectedly reduced to their level. It's beyond my powers of endurance. I'm afraid of it.

"Do you understand what I'm saying? *I'm terrified.*"

"The other day - it was Saturday, still quite early - the nightmarish impression was so very strong that it became quite insupportable. I'd taken the tram from the Louvre to Sèvres, and the distressing effect of the suburban landscape, perhaps exacerbated by the desolation of the Avenue de Versailles, brought me to such a pitch of anguish while I watched all those ugly faces, that I had to get off near the Pont-du-Jour. I couldn't bear it any longer; I was possessed, so sharply that I could have cried out for merciful relief, by the conviction that all the people facing and sitting to either side of me were beings of some alien race, half-beast and half-man: the disgusting products of I don't know what monstrous copulations, anthropoid creatures far closer to the animal than to the human, with every foul instinct and all the viciousness of wolves, snakes and rats incarnate in their filthy flesh.

"Sitting between two others of the same kind, right in front of me, there was a cigarette-smoking hag with a long, mottled neck like a stork's, and hard, widely-spaced little teeth set in a mouth that gaped like the mouth of a fish. The pupils of her staring, startled eyes were extraordinarily dilated. That foolish woman seemed to me to be the archetype of an entire species, and as I looked at her, an unreasoning dread took hold of me that if she should open her mouth to speak, no human language would emerge, but only the clucking and cackling of a hen. I knew that she was in truth a creature of the poultry-yard, and I was seized by a great sorrow and an infinite grief to think that a human being might degenerate so. To cap it all, she wore a hat of purple velvet, secured by a cameo brooch.

"I had to get off!

"Every day on the tramway, inside the tram, in that same carriage, the horror of the faces of all those living spectres emerges, further increased in the evening by the harsh light of the streetlamps. The same animal profiles are slowly set free from the glimpsed faces, for my eyes only, visible to no one except myself.

It is a kind of possession, do you see?

"But I know that I play my part too. I make that dreadful hell myself; I, and I alone, provide its trappings."

****

11.

SPLEEN
by Paul Verlaine

The roses were so very red,
And the ivy so intensely black.

My love, you have only to turn your head
And all my hopelessness floods back!

The vault of the sky was so deeply blue,
The sea so green and the air so mild.

I fear and hope to win from you
A curse that I might be defiled.

Of the gloss upon the holly leaf,
And the sunlit bush I can take no more,

Through all my far-flung fields of grief,
Your memory has passed before.

****

12.

THE FAUN
by Remy de Gourmont

She had retired early after the evening meal, weary of the innocent laughter of the little children and the forced joviality which was required of all parents at this season of the year. She felt wretched, and more than a little unhappy.

What had annoyed and upset her most of all was the way that her husband took care to put on a hypocritical show of affection whenever the eyes of the world were upon them; like all other wives, she would have preferred it if he had treated her badly in public and behaved in a loving manner when they were alone.

After dismissing her maid she drew the bolt; then, secure in the knowledge that she would not be disturbed, she was able to feel a little less unhappy.

She undressed slowly and gracefully, imagining as she did so how pleasant it would be if there were someone into whose loving arms she might melt, someone who would murmur endearments as they embraced, complimenting the slope of her shoulder and the delicacy of her knee, thus renewing the assurance that she was desirable in body and soul. She amused herself with this melancholy pretence, quite content to languish for a while in the realm of the imagination, which surely held no surprises for such as she.

Though she continued to touch herself, innocence was eventually overtaken by shame, or at least by delicacy.

She stopped and picked up her dress - although, like Arlette when Robert the Devil had favoured her with his intimacies, she would just as soon have torn the garment apart instead of hanging it up. But regrets were no use; there were bad times and there were good times, and that was the way of things. She gathered a fur-trimmed gown about herself, and knelt down demurely before the fireplace.

She took up the poker and stirred the fire, rearranging and reinvigorating the incandescent logs. She soaked up the warmth, still restless with annoyance.

Why, she wondered, did she allow the hypocritical attentions of her husband to upset her so much? Could she not be more dignified? Was she not capable of sensible self-control, of keeping herself calm - on this of all nights. Why was it that she had to make herself unhappy, until she was so vexed, so overwrought and so sick at heart that she was on the brink of tears? If she could not contrive to console and control herself better than this she would soon be a nervous wreck.

The fact that it was Christmas Eve made everything seem worse; this was one of those magical days when it became a crime to be alone, when the company of others was so very necessary to stave off remorse and painful thoughts. She must try to be constructive, to make herself better - but she had not the strength of will to do it. Her thoughts wandered again, and became confused; and within that confusion there remained only one word on which she could focus her attention: Christmas! Sad, stupid Christmas!

The image came into her mind of a little girl, not long returned from midnight mass, who lay asleep in her bed, dreaming of the gifts which were brought to the infant Jesus....

But no, it was all too banal! All the world gave way annually to such sentimental visions, but to what purpose? They were the meagre consolation of undistinguished souls who had not the power to evoke more satisfying illusions. Such commonplace and vulgar thoughts were insipid and silly, unworthy of the investment of *her* desire!

Rebelling against her memories of youth and innocence, she turned her thoughts instead to the delights of sensuality. The warmth which flooded the hearth now that the logs burned more brightly was changed by the alchemy of her imagination into a wicked titillation. She amused herself with the notion that peculiar caresses were flowing over her, like little angels without wings, hotter and more agile than the capering flames which played like demons about the burning logs.

She gave herself up to a dream of sumptuous fornication, imagining that she might sink into an unexpected stupor, a complaisant victim of desire, right there beside the fire with the fur about her - yes, with the complicity of that furry creature, of that amorous and devoted goat....

Some lascivious spirit which possessed that lukewarm chamber collected its atoms then, and began to materialise. A shadow shaped like the head of a faun fell upon the mirror which hung on the chimney-breast, and a curious draught stirred her hair, warming the nape of her neck.

She was afraid, but she was possessed by a perverse desire to inflame her fear; she did not, however, dare to lift her eyes to the looking-glass to see what might be reflected there. The feeling which flooded her being was achingly sweet; but that shadow of which she had caught the merest glimpse was alarming, strange and absurdly peculiar. She had had an impression of a solid and hairy head, of devouring eyes, of a mouth that was large and somewhat obscene, of a pointed beard...

She shivered.

He must be tall and broad, very handsome and very strong, this being who had emerged from her dream to make love to her! How she trembled within the compass of his arms! She continued to tremble, aware that she was possessed, aware that she had become the prey of some strange amorous monster which had lain in wait for her, had coveted her body.

The fur slid away from her shoulder, and immediately she felt a violent kiss scalding the bared flesh - a kiss so ardent and so powerful that she knew it would leave a visible mark like the brand of a red-hot iron. She tried to pull the mantle back to cover her shoulder - a belated gesture of modesty - but the Being would not let her do it; he seized her two arms with his own two hands. It did not displease her to be defeated so easily; the violence of the action was a tribute to her desirability. Her back and her shoulders had been made to be seen, to receive such fiercely courteous kisses; did she not owe it to herself to enjoy the fruits of her voluptuousness?

The weight of the other's huge body pressed down upon her, and she felt the panting breath of the incubus upon her, like the heat from a forge; it made her want to laugh recklessly. "What a vile imposition!" she thought. "He is atrociously, beautifully masterful...I can see from the corner of my eye how he looks at me...."

As she turned her head towards him, the bestial mask which was his face descended upon hers, and that mouth - so large, and certainly more than a little obscene! - crushed her lips.

She shut her eyes, but too late! For just an instant, she had seen the monster face to face, and knew that it was not the mere reflection of her self-indulgent dream - that in becoming real it had been deformed, into something so foul, so ugly, so intoxicated with a purely

134

bestial lust that....

She was suddenly overcome with shame, and instantly straightened herself. And when she looked at last into the mirror which was mounted on the chimney-breast...

....She saw herself, naked in body and in soul, all alone in her empty, dismal room.

****

13.

THE DRUNKEN BOAT
by Arthur Rimbaud

While I was borne along by the passionless flow,
I sensed that my halers had left me to float free;
They had become victims of some savage Redskin foe,
Stripped naked and nailed to some painted tree.

I could not care at all for the men I bore,
Or the cargoes of cotton and wheat they stowed below,
When, like the halers, they troubled me no more,
The rivers carried me on wherever I cared to go.

In the furious tidal races of the coast,
Last winter, while lost in childish thought,
I ran! And the peninsulas were never host
To such a clamour of triumphant sport.

My turbulent awakenings were tempest-blessed,
Ten nights upon the storm-tossed crests I danced,
By the power of the ever-rolling waves possessed,
And by the constant gleam of harbour lights romanced.

Children never found such sweetness in fallen fruit,
As was in the water leached into my pinewood hull,
Which washed away the blue wine spilt and spewed,
And left me rudderless and anchorless before the lull.

From that time on I bathed in the Poem of the Sea,
Heavy with milk and infused by the stars with light,
Devouring the blue pastures where, at last set free,
A drowning dreamer finds that deep and drear respite

Whose blueness by delirium is now remade,
Pulsating beneath the lightfall from above,
Stronger than alcohol, huger than harps displayed,
Fermenting the bitter rednesses of love!

I know the whirlpools and the lightning-riven sky
Of the sea enraged; but I know too the sea serene,
Launching the silver rays of dawn like doves on high;
And sights which men have sometimes dreamed, I've seen.

I have seen the setting sun, by horrid mists encaged
Painting with violet light the sullen clouds,
Like actors in a play which long ago was staged
Before the rolling waves and restless crowds.

I have dreamed of greenlit nights and dazzling snows,
Of kisses rising slowly to the sea's dark eyes,
Of the circulation of undreamed of flows,
And the phosphorescent glints of vivid dyes.

For months on end I have followed the swells
Which batter the coral reefs in maddened herds,
Never dreaming that the luminous conch-shells
Could quell the ocean's rage with murmurous words!

You little dream what Floridan landfalls I have made
Where I looked into the eyes of panthers with human skin,
And saw rainbows like bridles incredibly displayed
Beneath the sea's horizons where the shoals begin.

I have seen the stagnant marshlands like enormous snares
Among whose reeds the corpses of Leviathans decay,
While waterfalls disturb the calm of their abandoned lairs,
Exploring the abyssal depths where once they lay.

Glaciers and silver suns, pearly waves and skies afire!
And turbid gulfs with rotting wrecks upon their beds,
Where monstrous serpents extend their verminous empire
From the twisted trees to the darkness odorous with dreads!

I yearned to bring children to see the dolphins play
Upon the blue waves with the singing golden fish.
- As I drifted, the flowers of foam about me lay
Until wings lent by strange winds would carry me away.

Sometimes, that weary martyr of the poles and tropics,
The sea, whose sobbing rocked me like a gentle breeze
Would lift towards me some shadow-bloom with yellow calyx,
Beneath which I would rest like a woman on her knees...

Almost an island, with pale-eyed birds about my shore,
Which painted me with droppings while they clamorously
                                                    fought.
Still I sailed on, my rigging more tattered than before,
Touching the drowned men whose sleep was dearly bought!...

I lost myself amid the tresses of the ocean kelp,
Was thrown by a hurricane into that birdless space,
Where no warship or Hanseatic trader paused to help.
There my sodden hulk had reached its resting-place;

Free, fuming, enshrouded by clouds of violet light:
I who had breached the wall of the sky dyed red
Whose exquisite sweets tempt the poetic appetite:
Lichens of sunlight and blue mucus thread;

I who had run, tormented by St. Elmo's Fire,
A maddened board escorted by black seahorses,
When the summers crushed by cudgels would expire,
The Heavens split apart by thunderous forces;

I who had been shaken while fifty leagues away
By the rutting of Behemoths and the Maelstrom's moan,
An eternal spinner of the still cerulean display;
How I yearn for Europe's ancient parapets of stone!

I have seen the archipelagos of stars, and isles
Whose intoxicated skies belong to those who sail:
- Art thou among the endless throng of sleep's exiles,
O million golden birds, O future Holy Grail?

Still, I have wept too long! Dawn breaks my heart.
Moonlight is hateful, sunlight bitter to my taste:
Piercing love has swelled my every inebriate part.
O that my keel might be broken, my hull laid waste.

If there is any European water where I long to be,
It is a dark cold pool where a sad child might play
Launching into the scented twilight, upon an imagined sea
A paper boat as fragile as the butterflies of May.

Bathed by your caresses, O waves, I can no longer rise
To follow in the wake of cotton-clippers sailing home,
Nor chase the coloured pennants which decorate the skies
Nor leave behind the lightships' baleful glare, the seas to roam.

****

14.

THE PANTHER
by Rachilde

(A story designed to be read aloud to an audience)

From the subterranean regions beneath the circus the cage slowly climbed, bringing with it what seemed at first to be a fragment of the night incarnate.

A grille slid aside.

Released from her captivity into the resplendent light of day, the beast within came out on to the sand of the arena, glorying in the warmth and brightness as she passed before the cloth of gold, tasselled with purple.

The creature was young, handsomely clad in that regal mourning-dress which all black panthers wear. She carried herself very precisely on her long, lithe limbs. The gaze of her eyes, which were like enormous topazes, passed over those whom she did not care to contemplate, as though to stare at further horizons. Her great paws, powerful though seemingly gentle, made no sound as they fell.

Three smooth bounds took her to the middle of the arena; there she set herself down, and rolled herself over, all other matters apparently having become unimportant. There, under the curious examination of the people in the imperial box, she licked her private parts.

Close to her, the Christians who had as yet been spared were gathered beneath a high cross reddened with blood. The grey mass of a dead elephant lay before her like a colossal wall, blocking out a corner of the extraordinarily blue sky. In the far distance, arrayed upon the circular ranks of the stadium, was a blur of pale forms, from which arose a murmurous, intoxicated clamour.

The beast, having completed her toilet, paused a moment to puzzle over these furious noises, which were entirely new to her. She could not possibly have understood the reason for all the excitement; her way of killing was cold and methodical, quite devoid of all emotion, whether angry or lustful. The roar of the crowd was utterly unimportant to her - no more than the sound which a rainstorm made as it rattled the branches of the forest trees. She condescended to emit a few derisory mewling sounds in response to the uproar; then, without hurrying too much, she came to her feet.

Her instinct drew her automatically to the body of the stricken elephant, and that was where she went, utterly disdainful of the human offerings nearby. She dipped her tongue into the warm red liquid which was streaming from the monstrous cadaver, and then she tore away an ample strip of flesh from the wound.

Having secured her meal she camped down on top of the strip of flesh. Carefully, she licked it.

Two days before she had been brought to perform in the arena, while she waited in the darkness of her prison, they had given her vile meat seasoned with cumin and powdered saffron, intending to stir up a fierce fire in her belly; but her sense of smell had warned her to abstain. She had gone without food before, and knew that the world was full of dangerous temptations. Ignorant she might be, and virginal, but she knew the burning midday heat of her own land, where the melancholy crying of the birds sighed for the rain which rarely came; she knew the poisonous plants of the great impenetrable forests which snakes distilled into their venom; she knew the extremities of drought, and the ridiculous thinness of

141

whatever victims were then to be found, and the anxious waiting beneath the baleful eye of the moon before she launched herself forth in pursuit of some fleeting shadow.

The legacy of all her unsuccessful chases was a cunning wisdom which bade her always to conserve her strength, and that same careful judgement she now employed in this other - and seemingly delightful - world where carnivorous beasts were welcomed by men as brothers and invited to their solemn feasts. She took her own portion without undue avidity, only desirous that she should be fit company for those whose appetites were less natural than her own.

A Christian, naked and armed in derisory fashion with a crude club topped by a ball of iron, came towards her over the hindquarters of the elephant, pushed forward by attendants which she could not see. He slipped in the sticky blood and fell, dropping the club. He picked himself up, recovering his weapon with a taut smile on his pale lips. He had not the slightest wish to be forced into combat against the beast which would eventually eat him, but he moved towards her nevertheless, his staring eyes fixed upon his adversary.

She favoured him with a playful gesture of the paw, which said: "I am satisfied!..." Then she stretched herself out, her eyes half-closed, lazily switching her tail in perplexity as the other continued to approach. While their gazes interlocked the Christian discovered, in spite of the fact that he had already abandoned any hope of continued life, that he now seemed to possess the secret of subduing wild beasts by the imposition of his will.

The beast, meanwhile, exercised her own power of fascination over him.

They were awakened from their curious reverie by the increasing clamour of the crowd. The two of them had now become the central attraction of the festival of bloodshed, and the audience was avid for the kind of entertainment which they had come to see. Angered by the lack of action, the spectators called out to the mounted soldiers to make something happen.

Face to face, the unwilling adversaries continued to survey one another. The Christian had no heart for a fight; the panther, who neither knew nor cared about matters of courage, was no longer hungry. One of the soldiers galloped towards the pair, waving his sword.

With a graceful bound the animal avoided the blow, and the Christian simply stood there, smiling in a melancholy fashion. Then the anger of the crowd was unleashed in its full fury. The storm burst in fearful fashion, urging the soldiers on.

The horsemen rushed forward against the beast, who stubbornly refused to be moved to action by their threats. The horsemen went back to heat the heads of their spears in braziers, or to dip them in boiling oil. Then they came at her again, waving flaming torches, accompanied by dogs which had been trained to nip the heels of recalcitrant bulls.

All the hatred of the crowd was directed against the panther who would not play her allotted part in their carnival.

The panther, sorely annoyed by these provocations, beat her flanks with her tail as she retreated, uncertain what to do. The soldiers, insistent that she should prepare herself for the battle which she was supposed to fight, continued to harry her, shooting arrows after her fleeing form. They rode at her with their fearful goads, and she retreated more hastily, leaping over the dead bodies of men and animals which were strewn all around.

The uncomprehending panther was now seized by a superstitious terror; surely this was the end of the world! As she was chased around the arena the spectators rose in their seats, their anger increased by her foolish reluctance to amuse them. From every side there fell upon the hapless beast a rain of missiles: stones, rotten fruits, any weapon which came to hand. Patricians hurled ornaments which whistled as they flew through the air; and the emperor, standing up in his box, joined in by hurling silver coins.

With one last desperate bound, the panther - crazed by fear of the flames which surrounded her and tormented by arrows which had struck into her flesh - took refuge in the open cage from which she had come.

It was over. The grille slid back into place, and the mysterious mechanism drew the cage down once again into the underworld beneath the circus.

For the panther, the days and nights which followed were agonized and terrible. Time and time again she lamented her fate, mewling her desperate appeals to the sun which she might never be allowed to see again. But in the eyes of those who patronized the circus, she deserved all the pain which had been inflicted upon her. She was cowardly, they said; she had refused to take part in combat, and was no longer entitled to lay claim to the rank of a noble animal.

The keeper who looked after the captive beasts was an ancient slave, who had no pity at all for her, and did not care that she could not eat properly because her mouth had been ripped open by the blade of a sword which she had bitten. He did not feed her proper meat, but only threw her bones which had already been gnawed, leftovers from the neighbouring cages, and rotten pieces of infected meat. These foul remains were not cleared away, but were heaped up all around her, as though her cage was some kind of sewer.

Her fur was scarred by burns, and covered with sores; a group of young boys, in order to mock her, pinned

144

her tail to the ground with a nail - where it remained secured until, by means of a very painful effort, she contrived to tear it out. The old slave, amused by his apparent bravery, would offer to her an empty hand, while in the other, out of reach, he would hold up some tempting morsel. Once he scorched her ear with the crackling fire of a torch. Deprived of air, deprived of light, her injured mouth always full of her own leaking blood, she howled out her lamentations, battering the bars of her cage with her head and tearing the floor with her claws, hopelessly seeking release. Some mysterious illness began to torment her guts.

Because she growled in such a very sinister fashion the order was given out that she should be left to die of hunger; such worthy deaths as the thrust of a spear into her heart were not for the likes of her. She was simply neglected, and the old keeper ceased to pass before her with his torch.

The panther understood that she was to die, and she arranged herself in a proud position, wrapping her injured tail around her and crossing her gangrenous paws so that she might rest her head upon them. Closing her eyes of fire, she lost herself in dreams.

As she awaited the end of her agony she dreamed of the forests which rattled beneath the beat of the rain storm; of the sun high in the sky; of the moon when it was the colour of roses; of the birds sighing for the rain; of the limitless greenery; of the freshwater springs; of young and easy prey; of great rivers where the stooping wild beasts might see themselves mirrored with haloes of stars...

Little by little, the thoughts of the panther decayed into incoherence, and her mind was possessed by ancient memories of happiness and freedom. But one single moment of mad despair recalled her to the sadness of her fate, and she saw again the cloth of gold, tasselled with purple, the sand of the arena, the grey mass of the fallen elephant, the smile on the Christian's face - and, finally, the furious cries of the mounted soldiers, and the tortures...all the tortures...

With her head lowered on to her crossed paws, she lay quite still; she only slept, but it was as if she were already dead.

Then, suddenly the darkness of her prison was dispelled. A trapdoor in the roof of the cage slid aside and there appeared the slender white form of a young girl, who descended from above into that private hell where the damned beast crouched. In a flap of her tunic she carried a piece of soft leather, and balanced on her right shoulder, supported by her arms, was a jug, full to the brim.

The panther slowly raised herself up. This wonderful white-skinned child, with her blonde hair catching the light as it streamed behind her, must surely have come from the Eden of the wild beasts!

"Beast," said the marvellous girl, "I feel sorry for you. You should not be left to die like this."

Detaching the chain which held it, the little girl pushed aside the grille which secured the cage. On to the threshold, she let fall the piece of soft leather, and then she calmly lowered the vessel from her shoulder.

The panther flexed her supple haunches, and lowered her head to make herself small, so as not to frighten the child, hiding the glare of her phosphorescent eyes.

Then, with one bound, the predator surged upon her prey, seized the child by the throat, and made a meal of her.

****

146

15.

SPLEEN
by Charles Baudelaire

Had I lived a thousand years I could not remember more.

An enormous chest of drawers could not hold in store,
Despite that it be crammed with love-letters, verses,
                                                    tales,
Hanks of hair and records of obsolete entails,
More secrets than I harbour in my wretched mind.
It is a pyramid, a space by stone confined,
Where the bodies of the dead are vilely pressed.
- I am a cemetery by the moon unblessed
Where graveworms carry the slime of dim remorses
Relentlessly into the heart of cherished corpses.
I am an ancient bedroom decked with faded blooms,
Scattered with outdated gowns and tattered plumes,
Where only faded prints and painted faces,
Remain to breathe the perfumed airs and graces.

Nothing is as tedious as the limping days,
When snowdrifts yearly cover all the ways,
And ennui, sour fruit of incurious gloom,
Assumes control of fate's immortal loom.
- Henceforth, my living flesh, thou art no more,
Than a shroud of unease about a stony core,
Listlessly sunk beneath the desert sand;
A sphinx forgotten by the innocent and bland,
Banished from the map that she might gaze
Silently upon the setting sun's last rays.

16.

OLD FURNITURE
by Catulle Mendès

When the bed was broken:

"Look at that!" she said. "I ask you - what will they think of me when they see it tomorrow, with the mattress in that state and everything else you have managed to do? This is a respectable hotel! It must be said, sir, that your treatment of me has been singularly brutal; do you not realise how careful I must be to make sure that my husband never finds out that I have come away with you? The poor man believes that I have gone to see my aunt in the country. At this hour, he is probably fast asleep, in a bed which he has certainly never broken. Why could you not have been as calm and gentle as he always is? How I shall blush when the hotel manager and the servants find out what has happened. Because I was ignorant of your faults I permitted myself to entertain the tenderest feelings for you, but what you have contrived to do obliges me to recognise that I was entirely wrong to trust you. If I ever loved you at all, I love you no longer! I must ask you to forget the favours which I have already granted you, and to give up any hope that they will ever be renewed."

While she spoke these words, from the middle of the room, Roberta put on a fine show of controlled anger; her gestures were dignified, her manner was almost tragic. As she put on her clothes her movements were perfectly graceful, and she maintained her composure until the last button was fastened and the last lace tied.

The breaker of the bed was enthusiastic to excuse himself.

"But, darling...." he said.

She was quick to interrupt him.

"Oh, I know exactly what you are going to say. You were not in control of yourself; you have waited so long, thanks to the virtuous resistance which I have exerted against your entreaties, that as soon as I ceased to be cruel you lost your head. When at last the moment came and you were permitted to proceed, you were incapable of moderation. And now, I suppose, I should be overcome by happiness! One always cuts the most beautiful roses too quickly! You will also suggest, no doubt, that in the older houses of this region the furniture is of dubious solidity, and that it is no fault of yours that I should happen to lay my young body down in a bed which is a hundred years old, or more. None of these excuses, I assure you, can make the slightest difference. It does not alter the incontestable fact that the bed is broken - oh, what a mess! It is enough to make one die of shame! Tomorrow the servants will all have smiles upon their lips when they see me come downstairs, blushing to the roots of my hair."

He did not try to make any more excuses; his offence was all-too-evident; but he had an idea.

"But my dear," he said, "things are not as bad as they seem. The disengaged mattress, the broken springs, the cracked frame - all this can be repaired; given time and a little cleverness I can put things back in such good order that no one would ever imagine how wildly I was excited by the sight of your perfect teeth and your rosy cheeks."

She collected herself.

Yes, certainly, that would be the best thing. Repair the bed, and lose no time in doing so. And so they both set about it, determinedly. There were a few interruptions in the work, of course, because he had occasionally to touch her soft white arms or kiss her bee-stung lips, but in the end they completed the task - by which time they were quite reconciled, as firmly united in one purpose as they had ever been. Next day, the servants would be certain that the guests had slept very peacefully indeed.

On the other hand, the perilous scaffolding of the bed could not be expected to endure any further strain; the lightest jolt might easily make it collapse all over again. There was, however, a large chaise longue positioned between the two windows, beneath an old tapestry which depicted Tiresias explaining how the tearful Alcmene had come to be seduced by the god Zeus. There was plenty of room on the chaise longue for both of them, and they retired to it gratefully.

****

When that also was broken:

"Look what you've done now!" cried Roberta. "I have to say, sir, that you are the most insupportable man that one could possibly imagine. Insupportable, do you hear? Even the clumsiest of giants - Gargantua and Pantagruel, and all the colossuses displayed in the fair at Neuilly - could not have contrived such extraordinary breakages. Even Hercules never broke the couch where Omphale forced him to spin the wool of the golden fleece! You have not even the excuse of being obese nor enormous; you are, indeed, rather slim, although you have the manners and appetite of a peasant. My God, wasn't it sufficient to break the bed? Why couldn't you take no for an answer? Haven't I told you how important it is that I do not appear to be undeserving of my husband's trust? My husband - who thinks that I have gone to see my aunt in the country! You seem to think that my refusals are simply to be construed as an inducement to redouble the

150

effort of your assaults. I was content to assume that the tumult of the battle on the bed was a consequence of the novelty of your victory - and so you assured me. The chaise longue was supposed to be the rest camp to which combatants retire when the battle is over, and I cannot see that you have any excuse at all for sacking those positions which you had already conquered! I can hardly bear to think about what might happen in the morning. A maid, perhaps an entirely innocent girl - anything is possible in the country! - will come into the room and immediately behold a broken chaise longue beneath a picture in which blind Tiresias looks so lovingly at Alcmene's legs. You can be certain that I shall never forgive you for the blushes with which you have stained my innocence; I have no more feelings for you, save for the hateful and unhappy legacy of shattered illusions."

While she spoke these words from the middle of the room, Roberta had tears in her eyes. They were little tears, no larger than tiny pearls - if only they could have been tears of happiness, the pearls would surely have been real - and, given that she was undressed, palely desolate and quivering from head to toe, she could never before have presented such a beautiful sight.

The breaker of chaises longues tried to excuse himself.

"But, darling..." he said.

She was quick to interrupt him.

"Oh! I know exactly what you are going to say. The fault, this time, was not all yours. You little realise how hateful you are making yourself with these terrible accusations. My excesses have been as great as your own in pursuit of our mutual goal, you declare, and you dare to give me to understand that is is I who am responsible for the breaking of the chaise longue. Well, I will not entertain such an idea for an instant, and I find the very

151

suggestion offensive. From the very beginning, I could see myself in the mirror which hangs on the opposite wall - and I am sure that I did not abandon for a single instant, despite certain appearances of complaisance, the attitude of disinterest which propriety commanded me to maintain. But what does it matter? The fact remains, real and undeniable: the chaise longue is a ruin! How can you possibly expect me to endure the humiliation which will be heaped upon me by the sly laughter of the servants?"

"Oh, my love," he said, "let us simply repair the sofa, just as we have repaired the bed."

****

But, when the task was completed - when the chaise longue once again had the appearance of an honest sofa on which one would not hesitate to seat oneself; when the cushions were placed as neatly as any bourgeois visitor could possibly wish - there was further embarrassment to come. Where, now could they possibly spend the remainder of the night? They could not possibly use the bed, which was as fragile now as a house of cards, nor the couch which they had just repaired, which would fall to pieces at the slightest shock.

The lovers - content at last to think only of sleep - dolefully studied the narrow armchairs and considered the dimensions of the marble top on the chest of drawers, until Roberta, in the end, could not help but shake with suppressed laughter, rippling the long fair hair which she had bound up in a gold ribbon.

Then, quickly putting on a dressing-gown, she pulled violently on the bell-cord.

The bellboy, summoned uncomfortably from his bed, finally opened the door. "Madame rang?" he inquired.

She was still laughing.

"Oh yes, I rang," she answered.

Then, very charmingly, with the light of mischief in her eyes and a smile upon her lips, she said: "This is a dreadful room. It is terribly uncomfortable, and there is a draught from the window. Can you let us have another - one with more solid furniture, perhaps?"

****

17.

DON JUAN IN HELL
by Charles Baudelaire

(translated by James Elroy Flecker)

The night Don Juan came to pay his fees
  To Charon, by the caverned water's shore,
A beggar, proud-eyed as Antisthenes,
  Stretched out his knotted fingers on the oar.

Mournful, with drooping breasts and robes unsewn
  The shapes of women swayed in ebon skies,
Trailing behind him with a restless moan
  Like cattle herded for a sacrifice.

Here, grinning for his wage, stood Sganarelle,
  And here Don Luis pointed, bent and dim,
To show the dead who lined the holes of Hell,
  This was that impious son who mocked at him.

The hollow-eyed, the chaste Elvira came,
  Trembling and veiled, to view her traitor spouse.
Was it one last bright smile she thought to claim,
  Such as made sweet the morning of his vows?

A great stone man rose like a tower on board,
  Stood at the helm and cleft the flood profound:
But the calm hero, leaning on his sword,
  Gazed back, and would not offer one look round.

****

18.

DON JUAN'S SECRET
by Remy de Gourmont

Devoid of soul and avid in the flesh, Don Juan prepared himself from earliest adolescence for the vocation that would make his name legendary. His cunning foresight had revealed to him the shape of things to come, and he entered upon his career armed and armoured by the motto:

To please yourself, you must take what you please from she who pleases you.

****

From one of his fair-haired conquests he took a deft gesture of the hand, which echoed the painful beating of an empty heart;

From another he took an ironic fall of the eyelid, which conveyed an illusion of impertinence and which was certainly no mere reflex of a feeble eye before the light;

From another, he took the petulant stamp of her pretty and impatient foot;

From another, soft and pure, he took a smile in which he had previously seen, as if in a magical mirror, the contentment of satisfaction; and afterwards, the pleased renewal of desire.

From another, not so pure and without softness, but ever vibrantly alive and as nervous as a kitten, he took a very different smile: the kind of smile which remembered kisses strong enough to stir the heart of a virgin;

From another, he took a sigh: a deep, tremulous and timid sigh; a sigh like the hectically fluttering wings of a frightenened bird in flight;

From another he took the slow and unsteady gait of one overwhelmed by an excess of love;

From another, he took the loving voice whose whispered endearments were like the weeping of angels.

From all of them he took the expressions which showed upon their faces: the gentle, the imperious, the docile, the astonished, the combative, the envious, the lovely, the trusting, the devouring, the thunderous, and all the rest; and he built these one by one into a great garland of fascinating appearances. But the most beautiful of all expressions to Don Juan - a precious stone among countless beads of glass - was the expression of a ravished girl, hunted and caught and mortified by love and despair. That look he found so poignant that it became the motive force of his eternal search for more and more of the same wild gratification; it was the secret inspiration of his great carnal quest.

****

Time and time again, Don Juan triumphed over the female heart. He won hearts ingenuous and trusting, hearts tender and righteous, hearts which did not know their own secrets, hearts empty of innate desire, hearts deliciously naive; gentle seductresses and ardent seductresses all came alike to him, and were likewise beguiled.

The pattern of his seductions was always the same: his gentle touch, excused by a hint of laughter in the eye and a pleasant smile; her slow entrancement by his steady gaze; the first deep and fractured sigh wrung from his breast, accompanied by a subtly impatient tap of his foot, as if to say: "You have wounded my heart; that will not prevent me from loving you, but I am angry." Then, he would see the precious look of the hunted beast upon her face; then he would touch her playfully with his little finger.

After a pause, he would whisper, lovingly: "How beautiful it is tonight!" - and the young lady would instantly respond: "It is my heart and soul that you want, Don Juan! So be it! Take them, I give them to you freely."

Don Juan would accept this delicious offering, and would savour all the feminine charms of the new lover: her skin; her hair; her teeth; all of her beauty and all the perfumes of her secret places - and, having enjoyed to the full the fruits of her newly-awakened love, would then depart.

Around his own heart he built an inviolable shell, in which it was as comfortably encased as if it were enshrouded in white velvet - and with that armour to protect him, bolder than any giant-killer, more revered than the holiest of relics, he increased the number of his conquests vastly.

He took all of them: all those who might provide a new hint of pleasure, a delicate nuance of joy; he took all that he was allowed to take by those whose sisters had already given him all that he desired. His reputation went before him, and as it increased the women became all the more ready to bow down before him and kiss his hands submissively, overcome by the mere approach of their conqueror.

In the end, women competed with one another to be the first to submit to him or to be the one who would surrender most; intoxicated by the mere thought of their impending enslavement, they would begin to die for love of him before they had even tasted his love.

Through all the towns and all the chateaux, to the remotest parts of the land, there spread the cry of the fatally enamoured: "O my love! O desire of my flesh! He is irresistible."

****

But the time came, as it had to do, when Don Juan grew old. His strength was sapped by his luxurious indulgence and his appetites dried up. As is the inevitable way of things, he became a shadow of his former self.

To the last flowers of summer, Don Juan had given up the last grain of his pollen; there was not a drop of sap left in him. He had loved, but now could love no more - and he lay down on his bed to await the arrival of the one who was destined to claim him.

But when that one arrived, Don Juan - still unready to accept his fate - offered to him anything that he cared to take, out of all that had been so carefully stolen from those with whom the great lover had taken his pleasure.

"I offer to you the rewards of all my seductions," said Don Juan. "To you, O Ugly One, I offer all my gestures, all my looks, all my smiles, all my divers sights - all of that, and the armour which encases my soul: take it and go! I wish to relive my life in memory, knowing as I do now that memory is the true life."

"Relive your life if you wish," said Death. "I will see you again."

And Death departed, but left behind him a host of phantoms which he had raised from the shadows.

These phantoms were the forms of young and beautiful women, all of them naked and all incapable of speech, moving restlessly as though there were something which they were desperate to obtain. They arranged themselves in a great spiral around Don Juan's bed, and

158

though the first of them was close enough to take his hand and place it on her breast, the last was so far away that she seemed as distant as the stars.

She who had placed his hand on her breast took back from him a deft gesture of the hand which echoed the anguish of an empty heart;

Another took back from him the ironic fall of a white eyelid;

Another took back from him the petulant stamp of her foot;

Another took back from him the subtle smile which spoke of satisfaction obtained and the renewal of desire;

Another took back from him a different smile, which reflected the pleasure of secret delights;

Another took back from him a sigh like the flutter of a frightened bird;

And then there approached another, who moved with the slow and unsteady gait of one overwhelmed by an excess of love; and another whose sad and loving whispers were like the weeping of angels; and the great garland of the expressions which he had gathered one by one - the imperious and the thunderous, the astonished and the trusting, the gentle and the beguiled - all were retaken from him; and every one of those whom he had carefully violated came in her turn to take back from him her illimitably precious and fugitive expression of love and despair.

Another, finally, took from him his own heart, whose delicious innocence he had so carefully preserved within its cloak of white velvet; and then he was no longer the great Don Juan, but only a senseless phantom.

Like a rich man robbed of his wealth, or a flyer without wings, he was the merest echo of a human being, reduced to elementary truth, without his inspiration,

without his secret!

****

1.

THEORETIKOS
by Oscar Wilde

This mighty empire hath but feet of clay:
  Of all its ancient chivalry and might
  Our little island is forsaken quite:
Some enemy hath stolen its crown of bay,
And from its hills that voice hath passed away
  Which spake of Freedom: O come out of it,
  Come out of it, my Soul, thou art not fit
For this vile traffic-house, where day by day
  Wisdom and reverence are sold at mart,
  And the rude people rage with ignorant cries
Against an heritage of centuries.
  It mars my calm: wherefore in dreams of Art
  And loftiest culture I would stand apart,
Neither for God, nor for his enemies.

****

2.

THE COURT OF VENUS
by Aubrey Beardsley
(From *Under the Hill*)

I

Before a toilet that shone like the altar of Nôtre Dame des Victoires, Venus was seated in a little dressing-gown of black and heliotrope. The coiffeur Cosmé was caring for her scented chevelure, and with tiny silver tongs, warm from the caresses of the flame, made delicious intelligent curls that fell as lightly as a breath about her forehead and over her eyebrows, and clustered like tendrils about her neck. Her three favourite girls, Pappelarde, Blanchemains, and Loreyne, waited immediately upon her with perfume and powder in delicate flaçons and frail cassolettes, and held in porcelain jars the ravishing paints prepared by Chateline for those cheeks and lips that had grown a little pale with anguish of exile. Her three favourite boys, Claude, Clair, and Sarrasine, stood amorously about with salver, fan and napkin. Millamant held a slight tray of slippers, Minette some tender gloves, La Popelinière, mistress of the robes, was ready with a frock of yellow and yellow. La Zambinella bore the jewels, Florizel some flowers, Amadour a box of various pins, and Vadius a box of sweets. Her doves, ever in attendance, walked about the room that was panelled with the gallant paintings of Jean Baptiste Dorat, and some dwarfs and doubtful creatures sat here and there, lolling out their tongues, pinching each other, and behaving oddly enough. Sometimes Venus gave them little smiles.

162

As the toilet was in progress, Priapusa, the fat manicure and fardeuse, strode in and seated herself by the side of the dressing-table, greeting Venus with an intimate nod. She wore a gown of white watered silk with gold lace trimmings, and a velvet necklet of false vermilion. Her hair hung in bandeaux over her ears, passing into a huge chignon at the back of her head, and the hat, wide-brimmed and hung with a vallance of pink muslin, was floral with red roses.

Priapusa's voice was full of salacious unction; she had terrible little gestures with the hands, strange movements with the shoulders, a short respiration that made surprising wrinkles in her bodice, a corrupt skin, large horny eyes, a parrot's nose, a small loose mouth, great flaccid cheeks, and chin after chin. She was a wise person, and Venus loved her more than any of her other servants, and had a hundred pet names for her, such as, Dear Toad, Pretty Pol, Cock-robin, Dearest Lip, Touchstone, Little Cough-drop, Bijou, Buttons, Dear Heart, Dick-dock, Mrs Manly, Little Nipper, Cochon-de-lait, Naughty-naughty, Blessèd Thing, and Trump.

The talk that passed between Priapusa and her mistress was of that excellent kind that passes between old friends, a perfect understanding giving to scraps of phrases their full meaning, and to the merest reference, a point. Naturally Tannhauser, the new comer, was discussed a little. Venus had not seen him yet, and asked a score of questions on his account that were delightfully to the point.

Priapusa told the story of his sudden arrival, his curious wandering in the gardens, and calm satisfaction with all he saw there, his impromptu affection for a slender girl upon the first terrace, of the crowd of frocks that gathered round and pelted him with roses, of the graceful way he defended himself with his mask, and of

163

the queer reverence he made to the statue of the God of all gardens, kissing that deity with a pilgrim's devotion. Just now Tannhauser was at the baths, and was creating a most favourable impression.

The report and the coiffing were completed at the same moment.

"Cosmé," said Venus, "you have been quite sweet and quite brilliant, you have surpassed yourself to-night."

"Madam flatters me," replied the antique old thing, with a girlish giggle under his black satin mask. "Gad, Madam; sometimes I believe I have no talent in the world, but to-night I must confess to a touch of the vain mood."

It would pain me horribly to tell you about the painting of her face; suffice it that the sorrowful work was accomplished frankly, magnificently, and without a shadow of deception.

Venus slipped away the dressing-gown, and rose before the mirror in a flutter of frilled things. She was adorably tall and slender. Her neck and shoulders were so wonderfully drawn, and the little malicious breasts were full of the irritation of loveliness that can never be entirely comprehended, or ever enjoyed to the utmost. Her arms and hands were loosely but delicately articulated, and her legs were divinely long. From the hip to the knee, twenty-two inches; from the knee to the heel, twenty-two inches, as befitted a Goddess.

I should like to speak more particularly about her, for generalities are not of the slightest service in a description. But I am afraid that an enforced silence here and there would leave such numerous gaps in the picture that it had better not be begun at all than left unfinished.

Those who have only seen Venus in the Vatican, in the Louvre, in the Uffizi, or in the British Museum, can have no idea of how very beautiful and sweet she looked. Not at all like the lady in "Lemprière."

Priapusa grew quite lyric over the dear little person, and pecked at her arms with kisses.

"Dear Tongue, you must really behave yourself," said Venus, and called Millamant to bring her the slippers.

The tray was freighted with the most exquisite and shapely pantoufles, sufficient to make Cluny a place of naught. There were shoes of grey and black and brown suède, of white silk and rose satin, and velvet and sarcenet; there were some of sea-green sewn with cherry blossoms, some of red with willow branches, and some of grey with bright-winged birds. There were heels of silver, of ivory, and of gilt; there were buckles of very precious stones set in most strange and esoteric devices; there were ribands tied and twisted into cunning forms; there were buttons so beautiful that the button-holes might have no pleasure till they closed upon them; there were soles of delicate leathers scented with maréchale, and linings of soft stuffs scented with the juice of July flowers. But Venus, finding none of them to her mind, called for a discarded pair of blood-red maroquin, diapered with pearls. These looked very distinguished over her white silk stockings.

As the tray was being carried away, the capricious Florizel snatched as usual a slipper from it, and fitted the foot over his penis, and made the necessary movements. That was Florizel's little caprice. Meantime, La Popelinière stepped forward with the frock.

"I shan't wear one to-night," said Venus. Then she slipped on her gloves.

When the toilet was at an end all her doves clustered round her feet, loving to frôler her ankles with their plumes, and the dwarfs clapped their hands, and put their fingers between their lips and whistled. Never before had Venus been so radiant and compelling. Spiridion, in the corner, looked up from his game of Spellicans and trembled. Claude and Clair, pale with pleasure, stroked and touched her with their delicate hands, and wrinkled her stockings with their nervous lips, and smoothed them with their thin fingers; and Sarrasine undid her garters and kissed them inside and put them on again, pressing her thighs with his mouth. The dwarfs grew very daring, I can tell you. There was almost a mêlée. They illustrated pages 72 and 73 of Delvau's Dictionary.

In the middle of it all, Pranzmungel announced that supper was ready upon the fifth terrace. "Ah!" cried Venus, "I'm famished!"

II

She was quite delighted with Tannhauser, and, of course, he sat next her at supper.

The terrace, made beautiful with a thousand vain and fantastical devices, and set with a hundred tables and four hundred couches, presented a truly splendid appearance. In the middle was a huge bronze fountain with three basins. From the first rose a many-breasted dragon, and four little Loves mounted upon swans, and each Love was furnished with a bow and arrow. Two of them that faced the monster seemed to recoil in fear, two that were behind made bold enough to aim their shafts at him. From the verge of the second sprang a circle of slim golden columns that supported silver doves, with tails and wings spread out. The third, held by a group of grotesquely attenuated satyrs, was centred with a thin pipe hung with masks and roses, and capped with children's heads.

From the mouths of the dragon and the Loves,

from the swans' eyes, from the breasts of the doves, from the satyrs' horns and lips, from the masks at many points, and from the childrens' curls, the water played profusely, cutting strange arabesques and subtle figures.

The terrace was lit entirely by candles. There were four thousand of them, not numbering those upon the tables. The candlesticks were of a countless variety, and smiled with moulded cochônneries. Some were twenty feet high, and bore single candles that flared like fragrant torches over the feast, and guttered till the wax stood round the tops in tall lances. Some, hung with dainty petticoats of shining lustres, had a whole bevy of tapers upon them, devised in circles, in pyramids, in squares, in cuneiforms, in single lines regimentally and in crescents.

Then on quaint pedestals and Terminal Gods and gracious pilasters of every sort, were shell-like vases of excessive fruits and flowers that hung about and burst over the edges and could never be restrained. The orange-trees and myrtles, looped with vermilion sashes, stood in frail porcelain pots, and the rose-trees were wound and twisted with superb invention over trellis and standard. Upon one side of the terrace, a long gilded stage for the comedians was curtained off with Pagonian tapestries, and in front of it the music-stands were placed. The tables arranged between the fountain and the flight of steps to the sixth terrace were all circular, covered with white damask, and strewn with irises, roses, kingcups, colombines, daffodils, carnations and lilies; and the couches, high with soft cushions and spread with more stuffs than could be named, had fans thrown upon them, and little amorous surprise packets.

Beyond the escalier stretched the gardens, which were designed so elaborately and with so much splendour that the architect of the Fetes d'Armailhacq could have found in them no matter for cavil, and the still lakes strewn with profuse barges full of gay flowers and wax marionettes, the alleys of tall trees, the arcades and cascades, the pavilions, the grottoes, and the garden-gods - all took a strange tinge of revelry from the glare of the light that fell upon them from the feast.

The frockless Venus and Tannhauser, with Priapusa and Claude and Clair, and Farcy, the chief comedian, sat at the same table. Tannhauser, who had doffed his travelling suit, wore long black silk stockings, a pair of pretty garters, a very elegant ruffled shirt, slippers and a wonderful dressing-gown. Claude and Clair wore nothing at all, delicious privilege of immaturity, and Farcy was in ordinary evening clothes. As for the rest of the company, it boasted some very noticeable dresses, and whole tables of quite delightful coiffures. There were spotted veils that seemed to stain the skin with some exquisite and august disease, fans with eye-slits in them through which their bearers peeped and peered; fans painted with postures and covered with the sonnets of Sporion and the short stories of Scaramouche, and fans of big living moths stuck upon mounts of silver sticks. There were masks of green velvet that make the face look trebly powdered; masks of the heads of birds, of apes, of serpents, of dolphins, of men and women, of little embryons and of cats; masks like the faces of gods; masks of coloured glass, and masks of thin talc and of india-rubber. There were wigs of black and scarlet wools, of peacocks' feathers, of gold and silver threads, of swansdown, of the tendrils of the vine, and of human hairs; huge collars of stiff muslin rising high above the head; whole dresses of ostrich feathers curling inwards; tunics of panthers' skins that looked beautiful over pinktights; capotes of crimson satin trimmed with the wings of owls; sleeves cut into the shapes of apocryphal animals; drawers flounced down to the ankles, and

168

tiny, red roses; stockings with fetes galantes, and curious designs, and petticoats cut like artificial flowers. Some of the women had put on delightful little moustaches dyed in purples and bright greens, twisted and waxed with absolute skill; and some wore great white beards after the manner of Saint Wilgeforte. Then Dorat had painted extraordinary grotesques and vignettes over their bodies, here and there. Upon a cheek, an old man scratching his horned head; upon a forehead, an old woman teased by an impudent amor; upon a shoulder, an amorous singerie; round a breast, a circlet of satyrs; about a wrist, a wreath of pale, unconscious babes; upon an elbow, a bouquet of spring flowers; across a back, some surprising scenes of adventure; at the corners of a mouth, tiny red spots; and upon a neck, a flight of birds, a caged parrot, a branch of fruit, a butterfly, a spider, a drunken dwarf, or, simply, some initials. But most wonderful of all were the black silhouettes painted upon the legs, and which showed through a white silk stocking like a sumptuous bruise.

The supper provided by the ingenious Rambouillet was quite beyond parallel. Never had he created a more exquisite menu. The *consommé impromptu* alone would have been sufficient to establish the immortal reputation of any chef. What, then, can I say of the *Dorade bouillie sauce maréchale*, the *ragoût aux langues de carpes*, the *ramereaux à la charnière*, the *ciboulette de gibier à l'espagnole*, the *paté de cuisses d'oie aux pois de Monsalvie*, the *queues d'agneau au clair de lune*, the *artichauts à la Grecque*, the *charlotte de pommes à Lucy Waters*, the *bombes à la marée*, and the *glaces aux rayons d'or?* A veritable tour de cuisine that surpassed even the famous little suppers given by the Marquis de Réchale at Passy, and which the Abbé Mirliton pronounced "impeccable, and too good to be eaten."

Ah! Pierre Antoine Berquin de Rambouillet; you

are worthy of your divine mistress!

Mere hunger quickly gave place to those finer instincts of the pure gourmet, and the strange wines, cooled in buckets of snow, unloosed all the décolleté spirits of astonishing conversation and atrocious laughter.

III

At first there was the fun with the surprise packets that contained myriads of amusing things, then a general criticism of the decorations, everyone finding a delightful meaning in the fall of festoon, turn of twig, and twist of branch. Pulex, as usual, bore the palm for insight and invention, and to-night he was more brilliant than ever. He leant across the table and explained to the young page, Macfils de Martaga, what thing was intended by a certain arrangement of roses. The young page smiled and hummed the refrain of "La petite balette." Sporion, too, had delicate perceptions, and was vastly entertained by the disposition of the candelabra.

As the courses advanced, the conversation grew bustling and more personal. Pulex and Cyril and Marisca and Cathelin opened a fire of raillery. The infidelities of Cerise, the difficulties of Brancas, Sarmean's caprices that morning in the lily garden, Thorilliere's declining strength, Astarte's affection for Roseola, Felix's impossible member, Cathelin's passion for Sulpilia's poodle, Sola's passion for herself, the nasty bite that Marisca gave Chloe, the épilatiere of Pulex, Cyril's diseases, Butor's illness, Maryx's tiny cemetery, Lesbia's profound fourth letter, and a thousand amatory follies of the day were discussed.

From harsh and shrill and clamant, the voices grew blurred and inarticulate. Bad sentences were helped out by worse gestures, and at one table Scabius could only express himself with his napkin, after the manner of Sir Jolly Jumble in the "Soldier's Fortune" of Otway. Basalissa and Lysistrata tried to pronounce each other's names, and became very affectionate in the attempt, and Tala, the tragedian, robed in ample purple, and wearing plume and buskin, rose to his feet, and with swaying gestures began to recite one of his favourite parts. He got no further than the first line, but repeated it again and again, with fresh accents and intonations each time, and was only silenced by the approach of the asparagus that was being served by satyrs costumed in white muslin.

Clitor and Sodon had a violent struggle over the beautiful Pella, and nearly upset a chandelier. Sophie became very intimate with an empty champagne bottle, swore it made her enceinte, and ended by having a mock accouchment on the top of the table; and Belamour pretended to be a dog, and pranced from couch to couch on all fours, biting and barking and licking. Mellefont crept about dropping love philtres into glasses. Juventus and Ruella stripped and put on each other's things, Spelto offered a prize for whoever should come first, and Spelto won it! Tannhauser, just a little grisé, lay down on the cushions and let Julia do whatever she liked.

I wish I could be allowed to tell you what occurred round table 15, just at this moment. It would amuse you very much, and would give you a capital idea of the habits of Venus' retinue. Indeed, for deplorable reasons, by far the greater part of what was said and done at this supper must remain unrecorded and even unsuggested.

Venus allowed most of the dishes to pass untasted, she was so engaged with the beauty of Tannhauser. She laid her head many times on his robe, kissing him passionately; and his skin at once firm and yielding, seemed to those exquisite little teeth of hers, the most incomparable pasture. Her upper lip curled and trembled with excitement, showing the gums. Tannhauser, on his side, was no less devoted. He adored her all over and all the things she had on, and buried his face in the folds and flounces of her linen, and ravished away a score of frills in his excess. He found her exasperating, and crushed her in his arms, and slaked his parched lips at her mouth. He caressed her eyelids softly with his finger tips, and pushed aside the curls from her forehead, and did a thousand gracious things, tuning her body as a violinist tunes his instrument before he plays upon it.

Priapusa snorted like an old war horse at the sniff of powder, and tickled Tannhauser and Venus by turns, and slipped her tongue down their throats, and refused to be quiet at all until she had had a mouthful of the Chevalier. Claude, seizing his chance, dived under the table and came up the other side just under the queen's couch, and before she could say "One!" he was taking his coffee "aux deux colonnes." Clair was furious at his friend's success, and sulked for the rest of the evening.

IV

After the fruits and fresh wines had been brought in by a troop of woodland creatures, decked with green leaves and all sorts of Spring flowers, the candles in the orchestra were lit, and in another moment the musicians bustled into their places. The wonderful Titurel de Schentefleur was the chef d'orchestre, and the most insidious of conductors. His bâton dived into a phrase and brought out the most magical and magnificent things, and seemed rather to play every instrument than to lead it. He could add a grace even to Scarlatti and a wonder to Beethoven. A delicate, thin, little man with thick lips and a nez retroussé, with long black hair and curled moustache, in the manner of Molière. What were his amatory tastes, no one in the Venusberg could tell. He generally passed for a virgin, and Cathos had nicknamed him "The Solitaire."

To-night, he appeared in a court suit of white silk, brilliant with decorations. His hair was curled into resplendent ringlets that trembled like springs at the merest gesture of his arm, and in his ears swung the diamonds given him by Venus.

The orchestra was, as usual, in its uniform of red vest and breeches trimmed with gold lace, white stockings and red shoes. Titurel had written a ballet for the evening's divertissement, founded upon De Bergerac's comedy of "Les Bacchanales de Fanfreluche," in which the action and dances were designed by him as well as the music.

V

The curtain rose upon a scene of rare beauty, a remote Arcadian valley and watered with a dear river as fresh and pastoral as a perfect fifth of this scrap of Tempe. It was early morning, and the rearisen sun, like the prince in the "Sleeping Beauty," woke all the earth with his lips. In that golden embrace the night dews were caught up and made splendid, the trees were awakened from their obscure dreams, the slumber of the birds was broken, and all the flowers of the valley rejoiced, forgetting their fear of the darkness.

Suddenly, to the music of pipe and horn, a troop of satyrs stepped out from the recesses of the woods, bearing in their hands nuts and green boughs and flowers and roots and whatsoever the forest yielded, to heap upon the altar of the mysterious Pan that stood in the middle of the stage; and from the hills came down the shepherds and shepherdesses, leading their flocks and carrying garlands upon their crooks. Then a rustic priest, white-robed and venerable, came slowly across the valley followed by a choir of radiant children.

The scene was admirably stage-managed, and nothing could have been more varied yet harmonious than this Arcadian group. The service was quaint and simple, but with sufficient ritual to give the corps-de-ballet an opportunity of showing its dainty skill. The dancing of the satyrs was received with huge favour, and when the priest raised his hand in final blessing, the whole troop of worshippers made such an intricate and elegant exit that it was generally agreed that Titurel had never before shown so fine an invention.

Scarcely had the stage been empty for a moment, when Sporion entered, followed by a brilliant rout of dandies and smart women. Sporion was a tall, slim, depraved young man with a slight stoop, a troubled walk, an oval impassable face, with its olive skin drawn tightly over the bone, strong scarlet lips, long Japanese eyes, and a great gilt toupet. Round his shoulders hung a high-collared satin cape of salmon pink, with long black ribands untied and floating about his body. His coat of sea-green spotted muslin was caught in at the waist by a scarlet sash with scalloped edges, and frilled out over the hips for about six inches. His trousers, loose and wrinkled, reached to the end of the calf, and were brocaded down the sides, and ruched magnificently at the ankles. The stockings were of white kid, with stalls for the toes, and had delicate red sandles strapped over them. But his little hands, peeping out from their frills, seemed quite the most insinuating things, such supple fingers tapering to the point, with tiny nails stained pink, such unquenchable palms, lined and mounted like Lord Fanny's in "Love at all Hazards," and such blue-veined, hairless backs! In his left hand he carried a small lace handkerchief broidered with a coronet.

As for his friends and followers they made the most superb and insolent crowd imaginable, but to catalogue the clothes they had on would require a chapter as long as the famous tenth in Pénillière's history of underlinen. On the whole they looked a very distinguished chorus.

Sporion stepped forward and explained with swift and various gesture that he and his friends were tired of the amusements, wearied with the poor pleasures offered by the civil world, and had invaded the Arcadian valley hoping to experience a new frisson in the destruction of some shepherd's or some satyr's naiveté, and the infusion of their venom among the dwellers of the woods.

The chorus assented with languid but expressive movements.

Curious, and not a little frightened, at the arrival of the wordly company, the sylvans began to peep nervously at those subtle souls through the branches of the trees, and one or two fauns and a shepherd or so crept out warily. Sporion and all the ladies and gentlemen made enticing sounds and invited the rustic creatures with all the grace in the world to come and join them. By little batches they came, lured by the strange looks, by the scents and the doings, and by the brilliant clcthes, and some ventured quite near, timorously fingering the delicious textures of the stuffs. Then Sporion and each of his friends took a satyr or a shepherd or something by the hand, and made the preliminary steps of a courtly

175

measure, for which the most admirable combinations had been invented, and the most charming music written.

The pastoral folk were entirely bewildered when they saw such restrained and graceful movements, and made the most grotesque and futile efforts to imitate them.

Dio mio, a pretty sight! A charming effect too was obtained by the intermixture of stockinged calf and hairy leg, of rich brocade bodice and plain blouse, of tortured head-dress and loose untutored locks.

When the dance was ended, the servants of Sporion brought on champagne, and, with many pirouettes, poured it magnificently into slender glasses, and tripped about plying those Arcadian mouths that had never before tasted such a royal drink.

****

Then the curtain fell with a pudic rapidity.

VI

'Twas not long before the invaders began to enjoy the first fruits of their expedition, plucking them in the most seductive manner with their smooth fingers, and feasting lip and tongue and tooth, whilst the shepherds and satyrs and shepherdesses fairly gasped under the new joys, for the pleasure they experienced was almost too keen and too profound for their simple and untilled natures. Fanfreluche and the rest of the rips and ladies tingled with excitement and frolicked like young lambs in a fresh meadow. Again and again the wine was danced round, and the valley grew as busy as a market day.

Attracted by the noise and merrymaking, all those sweet infants I told you of, skipped suddenly on to the stage, and began clapping their hands and laughing immoderately at the passion and the disorder and commotion, and mimicking the nervous staccato movements they saw in their pretty childish way.

In a flash, Fanfreluche disentangled himself and sprang to his feet, gesticulating as if he would say, "Ah, the little dears!" "Ah, the rorty little things!" "Ah, the little ducks!" for he was so fond of children. Scarcely had he caught one by the thigh than a quick rush was made by everybody for the succulent limbs; and how they tousled them and mousled them! The children cried out, I can tell you. Of course there were not enough for everybody, so some had to share, and some had simply to go on with what they were doing before.

I must not, by the way, forget to mention the independent attitude taken by six or seven of the party, who sat and stood about with half-closed eyes, inflated nostrils, clenched teeth, and painful, parted lips, behaving like the Duc de Broglio when he watched the amours of the Regent d'Orleans.

Now as Fanfreluche and his friends began to grow tired and exhausted with the new debauch, they cared no longer to take the initiative, but, relaxing every muscle, abandoned themselves to passive joys, yielding utterly to the ardent embraces of the intoxicated satyrs, who waxed fast and furious, and seemed as if they would never come to the end of their strength. Full of the new tricks they had learnt that morning, they played them passionately and roughly, making havoc of the cultured flesh, and tearing the splendid frocks and dresses into ribands. Duchesses and Maréchales, Marquises and Princesses, Dukes and Marshalls, Marquesses and Princes, were ravished and stretched and rumpled and crushed beneath

177

the interminable vigour and hairy breasts of the inflamed
woodlanders. They bit at the white thighs and nozzled
wildly in the crevices. They sat astride the women's
chests and consummated frantically with their bosoms;
they caught their prey by the hips and held it over their
heads, irrumating with prodigious gusto. It was the
triumph of the valley.

High up in the heavens the sun had mounted and
filled all the air with generous warmth, whilst shadows
grew shorter and sharper. Little light-winged papillons
flitted across the stage, the bees made music on their
flowery way, the birds were very gay and kept up a
jargoning and refraining, the lambs were bleating upon
the hill side, and the orchestra kept playing, playing the
uncanny tunes of Titurel.

VII

Venus and Tannhauser had retired to the exquisite
little boudoir or pavilion Le Con had designed for the
queen on the first terrace, and which commanded the
most delicious view of the parks and gardens. It was a
sweet little place, all silk curtains and soft cushions.
There were eight sides to it, bright with mirrors and
candelabra, and rich with pictured panels, and the ceiling,
dome shaped and some thirty feet above the head, shone
obscurely with gilt mouldings through the warm haze of
candle light below. Tiny wax statuettes dressed
theatrically and smiling with plump cheeks, quaint
magots that looked as cruel as foreign gods, gilded
monticules, pale celadon vases, clocks that said nothing,
ivory boxes full of secrets, china figures playing whole
scenes of plays, and a world of strange preciousness

178

crowded the curious cabinets that stood against the walls. On one side of the room there were six perfect little card tables, with quite the daintiest and most elegant chairs set primly round them; so, after all, there may be some truth in that line of Mr. Theodore Watts, - "I played at picquet with the Queen of Love".

Nothing in the pavilion was more beautiful than the folding screens painted by De La Pine, with Claudian landscapes - the sort of things that fairly make one melt, things one can lie and look at for hours together, and forget the country can ever be dull and tiresome. There were four of them, delicate walls that hem in an amour so cosily, and make room within room.

The place was scented with huge branches of red roses, and with a faint amatory perfume breathed out from the couches and cushions - a perfume Chateline distilled in secret and called L'Eau Lavante.

Those who have only seen Venus at the Louvre or the British Museum, at Florence, at Naples, or at Rome, can have not the faintest idea how sweet and enticing and gracious, how really exquisitely beautiful she looked lying with Tannhauser upon rose silk in that pretty boudoir.

Cosmé's precise curls and artful waves had been finally disarranged at supper, and strayed ringlets of the black hair fell loosely over her soft, delicious, tired, swollen eyelids. Her frail chemise and dear little drawers were torn and moist, and clung transparently about her, and all her body was nervous and responsive. Her closed thighs seemed like a vast replica of the little bijou she held between them; the beautiful tétons du derrière were as firm as a plump virgin's cheek, and promised a joy as profound as the mystery of the Rue Vendôme, and the minor chevelure, just profuse enough, curled as prettily as the hair upon a cherub's head.

179

Tannhauser, pale and speechless with excitement, passed his gem-girt fingers brutally over the divine limbs; tearing away smock and pantaloon and stocking, and then, stripping himself of his own few things, fell upon the splendid lady with a deep-drawn breath!

It is, I know, the custom of all romancers to paint heroes who can give a lady proof of their valliance at least twenty times a night. Now Tannhauser had no such Gargantuan facility, and was rather relieved when, an hour later, Priapusa and Doricourt and some others burst drunkenly into the room and claimed Venus for themselves. The pavilion soon filled with a noisy crowd that could scarcely keep its feet. Several of the actors were there, and Lesfesses, who had played Fanfreluche so brilliantly, and was still in his makeup, paid tremendous attention to Tannhauser. But the Chevalier found him quite uninteresting off the stage, and rose and crossed the room to where Venus and the manicure were seated.

"How tired the dear baby looks," said Priapusa. "Shall I put him in his little cot?"

"Well, if he's as sleepy as I am," yawned Venus, "you can't do better."

Priapusa lifted her mistress off the pillows, and carried her in her arms in a nice, motherly way.

"Come along, children," said the fat old thing, "come along, it's time you were both in bed."

****

3.

SATIA TE SANGUINE
by Algernon Charles Swinburne

If you loved me ever so little,
  I could bear the bonds that gall,
I could dream the bonds were brittle;
  You do not love me at all.

O beautiful lips, O bosom
  More white than the moon's and warm,
A sterile, ruinous blossom
  Is blown your way in a storm.

As the lost white feverish limbs
  Of the Lesbian Sappho, adrift
In foam where the sea-weed swims,
  Swam loose for the streams to lift,

My heart swims blind in a sea
  That stuns me; swims to and fro,
And gathers to windward and lee
  Lamentation, and mourning, and woe.

A broken, an emptied boat,
  Sea saps it, winds blow apart,
Sick and adrift and afloat,
  The barren waif of a heart.

Where, when the gods would be cruel,
  Do they go for a torture? where
Plant thorns, set pain like a jewel?
  Ah, not in the flesh, not there!

The racks of earth and the rods
  Are weak as foam on the sands:
In the heart is the prey for gods,
  Who crucify hearts, not hands.

Mere pangs corrode and consume,
  Dead when life dies in the brain;
In the infinite spirit is room
  For the pulse of an infinite pain.

I wish you were dead, my dear;
  I would give you, had I to give,
Some death too bitter to fear;
  It is better to die than live.

I wish you were stricken of thunder
  And burnt with a bright flame through.
Consumed and cloven in sunder,
  I dead at your feet like you.

If I could but know after all,
  I might cease to hunger and ache,
Though your heart were ever so small,
  If it were not a stone or a snake.

You are crueller, you that we love,
  Than hatred, hunger, or death;
You have eyes and breasts like a dove,
  And you kill men's hearts with a breath.

As plague in a poisonous city
  Insults and exults on her dead,
So you, when pallid for pity
  Comes love, and fawns to be fed.

As a tame beast writhes and wheedles,
  He fawns to be fed with wiles;
You carve him a cross of needles,
  And whet them sharp as your smiles.

He is patient of thorn and whip,
  He is dumb under axe or dart;
You suck with a sleepy red lip
  The wet red wounds in his heart.

You thrill as his pulses dwindle,
  You brighten and warm as he bleeds,
With insatiable eyes that kindle
  And insatiable mouth that feeds.

Your hands nailed love to the tree,
  You stript him, scourged him with rods,
And drowned him deep in the sea
  That hides the dead and their gods.

And for all this, die will he not;
  There is no man sees him but I;
You came and went and forgot;
  I hope he will some day die.

****

4.

THE DYING OF FRANCIS DONNE
by Ernest Dowson

I

He had lived so long in the meditation of death, visited it so often in others, studied it with such persistency, with a sentiment in which horror and fascination mingled; but it had always been, as it were, an objective, alien fact, remote from himself and his own life. So that it was in a sudden flash, quite too stupefying to admit in the first instance of terror, that knowledge of his mortality dawned on him. There was an absurdity in the idea too.

"I, Francis Donne, thirty-five and some months old, am going to die," he said to himself; and fantastically he looked at his image in the glass, and sought, but quite vainly, to find some change in it which should account for this incongruity, just as, searching in his analytical habit into the recesses of his own mind, he could find no such alteration of his inner consciousness as would explain or justify his plain conviction. And quickly, with reason and casuistry, he sought to rebut that conviction.

The quickness of his mind - it had never seemed to him so nimble, so exquisite a mechanism of syllogism and deduction - was contraposed against his blind instinct of the would-be self-deceiver, in a conflict to which the latter brought something of desperation, the fierce,

184

agonized desperation of a hunted animal at bay. But piece by piece the chain of evidence was strengthened. That subtile and agile mind of his, with its special knowledge, cut clean through the shrinking protests of instinct, removing them as surely and as remorselessly, he reflected in the image most natural to him, as the keen blades of his surgical knives had removed malignant ulcers.

"I, Francis Donne, am going to die," he repeated, and, presently, "*I am going to die soon*; in a few months, in six perhaps, certainly in a year."

Once more, curiously, but this time with a sense of neutrality, as he had often diagnosed a patient, he turned to the mirror. Was it his fancy, or, perhaps, only for the vague light that he seemed to discover a strange grey tone about his face?

But he had always been a man of a very sallow complexion.

There were a great many little lines, like penscratches, scarring the parchment-like skin beneath the keen eyes: doubtless, of late, these had multiplied, become more noticeable, even when his face was in repose.

But, of late, what with his growing practice, his lectures, his writing; all the unceasing labour, which his ambitions entailed, might well have aged him somewhat. That dull, immutable pain, which had first directed his attention from his studies, his investigations, his profession, to his corporal self, the actual Francis Donne, that pain which he would so gladly have called inexplicable, but could explain so precisely, had ceased for the moment. Nerves, fancies! How long it was since he had taken any rest! He had often intended to give himself a holiday - he would grudge nothing - somewhere quite out of the way, somewhere, where there was fishing; in Wales, or perhaps in Brittany; that would surely set him

185

right.

And even while he promised himself this necessary relaxation in the immediate future, as he started on his afternoon round, in the background of his mind there lurked the knowledge of its futility; rest, relaxation, all that, at this date, was, as it were, some tardy sacrifice, almost hypocritical, which he offered to powers who might not be propitiated.

Once in his neat brougham, the dull pain began again; but by an effort of will he put it away from him. In the brief interval from house to house - he had some dozen visits to make - he occupied himself with a medical paper, glanced at the notes of a lecture he was giving that evening at a certain Institute on the "Limitations of Medicine."

He was late, very late for dinner, and his man, Bromgrove, greeted him with a certain reproachfulness, in which he traced, or seemed to trace, a half-patronizing sense of pity. He reminded himself that on more than one occasion, of late, Bromgrove's manner had perplexed him. He was glad to rebuke the man irritably on some pretext, to dismiss him from the room, and he hurried, without appetite, through the cold or overdone food which was the reward of his tardiness.

His lecture over, he drove out to South Kensington, to attend a reception at the house of a great man - great not only in the scientific world, but also in the world of letters. There was some of the excitement of success in his eyes as he made his way, with smiles and bows, in acknowledgement of many compliments, through the crowded rooms. For Francis Donne's lectures - those of them which were not entirely for the initiated - had grown into the importance of a social function. They had almost succeeded in making science fashionable, clothing its dry bones in a garment of so elegantly literary a pattern. But even in the ranks of the profession it was only the envious, the unsuccessful, who ventured to say that Donne had sacrificed doctrine to popularity, that his science was, in their contemptuous parlance, "mere literature."

Yes, he had been very successful, as the world counts success, and his consciousness of this fact, and the influence of the lights, the crowd, the voices, was like absinthe on his tired spirit. He had forgotten, or thought he had forgotten, the phantom of the last few days, the phantom which was surely waiting for him at home.

But he was reminded by a certain piece of news which late in the evening fluttered the now diminished assembly: the quite sudden death of an eminent surgeon, expected there that night, an acquaintance of his own, and more or less of each one of the little, intimate group which tarried to discuss it. With sympathy, with a certain awe, they spoke of him, Donne and others; and both the awe and the sympathy were genuine.

But as he drove home, leaning back in his carriage, in a discouragement, in a lethargy, which was only partly due to physical reaction, he saw visibly underneath their regret - theirs and his own - the triumphant assertion of life, the egoism of instinct. They were sorry, but oh, they were glad! royally glad, that it was another, and not they themselves whom something mysterious had of a sudden snatched away from his busy career, his interests, perhaps from all intelligence; at least, from all the pleasant sensuousness of life, the joy of the visible world, into darkness. And honestly dared not to blame it. How many times had not he, Francis Donne himself experienced it, that egoistic assertion of life in the presence of the dead - the poor, irremediable dead?.... And now, he was only good to give it to others.

Latterly, he had been in the habit of subduing

sleeplessness with injections of morphia, indeed in infinitesimal quantities. But to-night, although he was more than usually restless and awake, by a strong effort of reasonableness he resisted his impulse to take out the little syringe. The pain was at him again with the same dull and stupid insistence; in its monotony, losing some of the nature of pain and becoming a mere nervous irritation. But he was aware that it would not continue like that. Daily, almost hourly, it would gather strength and cruelty; the moments of respite from it would become rarer, would cease. From a dull pain it would become an acute pain, and then a torture, and then an agony, and then a madness. And in those last days, what peace might be his would be the peace of morphia, so that it was essential that, for the moment, he should not abuse the drug.

And as he knew that sleep was far away from him, he propped himself up with two pillows, and by the light of a strong reading lamp settled himself to read. He had selected the work of a distinguished German savant upon the cardiac functions, and a short treatise of his own, which was covered with recent annotations, in his crabbed handwriting, upon "Aneurism of the Heart". He read avidly, and against his own deductions, once more his instinct raised a vain protest. At last he threw the volumes aside, and lay with his eyes shut, without, however, extinguishing the light. A terrible sense of helplessness overwhelmed him; he was seized with an immense and heartbreaking pity for poor humanity as personified in himself; and, for the first time since he had ceased to be a child, he shed puerile tears.

II

The faces of his acquaintance, the faces of the
students at his lectures, the faces of Francis Donne's
colleagues at the hospital, were altered; were, at least,
sensibly altered to his morbid self-consciousness. In
every one whom he encountered, he detected, or fancied
that he detected, an attitude of evasion, a hypocritical air
of ignoring a fact that was obvious and unpleasant. Was
it so obvious, then, the hidden horror which he carried
incessantly about him? Was his secret, which he would
still guard so jealously, become a by-word and an anecdote
in his little world? And a great rage consumed him
against the inexorable and inscrutable forces which had
made him to destroy him; against himself, because of his
proper impotence; and, above all, against the living, the
millions who would remain when he was no longer, the
living, of whom many would regret him (some of them his
personality, and more, his skill), because he could see
under all the unconscious hypocrisy of their sorrow, the
exultant self-satisfaction of their survival.

And with his burning sense of helplessness, of a
certain bitter injustice in things, a sense of shame mingled;
all the merely physical dishonour of death shaping itself
to his sick and morbid fancy into a violent symbol of what
was, as it were, an actual *moral* or intellectual dishonour.
Was not death, too, inevitable and natural an operation
as it was, essentially a process to undergo apart and hide
jealously, as much as other natural and ignoble processes
of the body?

And the animal, who steals away to an uttermost
place in the forest, who gives up his breath in a solitude
and hides his dying like a shameful thing, - might he not
offer an example that it would be well for the dignity of

poor humanity to follow?

Since Death is coming to me, said Francis Donne to himself, let me meet it, a stranger in a strange land, with only strange faces round me and the kind indifference of strangers, instead of the intolerable pity of friends.

III

On the bleak and wave-tormented coast of Finisterre, somewhere between Quiberon and Fouesnant, he reminded himself of a little fishing-village: a few scattered houses (one of them being an *auberge* at which ten years ago he had spent a night), collected round a poor little grey church. Thither Francis Donne went, without leave-takings or explanation, almost secretly, giving but the vaguest indications of the length or direction of his absence. And there for many days he dwelt, in the cottage which he had hired, with one old Breton woman for his sole attendant, in a state of mind which, after all the years of energy, of ambitious labour, was almost peace.

Bleak and grey it had been, when he had visited it of old, in the late autumn; but now the character, the whole colour of the country was changed. It was brilliant with the promise of summer, and the blue Atlantic, which in winter churned with its long crested waves so boisterously below the little white lighthouse, which warned mariners (alas! so vainly), against the shark-like cruelty of the rocks, now danced and glittered in the sunshine, rippled with feline caresses round the hulls of the fishing-boats whose brown sails floated so idly in the faint air.

Above the village, on a grassy slope, whose green

was almost lurid, Francis Donne lay, for many silent hours, looking out at the placid sea, which could yet be so ferocious, at the low violet line of the Island of Groix, which alone interrupted the monotony of sky and ocean.

He had brought many books with him but he read in them rarely; and when physical pain gave him a respite for thought, he thought almost of nothing. His thought was for a long time a lethargy and a blank.

Now and again he spoke with some of the inhabitants. They were a poor and hardy, but a kindly race: fishers and the wives of fishers, whose children would grow up and become fishermen and the wives of fishermen in their turn. Most of them had wrestled with death; it was always so near to them that hardly one of them feared it; they were fatalists, with the grim and resigned fatalism of the poor, of the poor who live with the treachery of the sea.

Francis Donne visited the little cemetery, and counted the innumerable crosses which testified to the havoc which the sea had wrought. Some of the graves were nameless; holding the bodies of strange seamen which the waves had tossed ashore.

"And in a little time I shall lie here," he said to himself; "and here as well as elsewhere," he added with a shrug, assuming, and, for once, almost sincerely, the stoicism of his surroundings, "and as lief to-day as to-morrow."

On the whole, the days were placid; there were even moments when, as though he had actually drunk in renewed vigour from that salt sea air, the creative force of the sun, he was tempted to doubt his grievous knowledge, to make fresh plans for life. But these were fleeting moments, and the reaction from them was terrible. Each day his hold on life was visibly more slender, and the people of the village saw, with a rough sympathy, which did not offend him, allowed him to perceive that they saw, the rapid growth and the inevitableness of his end.

IV

But if the days were not without their pleasantness, the nights were always horrible - a torture of the body and an agony of the spirit. Sleep was far away, and the brain, which has been lulled till the evening, would awake, would grow electric with life and take strange and abominable flights into the darkness of the pit, into the black night of the unknowable and the unknown.

And interminably, during those nights which seemed eternity, Francis Donne questioned and examined into the nature of that Thing, which stood, a hooded figure beside his bed, with a menacing hand raised to beckon him so peremptorily from all that lay within his consciousness.

He had been all his life absorbed in science; he had dissected, how many bodies? and in what anatomy had he ever found a soul? Yet if his avocations, his absorbing interest in physical phenomena had made him somewhat a materialist, it had been almost without his consciousness. The sensible, visible world of matter had loomed so large to him, that merely to know that had seemed to him sufficient. All that might conceivably lie outside it, he had, without negation, been content to regard as outside his province.

And now, in his weakness, in the imminence of approaching dissolution, his purely physical knowledge seemed but a vain possession, and he turned with a passionate interest to what had been said and believed from time immemorial by those who had concentrated their intelligence on that strange essence, which might

192

after all be the essence of one's personality, which might be that sublimated consciousness - the Soul - actually surviving the infamy of the grave?

> Animula, vagula, blandula!
> Hospes comesque corporis,
> Quae nunc abidis in loca?
> Pallidula, rigida, nudula.

Ah, the question! It was a harmony, perhaps (as, who had maintained? whom the Platonic Socrates in the "Phaedo" had not too successfully refuted), a harmony of life, which was dissolved when life was over? Or, perhaps, as how many metaphysicians had held both before and after a sudden great hope, perhaps too generous to be true, had changed and illuminated, to countless millions, the inexorable figure of Death - a principle, indeed, immortal, which came and went, passing through many corporal conditions until it was ultimately resolved into the great mind, pervading all things? Perhaps?....But what scanty consolation, in all such theories, to the poor body, racked with pain and craving peace, to the tortured spirit of self-consciousness so achingly anxious not to be lost.

And he turned from these speculations to what was, after all, a possibility like the others; the faith of the simple, of these fishers with whom he lived, which was also the faith of his own childhood, which, indeed, he had never repudiated, whose practices he had simply discarded, as one discards puerile garments when one comes to man's estate. And he remembered, with the vividness with which, in moments of great anguish, one remembers things long ago familiar, forgotten though they may have been for years, the triumphant declarations of the Church:

Omnes quidem resurgemus, sed non omnes immutabimur. In momento, in ictu oculi, in novissima tuba: canet enim tuba: et mortui resurgent incorrupti, et nos immutabimur. Oportet enim corruptibile hoc induere immortalitatem. Cum autem mortale hoc induerit immortalitatem tunc fiet sermo qui scriptus est: Absorpta est mors in victoria. Ubi est, mors, victoria tua? Ubi est, mors, stimulus tuus?

Ah, for the certitude of that! of that victorious confutation of the apparent destruction of sense and spirit in a common ruin....But it was a possibility like the rest; and had it not more need than the rest to be more than a possibility, if it would be a consolation, in that it promised more? And he gave it up, turning his face to the wall, lay very still, imagining himself already stark and cold, his eyes closed, his jaw closely tied (lest the ignoble changes which had come to him should be too ignoble), while he waited until the narrow boards, within which he should lie, had been nailed together, and the bearers were ready to convey him into the corruption which was to be his part.

And as the window-pane grew light with morning, he sank into a drugged, unrestful sleep, from which he would awake some hours later with eyes more sunken and more haggard cheeks. And that was the pattern of many nights.

V

One day he seemed to wake from a night longer and more troubled than usual, a night which had, perhaps, been many nights and days, perhaps even weeks; a night of an ever-increasing agony, in which he was only dimly conscious at rare intervals of what was happening, or of the figures coming and going around his bed: the doctor from a neighbouring town, who had stayed by him unceasingly, easing his paroxysms with the little merciful syringe; the soft, practised hands of a sister of charity about his pillow; even the face of Bromgrove, for whom doubtless he had sent, when he had foreseen the utter helplessness which was at hand.

He opened his eyes, and seemed to discern a few blurred figures against the darkness of the closed shutters through which one broad ray filtered in; but he could not distinguish their faces, and he closed his eyes once more. An immense and ineffable tiredness had come over him that this - *this* was Death; this was the thing against which he had cried and revolted; the horror from which he would have escaped; this utter luxury of physical exhaustion, this calm, this release.

The corporal capacity of smiling had passed from him, but he would fain have smiled.

And for a few minutes of singular mental lucidity, all his life flashed before him in a new relief; his childhood, his adolescence, the people whom he had known; his mother, who had died when he was a boy, of a malady from which, perhaps, a few years later, his skill had saved her; the friend of his youth who had shot himself for so little reason; the girl whom he had loved, but who had not loved him....All that was distorted in life was adjusted and justified in the light of his sudden knowledge. *Beati mortui*....and then the great tiredness swept over him once more, and a fainter consciousness, in which he could yet just dimly hear, as in a dream, the sound of Latin prayers, and feel the application of the oils upon all the issues and approaches of his wearied sense; then utter unconsciousness, while pulse and heart gradually grew fainter until both ceased. And that was all.

first meeting, when I had found her laden with flaming tendrils in the thinned woods of my heritage. A very Dryad, robed in grass colour, she was chanting to the sylvan deities. The invisible web took me, and I became her slave.

Her house lay two leagues from mine. It was a low-built mansion lying in a concave park. The thatch was gaudy with stonecrop and lichen. Amongst the central chimneys a foreign bird sat on a nest of twigs. The long windows blazed with heraldic devices; and paintings of kings and queens and nobles hung in the dim chambers. Here she dwelt with a retinue of aged servants, fantastic women and men half imbecile, who salaamed before her with eastern humility and yet addressed her in such terms as gossips use. Had she given them life they could not have obeyed with more reverence. Quaint things the women wrought for her - pomanders and cushions of thistledown; and the men were never happier than when they could tell her of the first thrush's egg in the thornbush or the sege of bitterns that haunted the marsh. She was their goddess and their daughter. Each day had its own routine. In the morning she rode and sang and played; at noon she read in the dusty library, drinking to the full of the dramatists and the platonists. Her own life was such a tragedy as an Elizabethan would have adored. None save her people knew her history, but there were wonderful stories of how she had bowed to tradition, and concentrated in herself the characteristics of a thousand wizard fathers. In the blossom of her youth she had sought strange knowledge, and had tasted thereof, and rued.

The morning after my declaration she rode across her part to the meditating walk I always paced till noon. She was alone, dressed in a habit of white lutestring with a loose girdle of blue. As her mare reached the yew hedge, she dismounted, and came to me with more lightness than I had ever beheld in her. At her waist hung a black glass mirror, and her half-bare arms were adorned with cabalistic jewels.

When I knelt to kiss her hand, she sighed heavily. "Ask me nothing," she said. "Life itself is too joyless to be more embittered by explanations. Let all rest between us as now. I will love coldly, you warmly, with no nearer approaching." Her voice rang full of a wistful expectancy: as if she knew that I should combat her half-explained decision. She read me well, for almost ere she had done I cried out loudly against it: - "It can never be so - I cannot breathe - I shall die?"

She sank to the low moss-covered wall. "Must the sacrifice be made?" she asked, half to herself. "Must I tell him all?" Silence prevailed a while, then turning away her face she said: "From the first I loved you, but last night in the darkness, when I could not sleep for thinking of your words, love sprang into desire."

I was forbidden to speak.

"And desire seemed to burst the cords that bound me. In that moment's strength I felt that I could give all for the joy of being once utterly yours."

I longed to clasp her to my heart. But her eyes were stern, and a frown crossed her brow.

"At morning light," she said, "desire died, but in my ecstasy I had sworn to give what must be given for that short bliss, and to lie in your arms and pant against you before another midnight. So I have come to bid you fare with me to the place where the spell may be loosed, and happiness bought."

She called the mare: it came whinnying, and pawed the ground until she had stroked its neck. She mounted, setting in my hand a tiny, satin-shod foot that seemed rather child's than woman's. "Let us go together

199

to my house," she said. "I have orders to give and duties to fulfil. I will not keep you there long, for we must start soon on our errand." I walked exultantly at her side, but, the grange in view, I entreated her to speak explicitly of our mysterious journey. She stooped and patted my head. "'Tis but a matter of buying and selling," she answered.

When she had arranged her household affairs, she came to the library and bade me follow her. Then, with the mirror still swinging against her knees, she led me through the garden and the wilderness down to a misty wood. It being autumn, the trees were tinted gloriously in dusky bars of colouring. The rowan, with his amber leaves and scarlet berries, stood before the brown black-spotted sycamore; the silver beech flaunted his golden coins against my poverty; firs, green and fawn-hued, slumbered in hazy gossamer. No bird carolled, although the sun was hot. Marina noted the absence of sound, and without prelude of any kind began to sing from the ballad of the Witch Mother: about the nine enchanted knots, and the trouble-comb in the lady's knotted hair, and the master-kid that ran beneath her couch. Every drop of my blood froze in dread, for whilst she sang her face took on the majesty of one who traffics with infernal powers. As the shade of the trees fell over her, and we passed intermittently out of the light, I saw that her eyes glittered like rings of sapphires. Believing now that the ordeal she must undergo would be too frightful, I begged her to return. Supplicating on my knees - "Let me face the evil alone!" I said, "I will entreat the loosening of the bonds. I will compel and accept any penalty." She grew calm. "Nay," she said, very gently, "if aught can conquer, it is my love alone. In the fervour of my last wish I can dare everything."

By now, at the end of a sloping alley, we had

reached the shores of a vast marsh. Some unknown quality in the sparkling water had stained its whole bed a bright yellow. Green leaves, of such a sour brightness as almost poisoned to behold, floated on the surface of the rush-girdled pools. Weeds like tempting veils of mossy velvet grew beneath in vivid contrast with the soil. Alders and willows hung over the margin. From where we stood a half-submerged path of rough stones, threaded by deep swift channels, crossed to the very centre. Marina put her foot upon the first step. "I must go first," she said. "Only once before have I gone this way, yet I know its pitfalls better than any living creature."

Before I could hinder her she was leaping from stone to stone like a hunted animal. I followed hastily, seeking, but vainly, to lessen the space between us. She was gasping for breath, and her heart-beats sounded like the ticking of a clock. When we reached a great pool, itself almost a lake, that was covered with lavender scum, the path turned abruptly to the right, where stood an isolated grove of wasted elms. As Marina beheld this, her pace slackened, and she paused in momentary indecision; but, at my first word of pleading that she should go no further, she went on, dragging her silken mud-bespattered skirts. We climbed the slippery shores of the island (for island it was, being raised much above the level of the marsh), and Marina led the way over lush grass to an open glade. A great marble tank lay there, supported on two thick pillars. Decayed boughs rested on the crust of stagnancy within, and divers frogs, bloated and almost blue, rolled off at our approach. To the left stood the columns of a temple, a round, domed building, with a closed door of bronze. Wild vines had grown athwart the portal; rank, clinging herbs had sprung from the overteeming soil; astrological figures were enchiselled on the broad stairs.

Here Marina stopped. "I shall blindfold you," she said, taking off her loose sash, "and you must vow obedience to all I tell you. The least error will betray us." I promised, and submitted to the bandage. With a pressure of the hand, and bidding me neither move nor speak, she left me and went to the door of the temple. Thrice her hand struck the dull metal. At the last stroke a hissing shriek came from within, and the massive hinges creaked loudly. A breath like an icy tongue leaped out and touched me, and in the terror my hand sprang to the kerchief. Marina's voice, filled with agony, gave me instant pause. *"Oh, why am I thus torn between the man and the fiend? The mesh that holds life in will be ripped from end to end! Is there no mercy?"*

My hand fell impotent. Every muscle shrank. I felt myself turn to stone. After a while came a sweet scent of smouldering wood: such an Oriental fragrance as is offered to Indian gods. Then the door swung to, and I heard Marina's voice, dim and wordless, but raised in wild deprecation. Hour after hour passed so, and still I waited. Not until the sash grew crimson with the rays of the sinking sun did the door open.

"Come to me!" Marina whispered. "Do not unblindfold. Quick - we must not stay here long. He is glutted with my sacrifice."

Newborn joy rang in her tones. I stumbled across and was caught in her arms. Shafts of delight pierced my heart at the first contact with her warm breasts. She turned me round, and bidding me look straight in front, with one swift touch untied the knot. The first thing my dazed eyes fell upon was the mirror of black glass which had hung from her waist. She held it so that I might gaze into its depths. And there, with a cry of amazement and fear, *I saw the shadow of the Basilisk.*

The Thing was lying prone on the floor, the

202

presentment of a sleeping horror. Vivid scarlet and sable feathers covered its gold-crowned cock's-head, and its leathern dragon-wings were folded. Its sinuous tail, capped with a snake's eyes and mouth, was curved in luxurious and delighted satiety. A prodigious evil leaped in its atmosphere. But even as I looked a mist crowded over the surface of the mirror: the shadow faded, leaving only an indistinct and wavering shape. Marina breathed upon it, and, as I peered and pored, the gloom went off the plate and left, where the Chimera had lain, the prostrate figure of a man. He was young and stalwart, a dark outline with a white face, and short black curls that fell in tangles over a shapely forehead, and eyelids languorous and red. His aspect was that of a wearied demon-god.

When Marina looked sideways and saw my wonderment, she laughed delightedly in one rippling running tune that should have quickened the dead entrails of the marsh. "I have conquered!" she cried. "I have purchased the fulness of joy!" And with one outstretched arm she closed the door before I could turn to look; with the other she encircled my neck, and, bringing down my head, pressed my mouth to hers. The mirror fell from her hand, and with her foot she crushed its shards into the dank mould.

The sun had sunk behind the trees now, and glittered through the intricate leafage like a charcoal-burner's fire. All the nymphs of the pools arose and danced, grey and cold, exulting at the absence of the divine light. So thickly gathered the vapours that the path grew perilous. "Stay, love," I said. "Let me take you in my arms and carry you. It is no longer safe for you to walk alone." She made no reply, but, a flush arising to her pale cheeks, she stood and let me lift her to my bosom. She rested a hand on either shoulder, and gave no sign of fear as I bounded from stone to stone. The way lengthened deliciously, and by the time we reached the plantation the moon was rising over the further hills. Hope and fear fought in my heart: soon both were set at rest. When I set her on the dry ground she stood a-tiptoe, and murmured with exquisite shame: "To-night, then, dearest. My home is yours now."

So, in a rapture too subtle for words, we walked together, arm-enfolded, to her house. Preparations for a banquet were going on within: the windows were ablaze, and figures passed behind them bowed with heavy dishes. At the threshold of the hall we were met by a triumphant crash of melody. In the musician's gallery bald-pated veterans stood to it with flute and harp and viol-de-gamba. In two long rows the antic retainers stood, and bowed, and cried merrily: "Joy and health to the bride and groom!" And they kissed Marina's hands and mine, and, with the players sending forth that half-forgotten tenderness which threads through ancient song-books, we passed to the feast, seating ourselves on the dais, whilst the servants filled the tables below. But we made little feint of appetite. As the last dish of confections was removing, a weird pageant swept across the further end of the banqueting-room: Oberon and Titania with Robin Goodfellow and the rest, attired in silks and satins gorgeous of hue, and bedizened with such late flowers as were still with us. I leaned forward to commend, and saw that each face was brown and wizened and thin-haired: so that their motions and their epithalamy felt goblin and discomforting; nor could I smile till they departed by the further door. Then the tables were cleared away, and Marina, taking my finger-tips in hers, opened a stately dance. The servants followed, and in the second maze a shrill and joyful laughter proclaimed that the bride had sought her chamber....

Ere the dawn I wakened from a troubled sleep. My

dream had been of despair: I had been persecuted by a host of devils, thieves of a price-less jewel. So I leaned over the pillow for Marina's consolation; my lips sought hers, my hand crept beneath her head. My heart gave one mad bound - then stopped.

****

7.

MAGIC
by Lionel Johnson

I.

BECAUSE I work not, as logicians work,
Who but to ranked and marshalled reason yield:
But my feet hasten through a faery field,
Thither, where underneath the rainbow lurk
Spirits of youth, and life, and gold, concealed:

Because by leaps I scale the secret sky,
Upon the motion of a cunning star:
Because I hold the winds oracular,
And think on airy warnings, when men die:
Because I tread the ground, where shadows are:

Therefore my name is grown a popular scorn,
And I a children's terror! Only now,
For I am old! O Mother Nature! thou
Leavest me not; wherefore, as night turns morn,
A magian wisdom breaks beneath my brow.

These painful toilers of the bounded way,
Chaired within cloister halls: can they renew
Ashes to flame? Can they of moonlit dew
Prepare the immortalizing draughts? Can they
Give gold for refuse earth, or bring to view

Earth's deepest doings? Let them have their school,
Their science, and their safety! I am he,
Whom Nature fills with her philosophy,
And takes for kinsman. Let me be their fool,
And wise man in the winds' society.

II.

THEY wrong with ignorance a royal choice,
Who cavil at my loneliness and labour:
For them, the luring wonder of a voice,
The viol's cry for them, the harp and tabour:
   For me divine austerity.
   And voices of philosophy.

Ah! light imaginations, that discern
No passion in the citadel of passion:
Their fancies lie on flowers; but my thoughts turn
To thoughts and things of an eternal fashion:
   The majesty and dignity
   Of everlasting verity.

Mine is the sultry sunset, when the skies
Tremble with strange, intolerable thunder:
And at the dead of an hushed night, these eyes
Draw down the soaring oracles winged with wonder:
   From the four winds they come to me,
   The Angels of Eternity.

Men pity me; poor men, who pity me!
Poor, charitable, scornful souls of pity!
I choose laborious loneliness: and ye
Lead Love in triumph through the dancing city:
   While death and darkness girdle me,
   I grope for immortality.

III.

POUR slowly out your holy balm of oil,
Within the grassy circle: let none spoil
Our favourable silence. Only I,
Winding wet vervain round mine eyes, will cry
Upon the powerful Lord of this our toil;
Until the first lark sing, the last star die.

Proud Lord of twilight, Lord of midnight, hear!
Thou hast forgone us; and hast drowsed thine ear,
When haggard voices hail thee: thou hast turned
Blind eyes, dull nostrils, when our vows have burned
Herbs on the moonlit flame, in reverent fear:
Silence is all, our love of thee hath earned.

Master! we call thee, calling on thy name!
Thy savoury laurel crackles: the blue flame
Gleams, leaps, devours apace the dewy leaves.
Vain! for not breast of labouring midnight heaves,
Nor chilled stars fall: all things remain the same,
Save this new pang, that stings, and burns, and cleaves.

Despising us, knowest not! We stand,
Bared for thine adoration, hand in hand:
Steely our eyes, our hearts to all but thee
Iron: as waves of the unresting sea,
The wind of thy least Word is our command:
And our ambition hails thy sovereignty.

Come, Sisters! for the King of night is dead:
Come! for the frailest star of stars hath sped:
And though we waited for the waking sun,
Our King would wake not. Come! our world is done:
For all the witchery of the world is fled,
And lost all wanton wisdom long since won.

8.

THE OTHER SIDE
by Count Stanislaus Eric Stenbock

"Not that I like it, but one does feel so much better after it - oh, thank you, Mère Yvonne, yes just a little drop more." So the old crones fell to drinking their hot brandy and water (although of course they only took it medicinally, as a remedy for their rheumatics), all seated round the big fire and Mère Pinquèle continued her story.

"Oh, yes, then when they get to the top of the hill, there is an altar with six candles quite black and a sort of something in between, that nobody sees quite clearly, and the old black ram with the man's face and long horns begins to say Mass in a sort of gibberish nobody understands, and two black strange things like monkeys glide about with the book and the cruets - and there's music too, such music. There are things the top half like black cats, and the bottom part like men only their legs are all covered with close black hair, and they play on the bag-pipes, and when they come to the elevation, then -" Amid the old crones there was lying on the hearth-rug, before the fire, a boy, whose large lovely eyes dilated and whose limbs quivered in the very ecstacy of terror.

"Is that all true, Mère Pinquèle?" he said. "Oh, quite true, and not only that, the best part is yet to come; for they take a child and - ." Here Mère Pinquèle showed her fang-like teeth.

"Oh! Mère Pinquèle, are you a witch too?"

"Silence, Gabriel," said Mère Yvonne, "how can you say anything so wicked? Why, bless me, the boy ought to have been in bed ages ago."

Just then all shuddered, and all made the sign of the cross except Mère Pinquèle, for they heard that most dreadful of dreadful sounds - the howl of a wolf, which begins with three sharp barks and then lifts itself up in a long protracted wail of commingled cruelty and despair, and at last subsides into a whispered growl fraught with eternal malice.

There was a forest and a village and a brook, the village was on one side of the brook, none had dared to cross to the other side. Where the village was, all was green and glad and fertile and fruitful; on the other side the trees never put forth green leaves, and a dark shadow hung over it even at noon-day, and in the nightime one could hear the wolves howling - the were-wolves and wolf-men and the men-wolves, and those very wicked men who for nine days in every year are turned into wolves; but on the green side no wolf was ever seen, and only one little running brook like a silver streak flowed between.

It was spring now and the old crones sat no longer by the fire but before their cottages sunning themselves, and everyone felt so happy that they ceased to tell stories of the "other side". But Gabriel wandered by the brook as he was wont to wander, drawn thither by some strange attraction mingled with intense horror.

His schoolfellows did not like Gabriel; all laughed and jeered at him, because he was less cruel and more gentle of nature than the rest, and even as a rare and beautiful bird escaped from a cage is hacked to death by the common sparrows, so was Gabriel among his fellows. Everyone wondered how Mère Yvonne, that buxom and worthy matron, could have produced a son like this, with strange dreamy eyes, who was as they said "pas comme les autres gamins." His only friends were the Abbé

Félicien whose Mass he served each morning, and one little girl called Carmeille, who loved him, no one could make out why.

The sun had already set, Gabriel still wandered by the brook, filled with vague terror and irresistible fascination. The sun set and the moon rose, the full moon, very large and very clear, and the moonlight flooded the forest both this side and "the other side," and just on the "other side" of the brook, hanging over, Gabriel saw a large deep blue flower, whose strange intoxicating perfume reached him and fascinated him even where he stood.

"If I could only make one step across," he thought, "nothing could harm me if I only plucked that one flower, and nobody would know I had been over at all," for the villagers looked with hatred and suspicion on anyone who was said to have crossed to the "other side," so summing up courage he leapt lightly to the other side of the brook. Then the moon breaking from a cloud shone with unusual brilliance, and he saw, stretching before him, long reaches of the same strange blue flowers each one lovelier than the last, till, not being able to make up his mind which one flower to take or whether to take several, he went on and on, and the moon shone very brightly, and a strange unseen bird, somewhat like a nightingale, but louder and lovelier, sang, and his heart was filled with longing for he knew not what, and the moon shone and the nightingale sang. But of a sudden a black cloud covered the moon entirely, and all was black, utter darkness, and through the darkness he heard wolves howling and shrieking in the hideous ardour of the chase, and there passed before him a horrible procession of wolves (black wolves with red fiery eyes), and with them men that had the heads of wolves and wolves that had the heads of men, and above them flew

211

owls (black owls with fiery eyes), and bats and long serpentine black things, and last of all seated on an enormous black ram with hideous human face the wolf-keeper on whose face was eternal shadow; but they continued their horrid chase and passed him by, and when they had passed the moon shone out more beautiful than ever, and the strange nightingale sang again, and the strange intense blue flowers were in long reaches in front to the right and to the left. But one thing was there which had not been before, among the deep blue flowers walked one with long gleaming golden hair, and she turned once round and her eyes were of the same colour as the strange blue flowers, and she walked on and Gabriel could not choose but follow. But when a cloud passed over the moon he saw no beautiful woman but a wolf, so in utter terror he turned and fled, plucking one of the strange blue flowers on the way, and leapt again over the brook and ran home.

When he got home Gabriel could not resist showing his treasure to his mother, though he knew she would not appreciate it; but when she saw the strange blue flower, Mère Yvonne turned pale and said, "Why child, where hast thou been? sure it is the witch flower"; and so saying she snatched it from him and cast it into the corner, and immediately all its beauty and strange fragrance faded from it and it looked charred as though it had been burnt. So Gabriel sat down silently and rather sulkily, and having eaten no supper went up to bed, but he did not sleep but waited and waited till all was quiet within the house. Then he crept downstairs in his long white night-shirt and bare feet on the square cold stones and picked hurriedly up the charred and faded flower and put it in his warm bosom next his heart, and immediately the flower bloomed again lovelier than ever, and he fell into a deep sleep, but through his sleep he seemed to hear a soft low voice singing underneath his window in a strange language (in which the subtle sounds melted into one another), but he could distinguish no word except his own name.

When he went forth in the morning to serve Mass, he still kept the flower with him next his heart. Now when the priest began Mass and said "Intriobo ad altar Dei,"[1] then said Gabriel "Qui nequiquam laetificavit juventutem meam."[2] And the Abbé Félicien turned round on hearing this strange response, and he saw the boy's face deadly pale, his eyes fixed and his limbs rigid, and as the priest looked on him Gabriel fell fainting to the floor, so the sacristan had to carry him home and seek another acolyte for the Abbé Félicien.

Now when the Abbé Félicien came to see after him, Gabriel felt strangely reluctant to say anything about the blue flower and for the first time he deceived the priest.

In the afternoon as sunset drew nigh he felt better and Carmeille came to see him and begged him to go out with her into the fresh air. So they went out hand in hand, the dark haired, gazelle-eyed boy, and the fair wavy haired girl, and something, he knew not what, led his steps (half knowingly and yet not so, for he could not but walk thither) to the brook, and they sat down together on the bank.

Gabriel thought at least he might tell his secret to Carmeille, so he took out the flower from his bosom and said, "Look here, Carmeille, hast thou seen ever so lovely a flower as this?" but Carmeille turned pale and faint and said, "Oh Gabriel what is this flower? I but touched it and I felt something strange come over me. No, no, I don't like its perfume, no, there's something not quite right about it, oh, dear Gabriel, do let me throw it away," and before

1 "I will go unto the altar of God"
2 "Who denies me the joy of my youth"

213

he had time to answer, she cast it from her, and again all its beauty and fragrance went from it and it looked charred as though it had been burnt. But suddenly where the flower had been thrown on this side of the brook, there appeared a wolf, which stood and looked at the children.

Carmeille said, "What shall we do," and clung to Gabriel, but the wolf looked at them very steadfastly and Gabriel recognized in the eyes of the wolf the strange deep intense blue eyes of the wolf-woman he had seen on the "other side", so he said, "Stay here, dear Carmeille, see she is looking gently at us and will not hurt us."

"But it is a wolf," said Carmeille, and quivered all over with fear, but again Gabriel said languidly. "She will not hurt us." Then Carmeille seized Gabriel's hand in an agony of terror and dragged him along with her till they reached the village, where she gave the alarm and all the lads of the village gathered together. They had never seen a wolf on this side of the brook, so they excited themselves greatly and arranged a grand wolf hunt for the morrow, but Gabriel sat silently apart and said no word.

That night Gabriel could not sleep at all nor could he bring himself to say his prayers; but he sat in his little room by the window with his shirt open at the throat and the strange blue flower at his heart and again this night he heard a voice singing beneath his window in the same soft, subtle, liquid language as before -

> Ma zála liràl va jé
> Cwamûlo zhajéla je
> Cárma urádi el javé
> Járma, symai, - carmé -
> Zhála javály thra je
> al vú al vlaûle va azré

Safralje vairálje va já?
Cárma serâja
Lâja lâja
Luxhà!

and as he looked he could see the silvern shadows slide
on the limmering light of golden hair, and the strange
eyes gleaming dark blue through the night and it seemed
to him that he could not but follow; so he walked half clad
and bare foot as he was with eyes fixed as in a dream
silently down the stairs and out into the night.

And ever and again she turned to look on him with
her strange blue eyes full of tenderness and passion and
sadness beyond the sadness of things human - and as he
foreknew his steps led him to the brink of the brook. Then
she, taking his hand, familiarly said, "Won't you help me
over Gabriel?"

Then it seemed to him as though he had known her
all his life - so he went with her to the "other side" but he
saw no one by him; and looking again beside him there
were *two wolves*. In a frenzy of terror, he (who had never
thought to kill any living thing before) seized a log of
wood lying by and smote one of the wolves on the head.

Immediately he saw the wolf-woman at his side
with blood streaming from her forehead, staining her
wonderful golden hair, and with eyes looking at him with
infinite reproach, she said - "Who did this?"

Then she whispered a few words to the other wolf,
which leapt over the brook and made its way towards the
village, and turning again towards him she said, "Oh,
Gabriel, how could you strike me, who would have loved
you so long and so well." Then it seemed to him again as
though he had known her all his life but he felt dazed and
said nothing - but she gathered a dark green strangely
shaped leaf and holding it to her forehead, she said -

215

"Gabriel, kiss the place all will be well again." So he kissed as she has bidden him and he felt the salt taste of blood in his mouth and then he knew no more.

****

Again he saw the wolf-keeper with his horrible troupe around him, but this time not engaged in the chase but sitting in strange conclave in a circle and the black owls sat in the trees and the black bats hung downwards from the branches. Gabriel stood alone in the middle with a hundred wicked eyes fixed on him. They seemed to deliberate about what should be done with him, speaking in that same strange tongue which he had heard in the songs beneath his window. Suddenly he felt a hand pressing in his and saw the mysterious wolf-woman by his side. Then began what seemed a kind of incantation where human or half human creatures seemed to howl, and beasts to speak with human speech but in the unknown tongue. Then the wolf-keeper whose face was ever veiled in shadow spake some words in a voice that seemed to come from afar off, but all he could distinguish was his own name Gabriel and her name Lilith. Then he felt arms enlacing him. -

Gabriel awoke - in his own room - so it was a dream after all - but what a dreadful dream. Yes, but was it his own room? Of course there was his coat hanging over the chair - yes but - the Crucifix - where was the Crucifix and the benetier and the consecrated palm branch and the antique image of Our Lady perpetuae salutis, with the little ever-burning lamp before it, before which he placed every day the flowers he had gathered, yet had not dared to place the blue flower? -

Every morning he lifted his still dream-laden eyes to it and said Ave Maria and made the sign of the cross, which bringeth peace to the soul - but how horrible, how maddening, it was not there, not at all. No surely he could not be awake, at least not *quite* awake, he would make the benedictive sign and he would be freed from this fearful illusion - yes but the sign, he would make the sign - oh, but what was the sign? Had he forgotten? or was his arm paralyzed? No he could move. Then he had forgotten - and the prayer - he must remember that. Avae-nunc-mortis-fructus.[3] No surely it did not run thus - but something like it surely - yes, he was awake he could move at any rate - he would reassure himself - he would get up - he would see the grey old church with the exquisitely pointed gables bathed in the light of dawn, and presently the deep solemn bell would toll and he would run down and don his red cassock and lace-worked cotta and light the tall candles on the altar and wait reverently to vest the good and gracious Abbé Félicien, kissing each vestment as he lifted it with reverent hands.

But surely this was not the light of dawn it was liker sunset! He leapt from his small white bed, and a vague terror came over him, he trembled and had to hold on to the chair before he reached the window. No, the solemn spires of the grey church were not to be seen - he was in the depths of the forest; but in a part he had never seen before - but surely he had explored every part, it must be the "other side". To terror succeeded a languor and lassitude not without charm - passivity, acquiescence indulgence - he felt, as it were, the strong caress of another will flowing over him like water and clothing him with invisible hands in an impalpable garment; so he dressed himself almost mechanically and walked downstairs, the same stairs it seemed to him down which it was his wont to run and spring. The broad square stones seemed singularly beautiful and irridescent with

3 *"Behold, now I am ripe for death"*

many strange colours - how was it he had never noticed this before - but he was gradually losing the power of wondering - he entered the room below - the wonted coffee and bread-rolls were on the table.

"Why, Gabriel, how late you are to-day." The voice was very sweet but the intonation strange - and there sat Lilith, the mysterious wolf-woman, her glittering gold hair tied loose in a loose knot and an embroidery whereon she was tracing strange serpentine patterns, lay over the lap of her maize coloured garment - and she looked at Gabriel steadfastly with her wonderful dark blue eyes and said, "Why, Gabriel, you are late to-day," and Gabriel answered, "I was tired yesterday, give me some coffee."

****

A dream within a dream - yes, he had known her all his life, and they dwelt together; had they not always done so? And she would take him through the glades of the forest and gather for him flowers, such as he had never seen before, and tell him stories in her strange, low deep voice, which seemed ever to be accompanied by the faint vibration of strings, looking at him fixedly the while with her marvellous blue eyes.

****

Little by little the flame of vitality which burned within him seemed to grow fainter and fainter, and his lithe lissom limbs waxed languorous and luxurious - yet was he ever filled with a languid content and a will not his own perpetually overshadowed him.

One day in their wanderings he saw a strange dark blue flower like unto the eyes of Lilith, and a sudden half remembrance flashed through his mind.

"What is this blue flower?" he said, and Lilith shuddered and said nothing; but as they went a little further there was a brook - *the* brook he thought and felt his fetters falling off him, and he prepared to spring over the brook; but Lilith seized him by the arm and held him back with all her strength, and trembling all over she said, "Promise me Gabriel that you will not cross over." But he said, "Tell me what is this blue flower, and why you will not tell me?" And she said, "Look Gabriel at the brook." And he looked and saw that though it was just like the brook of separation it was not the same, the waters did not flow.

As Gabriel looked steadfastly into the still waters it seemed to him as though he saw voices - some impression of the Vespers for the Dead. "Hei mihi quia incolatus sum,"[4] and again "De profundis clamavi ad te"[5] - oh, that veil, that overshadowing veil! Why could he not hear properly and see, and why did he only remember as one looking through a threefold semi-transparent curtain. Yes they were praying for him - but who were they? He heard again the voice of Lilith in whispered anguish, "Come away!"

Then he said, this time in monotone, "What is this blue flower, and what is its use?"

And the low thrilling voice answered, "It is called 'lûli uzhûri,' two drops pressed upon the face of the sleeper and he will *sleep*."

He was as a child in her hand and suffered himself to be led from thence, nevertheless he plucked listlessly one of the blue flowers, holding it downwards in his hand. What did she mean? Would the sleeper wake? Would the blue flower leave any stain? Could that stain be wiped off?

4 *"Woe unto me, for I am hedged in"*
5 *"Out of the depths have I cried unto thee"*
219

But as he lay asleep at early dawn he heard voices from afar off praying for him - the Abbé Félicien, Carmeille, his mother too, then some familiar words struck his ear: "Libera mea porta inferi"[6] Mass was being said for the repose of his soul, he knew this. No, he could not stay, he would leap over the brook, he knew the way - he had forgotten that the brook did not flow. Ah, but Lilith would know - what should he do? The blue flower - there it lay close by his bedside - he understood now; so he crept very silently to where Lilith lay asleep, her long hair glittering gold, shining like a glory round about her. He pressed two drops on her forehead, she sighed once, and a shade of praeternatural anguish passed over her beautiful face. He fled - terror, remorse, and hope tearing his soul and making fleet his feet. He came to the brook - he did not see that the water did not flow - of course this was the brook of separation; one bound, he should be with things human again. He leapt over and -

A change had come over him - what was it? He could not tell - did he walk on all fours? Yes surely. He looked into the brook, whose still waters were fixed as a mirror, and there, horror, he beheld himself; or was it himself? His head and face, yes; but his body transformed to that of a wolf. Even as he looked he heard a sound of hideous mocking laughter behind him. He turned round - there, in a gleam of red lurid light, he saw one whose body was human, but whose head was that of a wolf, with eyes of infinite malice; and while, this hideous being laughed with a loud human laugh, he, essaying to speak, could only utter the prolonged howl of a wolf.

****

But we will transfer our thoughts from the alien

6 *"Deliver me from the gates of hell"*

things on the "other side" to the simple human village where Gabriel used to dwell. Mère Yvonne was not much surprised when Gabriel did not turn up to breakfast - he often did not, so absent minded was he; this time she said, "I suppose he has gone with the others to the wolf hunt." Not that Gabriel was given to hunting, but, as she sagely said, "there was no knowing what he might do next." The boys said, "Of course that muff Gabriel is skulking and hiding himself, he's afraid to join the wolf hunt; why, he wouldn't even kill a cat," for their one notion of excellence was slaughter - so the greater the game the greater the glory. They were chiefly now confined to cats and sparrows, but they all hoped in after time to become generals of armies.

Yet these children had been taught all their life through with the gentle words of Christ - but alas, nearly all the seed falls by the wayside, where it could not bear flower or fruit; how little these know the suffering and bitter anguish or realise the full meaning of the words to those of whom it is written "Some fell among thorns."

The wolf hunt was so far a success that they did actually see a wolf, but not a success, as they did not kill it before it leapt over the brook to the "other side", where, of course, they were afraid to pursue it. No emotion is more inrooted and intense in the minds of common people than hatred and fear of anything "strange."

Days passed by, but Gabriel was nowhere seen - and Mère Yvonne began to see clearly at last how deeply she loved her only son, who was so unlike her that she had thought herself an object of pity to other mothers - the goose and the swan's egg. People searched and pretended to search, they even went to the length of dragging the ponds, which the boys thought very amusing, as it enabled them to kill a great number of water rats, and Carmeille sat in a corner and cried all day long. Mère

221

Pinquèle also sat in a corner and chuckled and said that she had always said Gabriel would come to no good. The Abbé Fèlicien looked pale and anxious, but said very little, save to God and those that dwelt with God.

At last, as Gabriel was not there, they supposed he must be nowhere - that is *dead*. (Their knowledge of other localities being so limited, that it did not even occur to them to suppose he might be living elsewhere than in the village.) So it was agreed that an empty catafalque should be put up in the church with tall candles round it, and Mère Yvonne said all the prayers that were in her prayer book, beginning at the beginning and ending at the end, regardless of their appropriateness - not even omitting the instructions of the rubrics. And Carmeille sat in the corner of the little side chapel and cried, and cried. And the Abbé Fèlicien caused the boys to sing the Vespers for the Dead (this did not amuse them so much as dragging the pond), and on the following morning, in the silence of early dawn, said the Dirge and the Requiem - *and this Gabriel heard*.

Then the Abbé Fèlicien received a message to bring the Holy Viaticum to one sick. So they set forth in solemn procession with great torches, and their way lay along the brook of separation.

****

Essaying to speak he could only utter the prolonged howl of a wolf - the most fearful of all bestial sounds. He howled and howled again - perhaps Lilith would hear him! Perhaps she could rescue him? then he remembered the blue flower - the beginning and end of all his woe. His cries aroused all the denizens of the forest - the wolves, the wolf-men, and the men-wolves. He fled before them in an agony of terror - behind him, seated on the black ram with human face, was the wolf-keeper, whose face was veiled in eternal shadow. Only once he turned to look behind - for among the shrieks and howls of bestial chase he heard one thrilling voice moan with pain. And there among them he beheld Lilith, her body too was that of a wolf, almost hidden in the masses of her glittering golden hair, on her forehead was a stain of blue, like in colour to her mysterious eyes, now veiled with tears she could not shed.

****

The way of the Most Holy Viaticum lay along the brook of separation. They heard the fearful howlings afar off, the torch bearers turned pale and trembled - but Abbé Fèlicien, holding aloft the Ciborium, said "They cannot harm us."

Suddenly the whole horrid chase came in sight. Gabriel sprang over the brook, the Abbé Fèlicien held the most Blessed Sacrament before him, and his shape was restored to him and he fell down prostrate in adoration. But the Abbé Fèlicien still held aloft the Sacres Ciborium, and the people fell on their knees in the agony of fear, but the face of the priest seemed to shine with divine effulgence. Then the wolf-keeper held up in his hands the shape of something horrible and inconceivable - a monstrance to the Sacrament of Hell, and three times he raised it, in mockery of the blessed rite of Benediction. And on the third time streams of fire went forth from his fingers, and all the "other side" of the forest took fire, and great darkness was over all.

All who were there and saw and heard it have kept the impress thereof for the rest of their lives - nor till in their death hour was the remembrance thereof absent from their minds. Shrieks, horrible beyond conception, were heard till nightfall - then the rain rained.

The "other side" is harmless now - charred ashes only; but none dares to cross but Gabriel alone - for once a year for nine days a strange madness comes over him.

****

9.

NON SUM QUALIS ERAM BONAE
SUB REGNO CYNARAE
by Ernest Dowson

Last night, ah, yesternight, betwixt her lips and mine
There fell thy shadow, Cynara! thy breath was shed
Upon my soul between the kisses and the wine;
And I was desolate and sick of an old passion,
  Yea, I was desolate and bowed my head:
I have been faithful to thee, Cynara! in my fashion.

All night upon mine heart I felt her warm heart beat,
Night-long within mine arms in love and sleep she lay;
Surely the kisses of her bought red mouth were sweet;
But I was desolate and sick of an old passion,
  When I awoke and found the dawn was gray:
I have been faithful to thee, Cynara! in my fashion.

I have forgot much, Cynara! gone with the wind,
Flung roses, roses riotously with the throng,
Dancing, to put thy pale, lost lilies out of mind;
But I was desolate and sick of an old passion,
  Yea, all the time, because the dance was long:
I have been faithful to thee, Cynara! in my fashion.

I cried for madder music and for stronger wine,
But when the feast is finished and the lamps expire,
Then falls thy shadow, Cynara! the night is thine;
And I am desolate and sick of an old passion,
  Yea hungry for the lips of my desire:
I have been faithful to thee, Cynara! in my fashion.

10.

A SOMEWHAT SURPRISING CHAPTER
by John Davidson

(From *The Wonderful Mission of Earl Lavende*r)

The cabman was having a hot altercation with a policeman when Earl Lavender and his companions left the Café Benvenuto. An oft-renewed altercation it had been, for the cabman had repeatedly taken his stand opposite the door; whenever, indeed, the approach to the restaurant was unoccupied by arrivals or departures: only to be warned away by the watchful constable. Both his patience and the policeman's were exhausted, and the latter was declaring that he believed the cabman had no engagement at all at the very moment his fare reappeared.

"Here; take my number," cried the cabman triumphantly to his tormentor; "Fifteen million three hundred and thirty-nine thousand five hundred and sixty-two and a half. I got no fare, haven't I? Oh, no; I'm one o' these wealthy private cabs that sneaks a livin' from the miserable toffs wot runs the 'ansoms. D'ye see my armorial bearin's, stoopid? Can't yer read Latin? *Vidget incendiary Virtus* and a Venux above a B. This yer's Lord Basinghoume's cab, and pretty sweetly I pay for it, I can tell you."

The policeman grinned but made no reply.

"Where to, sir?" asked the cabman.

The Veiled Lady, who sat between Earl Lavender and Lord Brumm, replied, -

"Trallidge's Hotel."

"Move on there," shouted the policeman, adding in

an aside to the Soudanese commissionaire, "incendiary vegetable or whatever you call yourself."

Rookwood Square, one side of which is occupied by Trallidge's is not far from Piccadilly Circus, and in less than five minutes the party arrived. The lady paid the fare, and the three entered the hotel.

In the hall Lord Brumm rebelled. He had heard of Trallidge's, and so, indeed, for the matter of that, had Earl Lavender. It had a very dubious reputation. No specific charge was ever brought against it, but ordinary people looked mighty knowing when it was mentioned.

"I'm not going to stay here," said Lord Brumm; "I have still some character to lose if you haven't."

"What's the matter?" said Earl Lavender.

"How do I know?" retorted Lord Brumm; "but you surely can't be ignorant of the ill-name this place has. We may all be arrested in the night and appear in tomorrow's evening papers among a herd of German Jews and Jewesses, needy swells and commercial travellers - "Raid on a West-end Night-house," or something of that kind."

The Lady of the Veil, who had vanished on entering the hotel, now reappeared from the clerk's office. She overheard the last of Lord Brumm's remarks, and, raising one hand to stay Earl Lavender's answer, beckoned a stalwart porter with the other. She then led the way to a stair which went down to the kitchen department. Earl Lavender followed closely, and so did Lord Brumm, for behind him came the stalwart porter smiling sardonically. Pursuing a passage in the sunk flat, the Lady of the Veil brought them to a second stair, very broad and well lit, at the foot of which they found themselves in a large room floored with cedar, hung with tapestry, and furnished with rugs, couches and cushions. A small fountain gurgled and lisped in a marble basin, and several doors admitted

227

muffled sounds of music and conversation. Four men and four women, stately in figure, and with grave, pleasant faces, were the inmates of this room; they were dressed in loose flowing robes, and from the books in their hands, or laid open on the couches, it was plain that they had been reading before the new arrivals disturbed their studies. Too amazed to speak or think, Earl Lavender and Lord Brumm stared about them, while the Veiled Lady, having dismissed the porter, conversed in whispers with the occupants of the room. Shortly the four men approached Earl Lavender and Lord Brumm, and led them towards one of the doors. Earl Lavender, submitting to the Evolutionary will, remained passive in the hands of the pair who had laid hold on him; but Lord Brumm was at first inclined to resent interference with his liberty. However, the powerful grasp which his captors laid upon him at his first struggle taught him to abandon all attempts at resistance.

They were conducted along a lofty carpeted passage to a room much larger than that they had left, which was also hung with tapestry and furnished with rugs, cushions and couches. In it a performance was going on which froze Lord Brumm with terror, and excited a very lively interest in the mind of Earl Lavender.

On the couches sat several middle-aged men and women, whose countenances, like those of the inmates of the first room, wore an agreeable expression of thoughtful gravity. These were superintending the operations of men and women of almost all ages, who entered sometimes in pairs and sometimes in groups. There were three couples present when Earl Lavender and Lord Brumm were led in; and two of the men and one of the women were being soundly flogged by the other three. The chastisers counted the lashes aloud, and in each case twelve were administered. As soon as the punishment had been inflicted, the seeming culprits gathered their robes about them, received the whips, which were of knotted cords, from the hands of those who had wielded them, and the punishers became the punished. Then the couples, having been thus reciprocally lashed, laid their whips on one of the couches, and tripped out of the room, dancing to a measure which was clearly heard, and evidently proceeded from a band of music in a neighbouring apartment.

Having tarried in this room for a minute or two, their captors led Earl Lavender and Lord Brumm along another passage to the toilet department of the Underground City. Here they were laved in warm water, then plunged into snow artifically prepared, and finally drenched in a shower bath of attar of roses. Robes similar to those worn by the other dwellers in the Underground World were given them, and they were taken back to the Whipping Room. Four couples were engaged in the extraordinary ceremony of this apartment when they re-entered it. As there could be no mistake about the actuality and severity of the chastisement, Lord Brumm, at the sight of two tall young women armed with whips, who rose from a couch to greet him and Earl Lavender, cried, -

"No, no! I won't have it, I -"

He got no further with his protest, for he was instantly gagged, his hands and feet tied, and his robe thrown from his shoulders. Then one of the young women, an athletic girl of about twenty, with a laughing face and a roguish eye, laid twelve lashes on his broad back with the heartiest goodwill.

In the meantime Earl Lavender, without waiting for instructions, bared his shoulders as he had seen the others do, clasped his hands on his breast and stood stock-still. The second woman, who possessed great beauty, and seemed to be about twenty-five years of age, at once inflicted with sufficient vigour a dozen lashes and one to the bargain. Earl Lavender winced at the first and second lash, and at the third he moved a step forward, but he took the rest of his punishment without a motion. His fair chastiser approved of his conduct with a charming smile, and having handed him the whip, exposed her own back. Lightly Earl Lavender brought down the scourge. How could he score the soft white shoulders of this beautiful woman! But she turned to him with a mortified look, and said, -

"You are unworthy of my friendship if you spare me. Put forth your strength, or I will leave you."

Convinced of the lady's sincerity, Earl Lavender then laid on lustily, and was astonished to find, when he gave himself to it, what enjoyable work it was.

Although, while in his company before, the Veiled Lady had not uncovered her face for an instant, Earl Lavender had no difficulty in recognising her as the robed beauty with whom he had just exchanged whippings. It was the individuality of her carriage, along with her unusual height, which betrayed her. All her motions were rapid, graceful and full of precision without being precise; and when she was at rest her stillness was like that of a statue - of Galatea wakening into life. Had any doubt remained in Earl Lavender's mind as to her identity the sound of the harp-like voice in which she had bidden him put forth his strength would have dispelled it.

"Come," she said, when she had covered her shoulders.

He took the hand she offered, and they left the Whipping Room, moving in time to the music, which sounded from the apartment they were about to enter. On the threshold he looked back to see how it fared with

Lord Brumm. His henchman had been unbound, and was just beginning to repay his chastiser, the roguish-looking girl, who had thrashed him mercilessly; and Earl Lavender, catching his eye, bowed and smiled to signify his approbation.

In the apartment from which the music came, a vast hall with pillars supporting a lofty roof, no light burned, but floods of the richest colour streamed in from lamps without through many Gothic windows filled with stained glass. The musicians, a hundred men and women, old and young, sat in a minstrels' gallery of carved oak, playing on all kinds of stringed instruments, on wind instruments of wood, with triangles, drums and cymbals. On the shining marble floor, dyed by the lamp-beams, a multitude of all ages moved to the slow measure, dancing in groups or couples; and every now and again a few of the musicians would leave the gallery, their places being taken by some of the dancers. An expression of radiant seriousness, as far removed from solemnity as from ordinary mirth, sat on the faces of all the dancers. Earl Lavender glanced quickly at his companion, and beheld in her the same high look. He touched her waist, and they joined the dance. For more than an hour, steeped in colour and sound, they circled among the pillars of the vast hall, unwearied, silent, without need to speak a word. Then the lady led the way to an ante-room where many couples reclined on couches conversing in undertones.

"Let us rest and talk a little," she said.

"Lady," said Earl Lavender, reclining opposite his companions, for the couches were arranged in pairs facing each other, with a little space between. "Lady," he said, "since I became aware that I am the fittest of men, and knew that it is incumbent on me to find and wed the fittest woman, my imagination has figured many ideals,

231

but not my most exquisite dream approached the reality. Most beautiful, most graceful, most lofty-spirited and fittest of women, let us go at once to the proper authority and be married according to the form of this subterranean land - if there be any form that is to say."

The Lady of the Veil gave him a piercing glance, and said coldly, -

"There is no marriage, nor giving in marriage here."

"Then let us return to the upper world," rejoined Earl Lavender, "for it becomes us to be married immediately."

"I shall never marry," said the lady. "But why do you keep up this foolish fantasy with me?"

"Foolish fantasy!" cried Earl Lavender, starting to his feet. "Foolish fantasy! Ah," he continued more quietly, resuming his couch, "you naturally wish to try me; I may have to pass through many ordeals before Evolution will permit our union. Your indifference is only apparent I am sure. Being the fittest of women, you must love me as I love you. And thus I pass at once the first ordeal. Lady, nothing you can do or say will persuade me that you do not love me, and are not as eager for our union as I am. Think what it means - the union of the fittest man and the fittest woman. Think of the ecstasy and glory of it - the need of it; the world waits for this event - has waited since its creation. The haste which Evolution has shown in bringing us together on the very first day of the new era points to the propriety of a speedy consummation. If we may not marry here, let us fly at once. Come, lady."

The lady surveyed him long before she spoke, gradually hiding with the deep fringe of her eyelashes the look of pity that dawned out of the blank amazement in her eyes.

"You do not ask," she said at length, making no

reference to his appeal and wishing to occupy his thoughts with something else, "for any explanation of the manners and customs of the underground world."

"I am no longer interested," he said. "I was at first astonished, but I am now absorbed entirely by my love for you, and my desire to fulfil at once the intention of Evolution. If there be another ordeal, submit me to it without further delay, oh, fittest among women!"

"I am not the fittest among women," rejoined the lady, with some resentment. "There are present here to-night many lovelier, handsomer, stronger, warmer-hearted, better-educated women than I am. Although you are mad, I beg you not to be foolish."

"Ah!" exclaimed Earl Lavender, a look of pain crossing his face. "Now, indeed, you put me to the test. But although at this moment you were to become old and shrivelled, weak and rheumatic, I should still maintain that you are the fittest of women, confident that the first kiss of love would restore you to youth and grace like the bewitched lady in the ballad. Were you to ransack the harems of the East, the palaces of Russia, the homes of the English nobility, and place before me the choice beauties of the world, I should still select you, for I can trust Evolution and read the signs provided. The moment I saw you sitting veiled in the Café Benvenuto, I said to Lord Brumm, "Behold the fittest among women!" And you, dear lady, whipered within yourself, I am certain, "Behold the man of men!" You see with what ease I pass this second ordeal. The third has no terrors for me. You accuse me coldly of being mad. I am as astonished that you make the accusation as I would have been had the twins not made it. I am not mad, and I know, although you act well, you are only pretending to think me insane. Some sterner ordeal, lady!"

Again the lady looked long at him through her

eyelashes before replying.

"I shall devise an ordeal," she said suddenly, as if ending a debate in her own mind. "But tell me in the meantime what you think of the new stimulant."

"The new stimulant?"

"Yes; whipping. Examine yourself. Has the intoxication worn off yet?"

"No," answered Earl Lavender; "the exalted mood continues. Was it the whipping? - Yes, I believe it was the whipping that roused all my senses."

"Not all your senses," rejoined the lady; "it sets the soul more broad awake than wine. Wine rouses the lower nature also, and the soul, only half-enlightened, continues still surrounded by the fleshly dream, which is the body. The scourge frees the soul and quells the body. You must have been drunk with wine when you came here, or you would not have talked to me of love."

"How is this?" began Earl Lavender, remembering some old passages in his reading, wherein whipping is said to rouse the animal passions; but the lady interrupted him.

"I anticipate your objection," she said. "Many novices make it, coming here for the first time full-fed and wine-flushed. If the body is already over-stimulated with food and drink, the effect of a moderate whipping is to intensify the existing excitment. Had you drunk much to-night?"

"Not very much," said Earl Lavender. "A little whisky, a little beer, and a fair quantity of champagne."

"Ah!" exclaimed the lady sitting up, "And your companion. Did he drink as much?"

"Yes, but that is not much. We had no port nor liqueurs."

"Let us find your friend," said the lady.

They returned to the Dancing Hall and searched

the eddying throng that now seemed to cover its vast floor; but Lord Brumm was not there. Before withdrawing they turned round on the threshold of the Whipping Room and watched the dancers. Their robes, arms, faces, hair, and twinkling feet, and the floor and the pillars of the hall were all embroidered and enamelled with rich hues and set with many-coloured jewels from the stained and warmly-lit windows. The slow, searching music of strings and wood-pipes seemed always about to open up some new secret of joy, but the cymbals and drums and triangles were unable to reveal it.

"Why have they no trumpets?" whipered Earl Lavender. "The music aches to burst bounds and soar."

"This music and this dance," replied the lady, "go on in this room endlessly. In the underground world we know neither night nor day. New-comers take the places continually of the players and the dancers who withdraw. The music itself is unresolved. Listen attentively, and it seems a softly-wailing question which haunts and troubles forever all who hear it. An answer, an illusive answer comes only in dancing to it. To play it is exquisite pain. See how often the players are changed. Watch their sad faces."

Earl Lavender looked and sighed.

"And what may this mean?" he said. "This must be some great allegory."

"Seek for no meaning in it; it has none. What meaning is there in pain and pleasure? They are twins; that is all we know. Seek no meaning in anything you see here. Images, ideas, flashes of purpose will peer out in all our ways and deeds, but there is no intention here below. Is there any intention anywhere?"

"Intention," cried Earl Lavender aloud, startling the dancers near him. "Intention is another name for Evolution; the great purpose that is in the universe. Ho!

235

all ye sad-souled players," he called out, ascending the steps of the minstrels' gallery, "and you self-deceived dancers! Is it purpose or is it meaning you cannot find? Behold in me the purpose of the ages, Earl Lavender, the fittest of men."

He was not permitted to say more. Five of the dancers, joined by the Lady of the Veil, seized him and led him along a passage he had not yet traversed to a lofty room which bore some resemblance to a court of justice. On a platform sat three reverend-looking men; before them a table covered with books and scrolls. He who occupied the middle seat was clad in a white robe; his co-mates, in red and blue respectively. Opposite the platform, and occupying more than half of the room, was a gallery which speedily filled on the entrance of Earl Lavender and those who accompanied him.

"Judgment, oh, sages!" said the Lady of the Veil.

"And again judgment, oh, sages! cried another voice.

Looking behind him, Earl Lavender beheld Lord Brumm, also conducted by six denizens of the Underworld, including the roguish damsel who had whipped him. Earl Lavender's henchman presented a very woebegone appearance. His robe was torn from his shoulders, and his hair tumbled. He was gagged, and his hands tied behind his back; tears stood in his eyes.

"Why, what have you done, my good Brumm?" asked Earl Lavender.

"Silence," said the white-robed sage in a stern voice.

Earl Lavender bowed in submission to the sage's decision, and he and Lord Brumm were placed at the bar.

In reply to a sign from the white-robed sage, the Lady of the Veil, making a profound obeisance, addressed the court.

"Oh, sages," she said, "of what the second misdemeanant is accused I cannot tell, but in charging the first, I must speak to the presence of both in this city. I saw these men in the Café Benvenuto, where I tasted a little macaroni after a railway journey of six hours. He, against whom I bear witness, seemed to me worthy of admission to the Underworld, and in accordance with our established custom, I brought him along with me; his comrade was apparently undetachable. Just now, as we passed through the Hall of Dancing, he ascended the steps of the gallery and cried aloud - I remember his exact words, - "Intention is another name for Evolution; the great purpose that is in the universe. Ho! all ye sad-souled players, and you self-deceived dancers! Is it purpose, is it meaning you cannot find? Behold in me the purpose of the ages, Earl Lavender, the fittest of men." Before he could proceed further, we seized him and brought him hither."

"Has she spoken truly in all points so far as you know?" asked the white-robed sage of those who had brought Earl Lavender before the judgment-seat. The dancers acquiesced silently in the lady's deposition.

When the sages had consulted together in whispers, their spokesman announced that they intended to proceed with the second case before sentencing Earl Lavender.

"Oh, sages," at once began the roguish damsel, making her obeisance, "you have heard already how this misdemeanant obtained entrance to the Underworld. Judging from his appearance and disinclination to be whipped, I thought him more fitted for the Hall of Fancy than for the Hall of Dancing. There he behaved well, and appeared to enjoy everything that was said. His conduct, however, became foolish during the narration of a love story. He cast what are called sheep's eyes at me, and furtively kissed my hand. I promptly revealed his crime, and we brought him hither. When we seized him he struggled and bellowed, afraid of another whipping, whereupon we gagged and bound him.

"Has she spoken truly in all points so far as you know?" asked the white-robed sage of the roguish girl's companions. They bowed an affirmative.

After a second whispered consultation, the white-robed sage announced the decision of the court, which was the same in both cases, viz., - that Earl Lavender and Lord Brumm should be taken at once to the dormitory, put to bed, and in the morning, expelled from the underground city.

"Well, what did I tell you?" said Earl Lavender, when he and Lord Brumm, hurried away before either could attempt a reply, had been locked into a spacious double-bedded apartment, one of a suite which formed the men's dormitory. "Here are the best beds in London, and changes of linen hanging ready aired."

Lord Brumm only groaned in reply.

****

11.

THE TRANSLATOR AND THE CHILDREN
by James Elroy Flecker

While I translated Baudelaire,
Children were playing out in the air.
Turning to watch, I saw the light
That made their clothes and faces bright.
I heard the tune they meant to sing
As they kept dancing in a ring;
But I could not forget my book,
And thought of men whose faces shook
When babies passed them with a look.

They are as terrible as death,
Those children in the road beneath.
Their witless chatter is more dread
Than voices in a madman's head:
Their dance more awful and inspired,
Because their feet are never tired,
Then silent revel with soft sound
Of pipes, on consecrated ground,
When all the ghosts go round and round.

****

12.

POPE JACYNTH
by Vernon Lee

It was Pope Jacynth who built anew the basilica over the bodies of the holy martyrs, Paul and John, brothers; and who wainscoted the choir, and laid down the flooring, and set up the columns of the nave, a row on either side, all of precious marble. And it was of his death and the marvellous thing which was seen afterward, showing indeed the justice of God and His infinite mercy, that the following tale is told.

This Jacynth, whose name in the world and in the cloister was Odo, was known all through Italy, and through the Marquisate of Tuscany and the County of Benevento, and the Kingdom of Sicily and such dominions as belonged to the Grecian Emperors, for his great and unparalleled humility and his exceeding ardent and exclusive love of God. And in these lay his ruin. For, even as is written in the book of the Prophet Job, which it were sin for any layman to read, and damnation for any clerk to translate, that the Lord allowed Satan to try his faithful servant with many plagues and doubts and evil incitements, so it pleased Him who is the Mirror of all Truth, to make a wager with Satan concerning the soul of this man Odo or otherwise Jacynth. And this when he was still in his mother's womb. For the Lord said to Satan: "I grant leave that thou tempt any man whatsoever at My choice among such as shall be born into the world before the sun, which turns for ever round earth, shall have gone back to the spot where it now is."

And Satan caused the man Odo, afterwards Jacynth, to be born to the greatest dignity in his land,

240

even to be firstborn of Averard, Marquis of Tusculum. But Odo cared not for the greatness of his birth, and the wealth of his father's house. And, being only fourteen years of age, he fled from his parents and went on the ship of a certain mariner, who brought even wine and tanned hides and fair white stone for building from Greece, Istria, and Salernum, to the port of Rome, which is below Mount Aventine, and took back the fleece of sheep and thin cheese, and slabs of porphyry and serpentine from the temples of the heathen. But Satan caused Odo to grow most marvellously in beauty and shapeliness of body and loveliness of countenance and sweetness of voice, so that pirates captured him and sold him, being eighteen years of age, to Alecto, Queen of the Amazons, which inhabit the isles beyond the pillars of Hercules, and are the most wondrously fair women. And Queen Alecto became enamoured of the beauty of Odo, otherwise Jacynth, and offered him her love and every delight. But Jacynth scourged himself with ropes of thistles, and ate only of the fruit of the prickly pear and drank only of water from the marshes; and he shaved his head and stained his face with certain herbs, and consorted with lepers, and spurned the queen and her delicates.

Then Satan caused Odo, otherwise Jacynth, to increase most mightily in strength and courage, so that he could wrestle with the lions in the desert and cleave a strong man in twain with one blow. So that the people, seeing his might and wondering greatly thereat, made him their captain, captain even over hundreds, that he might avenge them on certain wicked kings, their neighbours, and clear the country of robbers and wild beasts. But when he had put the kings in chains and thrown the robbers into dungeons, and exterminated the wild beasts, Jacynth, who was then called Odo, put up his

241

sword and allowed not that any man should be killed or sold into captivity, and bade them desist from slaying the hares and deer and wild asses, saying that these also were creatures of God and worthy of kindness. And he was at this time thirty-two years of age.

Then Satan caused Odo, later to be called Jacynth, to exceed all other men in subtlety of mind. And he learned all languages, both living and dead, as those of the Grecians, Romans, Ethiopians, and even of Armorica and Taprobane; and studied all books on philosophy, divine and natural astrology, medicine, music, alchemy, the properties of herbs and numbers, magic and poetry and rhetoric, whatsoever books have been written since the building of Babel, when all languages were dispersed. And he went from place to place teaching and disputing; and whithersoever he went, and mostly in Paris and at Salernum, did he challenge all doctors, rabbis, and men of learning to discuss with him on any subject of their choice, and always did he demonstrate before all men that their arguments were wrong and their science vain. But when Odo, otherwise Jacynth, had done this, he burned his books, save the gospels, and retired to a monastery of his founding. And he was at this time forty and five years of age.

Then Satan caused Odo, later called Jacynth, to become wondrously knowing of the heart of man and his wickedness, and wondrous full of unction and fervour, and all men came to his monastery, which was called Clear Streams, and listened to his preaching and reformed their ways, and many put themselves under his rule, and of these there were such multitudes that the monastery would not hold them, and others had to be built in all parts of the world. And kings and emperors confessed to him their sins, and stood at his bidding clothed in sackcloth at the church door, singing the penitential psalms and holding lighted tapers.

But Odo, later called Jacynth, instituted abbots and heads of the order, and for himself retired into the wild places of the mountains and built himself there a hermitage of stone quarried with his own hands, and planted fruit-trees and pot-herbs, and lived there alone, praying and meditating, high up near the well-head of the river which runs down through the woods to the Tyrrhene Sea. And he was sixty years of age.

And Satan went up before the Lord and said, "Verily I can tempt him yet. Grant me, I pray Thee, but the use of Thine own tools, and I will bring Thee the soul of this man bound in mortal sin." And the Lord answered, "I grant it." And at the prayer of Satan, God caused him to be acclaimed as pope. And the cardinals and prelates and princes of the earth journeyed to the hermitage, and sought for the man Odo, who henceforth was to be called Jacynth. And they found him in his orchard pruning a fig-tree, and by his side were the herbs for his supper in a clean platter, and the gospel lay on his lectern, and there stood by it a tame goat, ready to be milked; and on a hook hung his red hat, and a crucifix was by the lectern. And in the wall of his garden, which was small, with a well in the midst and set round with wooden pillars, was a window, with a pillar carved of stone in the middle, and through the window one could see the oak woods below, and the olive-yards, and the river winding through the valley, and the Tyrrhene Sea, with ships sailing, in the distance. Now when he saw the cardinals and prelates and princes of the earth, Odo, who was thenceforth called Jacynth, put down his pruning-hook; and when he heard their message he wept, and knelt before the crucifix, and wept again, and cried, "Woe's me! Terrible are the trials of Thy servants, O Lord, and great must be Thy mercy." But he went with them to be crowned Pope, because his heart was full of humbleness and the love of God. And Pope Jacynth, formerly Odo, was seventy-five years of age when they set him on his throne.

And the Lord called to him Satan, and was angered, and said, "What wilt thou do next, Accursed One?" And Satan replied, "I will do no more, O Lord. Suffer this man but to live the space of five years, and then watch we for our wager."

And they took Pope Jacynth, once called Odo, and carried him to the palace, which is over against the Church of St. Peter, and before which stands the pine cone of brass, made as a talisman by the Emperor Adrian. And they arrayed him in fine linen from Egypt, and silk from Byzantium, as befits a Pope; and his cope was of beaten gold, even gold beaten to the thinness of a leaf, wrought all over with the history of our Lord and His Apostles, with a border of lambs and lilies, a lamb and a lily all the way turn about. And his stole was likewise of gold, gold plates cunningly riveted, and it was set all round with precious stones, emeralds, and opals, and beryls and sardonyxes, and the stone called *Melitta*, all perfectly round and the size of a pigeon's egg; and two goodly graven stones of the ancients, one showing a chariot-race and the other the effigy of the Emperor Galba, most cunningly cut in relief. And his mitre also was of riveted gold, and inside it was fastened the lance-head of Longinus, which touched the flesh of our Lord; and on the outside it was bordered with pearls, and in its midst was a sapphire the size of a swan's egg, worked marvellously into a cup, which was the cup that the Angel brought to our Lord. And when they had arrayed Pope Jacynth in this apparel, they placed him in his chair, which was of cedar-wood covered with plates of gold, and they bore him, eight bearers, namely, three counts, three marquises, a duke and the Exarch of the

Pentapolis, on their shoulders; and the cushions of his chair were of silk. And over him they bore a canopy embroidered most marvellously with the signs of the Zodiac by the Matrons of Amalfi. And before him went two carrying fans of the feathers of the white peacock, and two bearing censers filled with burning ambergris, and six blowing on clarions of silver. And in this manner was he enthroned above the place where rests the body of the Apostle, behind the ambones of onion stone, and the railing of alabaster open-work showing peacocks and vine leaves, and under the dome where our Lord sits in judgment on a ground of purple and seagreen and gold, and the holy lambs pasture on green enamel, each with a palm-tree by his side, and the great gold vine rises on a ground of turquoise blue. And on either side of the throne was a column of precious marble taken from a temple of the heathen, even a column of red porphyry from the temple of Mars, and a column of alabaster cunningly fluted, from the temple of Apollo. And the bells in the belfry, which is set with discs of serpentine and platters from Majorca, began to ring, and the trumpets to sound, and all the people sang the psalm *Magnificat*. And the heart of Pope Jacynth, formerly called Odo, was filled with joy and pride, because in the midst of his glory he knew himself to be more humble than the lepers outside the city gate. And the people prostrated themselves before Pope Jacynth, and prayed for his blessing.

And Pope Jacynth slept on the rushes in his chamber, and drank only water from the well and ate only salad, and beneath his robe he wore a shirt of camel's hair, mightly rough to the body. And he gloried in this humbleness. And he took of the money of the jubilee year, which twenty priests raked with silver rakes where the pilgrims passed the bridge by the

245

Emperor Adrian's tomb, and would have none of it himself, but distributed half to the poor and the widows and orphans, and with the other he caused stonemasons to quarry for marble among the temples of the heathen, and draw thence the columns having flutings and sculptured capitals to set up in the nave, and to saw into slabs the pillars of porphyry and serpentine and Egyptian marble, for wainscoting and flooring. And in this fashion he did build the basilica by the Ostian gate. And he dedicated it to St. John and St. Paul, slaves and servants of Flavia, the sister of the Emperor Domitian, meaning to show thereby that in the love of God the lowest are highest; for he gloried in his humbleness. And they brought him blind men, and those with grievous sores, and lepers, to bless, that they might recover. And Pope Jacynth blessed them, and washed their sores and embraced them; and Pope Jacynth gloried in his humility.

Now when Satan saw this, he laughed; and the sound of his laughter was as a rushing wind, that burns the shoots of the wheat (for it was spring), and nipped the blossom of the almond-tree and plum-tree, causing it to fall in great profusion, as every man could testify. And Satan went before the Lord and said: "Behold, O Lord, I have won my wager. For the man Jacynth, once Odo, has sinned against Thee, even the sin of vaingloriousness; so do Thou give him to me, body and soul." And the Lord answered: "Take thou the man Jacynth, formerly Odo, his body and his soul, and do therewith whatsoever thou please, for he has sinned the sin of vaingloriousness; but for Myself I reserve that which remaineth."

So Satan departed. And he took the body of Pope Jacynth, and touched it with invisible fingers; and lo, it did gradually turn into stone; and he took the soul of Pope Jacynth, and blew on it, and behold, it shrank slowly and hardened, and became a stone, even a diamond, which, as all know, burns for ever.

Now the people and the pilgrims were so amazed at the humility of Pope Jacynth, that they clamoured to see him; and they attacked the gate of the palace over against the Church of St. Peter, the gate which has a gable, and in it our Lord clad in white, on a ground of gold, with a purple halo round his head, all done in mosaic by the Grecians. So the priests and the barons were afraid of the violence of the people and particularly of the pilgrims from the north, and they promised to bring Pope Jacynth for them to worship. And they dressed him in his vestments of beaten and riveted gold, set with precious stones and graven stones, and placed him on his throne of cedar-wood, and the eight bearers, three counts, two marquises, two dukes, and the Exarch of the Pentapolis, raised him on their shoulders and bore him through the square, with the censer-bearers before and the trumpeters and the fans of white peacock. And the people fell on their knees. Only there stood up one, who afterwards vanished, and was the Apostle Peter, and he cried, "Behold, Pope Jacynth has turned into an idol, even an idol of the heathen." But when the people had dispersed, and the procession had entered the church, the throne-bearers knelt down, and the throne was lowered, and behold, Pope Jacynth was dead.

But when the embalmers and the physicians took the body after three days that it had lain in state, surrounded by tapers, with lamps hung all round, under the mosaic of the dome, they found that it was uncorrupted, and had turned into marble, even marble of Paros, like the idols of the ancient Grecians. And they wondered greatly. And the learned men disputed, and decided that Pope Jacynth, formerly called Odo, must have been a wizard, for this certainly was devilry. So they caused his body to be taken and burned into lime, which, being turned to the finest marble, it readily did. Only, when they came to remove the lime, they found in the midst of it a burning diamond, that instantly vanished, nor was any man in time to seize it. And likewise a thing of the consistency of a dead leaf, and smelling wonderfully of violets, but it was shaped in the image of a heart. And it also vanished, nor was any man quick enough to seize it.

Now when he came down from the palace, hard by the pine cone of the Emperor Adrian, Satan did meet an angel of the Lord, even Gabriel, who was entering, wrapped round in wings of golden green. And Satan said, "Hail! brother, whither goest thou? for there remaineth of the man Jacynth, called formerly Odo, only a little lime, which was his body, and this stone that burneth eternally, which was his soul." And Satan laughed. But the angel answered, "Laugh not, most foolish fellow-servant of the Lord. For I go to seek of the man Odo, sometime called Pope Jacynth, only the heart, which the Lord has reserved for Himself for all eternity, because it was full of love and hope in His mercy." Now as Gabriel passed by, behold! a pomegranate tree along the wall, which had dried up and died in the frost ten years before, sprouted and put forth buds.

****

13.

INSOMNIA
by John Davidson

He wakened quivering on a golden rack
  Inlaid with gems: no sign of change, no fear
  Or hope of death came near;
Only the empty ether hovered black
  About him stretched upon his living bier,
Of old by Merlin's Master deftly wrought:
  Two Seraphim of Gabriel's helpful race
  In that far nook of space
With iron levers wrenched and held him taut.

The Seraph at his head was Agony;
  Delight, more terrible, stood at his feet:
  Their sixfold pinions beat
The darkness, or were spread immovably
  Poising the rack, whose jewelled fabric meet
To strain a god, did fitfully unmask
  With olive light of chrysoprases dim
  The smiling Seraphim
Implacably intent upon their task.

****

14.

THE NIGHTINGALE AND THE ROSE
by Oscar Wilde

"She said that she would dance with me if I brought her red roses," cried the young Student, "but in all my garden there is no red rose."

From her nest in the holm-oak tree the Nightingale heard him, and she looked out through the leaves and wondered.

"No red rose in all my garden!" he cried, and his beautiful eyes filled with tears. "Ah, on what little things does happiness depend! I have read all that the wise men have written, and all the secrets of philosophy are mine, yet for want of a red rose is my life made wretched."

"Here at last is a true lover," said the Nightingale. "Night after night have I sung of him, though I knew him not: night after night have I told his story to the stars and now I see him. His hair is dark as the hyacinth-blossom, and his lips are red as the rose of his desire; but passion has made his face like pale ivory, and sorrow has set her seal upon his brow."

"The Prince gives a ball to-morrow night," murmured the young student, "and my love will be of the company. If I bring her a red rose she will dance with me till dawn. If I bring her a red rose, I shall hold her in my arms, and she will lean her head upon my shoulder, and her hand will be clasped in mine. But there is no red rose in my garden, so I shall sit lonely, and she will pass me by. She will have no heed of me, and my heart will break."

"Here, indeed, is the true lover," said the Nightingale. "What I sing of, he suffers; what is joy to me, to him is pain. Surely love is a wonderful thing. It is more precious than emeralds and dearer than fine opals. Pearls and pomegranates cannot buy it, nor is it set forth in the market-place. It may not be purchased of the merchants, nor can it be weighed out in the balance for gold."

"The musicians will sit in their gallery," said the young Student, "and play upon their stringed instruments, and my love will dance to the sound of the harp and the violin. She will dance so lightly that her feet will not touch the floor, and the courtiers in their gay dresses will throng round her. But with me she will not dance, for I have no red rose to give her;" and he flung himself down on the grass, and buried his face in his hands, and wept.

"Why is he weeping?" asked a little Green Lizard, as he ran past him with his tail in the air.

"Why, indeed?" said a Butterfly, who was fluttering about after a sunbeam.

"Why, indeed?" whispered a Daisy to his neighbour, in a soft, low voice.

"He is weeping for a red rose," said the Nightingale.

"For a red rose?" they cried; "how very ridiculous!" and the little Lizard, who was something of a cynic laughed outright.

But the Nightingale understood the secret of the Student's sorrow, and she sat silent in the oak-tree, and thought about the mystery of Love.

Suddenly she spread her brown wings for flight, and soared into the air. She passed through the grove like a shadow, and like a shadow she sailed across the garden.

In the centre of the grass-plot was standing a beautiful rose-tree, and when she saw it she flew over to it, and lit upon a spray.

"Give me a red rose," she cried, "and I will sing you my sweetest song."

But the tree shook its head.

"My roses are white," it answered; "as white as the foam of the sea, and whiter than the snow upon the mountain. But go to my brother who grows round the old sun-dial, and perhaps he will give you what you want."

So the Nightingale flew over to the Rose-tree that was growing round the old sun-dial.

"Give me a red rose," she cried, "and I will sing you my sweetest song."

But the Tree shook its head.

"My roses are yellow," it answered; "as yellow as the hair of the mermaiden who sits upon an amber throne, and yellower than the daffodil that blooms in the meadow before the mower comes with his scythe. But go to my brother who grows beneath the Student's window, and perhaps he will give you what you want."

So the Nightingale flew over to the Rose-tree that was growing beneath the Student's window.

"Give me a red rose," she cried, "and I will sing you my sweetest song."

But the Tree shook its head.

"My roses are red," it answered, "as red as the feet of the dove, and redder than the great fans of coral that wave and wave in the ocean-cavern. But the winter has chilled my veins, and the frost has nipped my buds, and the storm has broken my branches, and I shall have no roses at all this year."

"One red rose is all I want," cried the Nightingale, "only one red rose! Is there no way by which I can get it?"

"There is a way," answered the Tree; "but it is so terrible that I dare not tell it to you."

"Tell it to me," said the Nightingale, "I am not afraid."

"If you want a red rose," said the Tree, "you must build it out of music by moonlight, and stain it with your own heart's-blood. You must sing to me with your breast against a thorn. All night long you must sing to me, and the thorn must pierce your heart, and your life-blood must flow into my veins, and become mine."

"Death is a great price to pay for a red rose," cried the Nightingale, "and Life is very dear to all. It is pleasant to sit in the green wood, and to watch the Sun in his chariot of gold, and the Moon in her chariot of pearl. Sweet is the scent of the hawthorn, and sweet are the bluebells that hide in the valley, and the heather that blows on the hill. Yet Love is better than Life, and what is the heart of a bird compared to the heart of a man?"

So she spread her brown wings for flight, and soared into the air. She swept over the garden like a shadow, and like a shadow she sailed through the grove.

The young Student was still lying on the grass, where she had left him, and the tears were not yet dry in his beautiful eyes.

"Be happy," cried the Nightingale, "be happy; you shall have your red rose. I will build it out of music by moonlight, and stain it with my own heart's-blood. All that I ask of you in return is that you will be a true lover, for Love is wiser than Philosophy, though he is wise, and mightier than Power, though he is mighty. Flame-coloured are his wings, and coloured like flame is his body. His lips are sweet as honey, and his breath is like frankincense."

The Student looked up from the grass, and listened, but he could not understand what the Nightingale was saying to him, for he only knew the things that are written down in books.

But the Oak-tree understood, and felt sad, for he was very fond of the little Nightingale who had built her nest in his branches.

"Sing me one last song," he whispered; "I shall feel lonely when you are gone."

So the Nightingale sang to the Oak-tree, and her voice was like water bubbling from a silver jar.

When she had finished her song, the Student got up, and pulled a note-book and a lead-pencil out of his pocket.

"She has form," he said to himself, as he walked away through the grove - "that cannot be denied to her; but has she got feeling? I am afraid not. In fact, she is like most artists; she is all style without any sincerity. She would not sacrifice herself for others. She thinks merely of music, and everybody knows that the arts are selfish. Still, it must be admitted that she has some beautiful notes in her voice. What a pity it is that they do not mean anything, or do any practical good!" And he went into his room, and lay down on his little pallet-bed, and began to think of his love; and, after a time, he fell asleep.

And when the moon shone in the heavens the Nightingale flew to the Rose-tree, and set her breast against the thorn. All night long she sang, with her breast against the thorn, and the cold crystal Moon leaned down and listened. All night long she sang, and the thorn went deeper and deeper into her breast, and her life-blood ebbed away from her.

She sang first of the birth of love in the heart of a boy and a girl. And on the topmost spray of the Rose-tree there blossomed a marvellous rose, petal following petal, as song followed song. Pale was it, at first, as the mist that hangs over the river - pale as the feet of the morning, and silver as the wings of the dawn. As the shadow of a rose in a mirror of silver, as the shadow of a rose in a water-pool, so was the rose that blossomed on the topmost spray of the Tree.

But the Tree cried to the Nightingale to press closer against the thorn. "Press closer, little Nightingale," cried the Tree, "or the Day will come before the rose is finished."

So the Nightingale pressed closer against the thorn, and louder and louder grew her song, for she sang of the birth of passion in the soul of a man and a maid.

And a delicate flush of pink came into the leaves of the rose, like the flush in the face of the bridegroom when he kisses the lips of the bride. But the thorn had not yet reached her heart, so the rose's heart remained white, for only a Nightingale's heart's-blood can crimson the heart of a rose.

And the Tree cried to the Nightingale to press closer against the thorn. "Press closer, little Nightingale," cried the Tree, "or the Day will come before the rose is finished."

So the Nightingale pressed closer against the thorn, and the thorn touched her heart, and a fierce pang of pain shot through her. Bitter, bitter, was the pain, and wilder and wilder grew her song, for she sang of the Love that is perfected by Death, of the Love that dies not in the tomb.

And the marvellous rose became crimson, like the rose of the eastern sky. Crimson was the girdle of petals, and crimson as a ruby was the heart.

But the Nightingale's voice grew fainter, and her little wings began to beat, and a film came over her eyes. Fainter and fainter grew her song, and she felt something choking her in her throat.

Then she gave one last burst of music. The white Moon heard it, and she forgot the dawn, and lingered on in the sky. The red rose heard it, and it trembled all over with ecstasy, and opened its petals to the cold morning air. Echo bore it to her purple cavern in the hills, and woke the sleeping shepherds from their dreams. It floated through the reeds of the river, and they carried its message to the sea.

"Look, look!" cried the Tree, "the rose is finished now;" but the Nightingale made no answer, for she was lying dead in the long grass, with the thorn in her heart. And at noon the Student opened his window and looked out.

"Why, what a wonderful piece of luck!" he cried; "here is a red rose! I have never seen any rose like it in all my life. It is so beautiful that I am sure it has a long Latin name;" and he leaned down and plucked it.

Then he put on his hat, and ran up to the Professor's house with the rose in his hand.

The daughter of the Professor was sitting in the doorway winding blue silk on a reel, and her little dog was lying at her feet.

"You said that you would dance with me if I brought you a red rose," cried the Student. "Here is the reddest rose in all the world. You will wear it to-night next your heart, and as we dance together it will tell you how I love you."

But the girl frowned.

"I am afraid it will not go with my dress," she answered; "and, besides, the Chamberlain's nephew has sent me some real jewels, and everybody knows that jewels cost far more than flowers."

"Well, upon my word, you are very ungrateful," said the Student angrily; and he threw the rose into the street, where it fell into the gutter, and a cartwheel went over it.

"Ungrateful!" said the girl. "I tell you what, you are very rude; and, after all, who are you? Only a Student. Why, I don't believe you have even got silver buckles to your shoes as the Chamberlain's nephew has;" and she got up from her chair and went into the house.

"What a silly thing Love is!" said the Student as he walked away. "It is not half as useful as Logic, for it does not prove anything, and it is always telling one of things that are not going to happen, and making one believe things that are not true. In fact, it is quite unpractical, and, as in this age to be practical is everything, I shall go back to Philosophy and study Metaphysics."

So he returned to his room and pulled out a great dusty book, and began to read.

****

15.

VINUM DAEMONUM
by Lionel Johnson

The crystal flame, the ruby flame,
Alluring, dancing, revelling!
See them: and ask me not, whence came
   This cup I bring.

But only watch the wild wine glow,
But only taste its fragrance: then,
Drink the wild drink I bring, and so
   Reign among men.

Only one sting, and then but joy:
One pang of fire, and thou art free.
Then, what thou wilt, thou canst destroy:
   Save only me!

Triumph in tumult of thy lust:
Wanton in passion of thy will:
Cry Peace! to conscience, and it must
   At last be still.

I am the Prince of this World: I
Command the flames, command the fires.
Mine are the draughts, that satisfy
   This World's desires.

Thy longing leans across the brink:
Ah, the brave thirst within thine eyes!
For there is that within this drink,
   Which never dies.

****

16.

ABSINTHIA TAETRA
by Ernest Dowson

Green changed to white, emerald to an opal: nothing was changed.

The man let the water trickle gently into his glass, and as the green clouded, a mist fell from his mind.

Then he drank opaline.

Memories and terrors beset him. The past tore after him like a panther and through the blackness of the present he saw the luminous tiger eyes of the things to be.

But he drank opaline.

And that obscure night of the soul, and the valley of humiliation, through which he stumbled were forgotten. He saw blue vistas of undiscovered countries, high prospects and a quiet, caressing sea. The past shed its perfume over him, to-day held his hand as it were a little child, and to-morrow shone like a white star: nothing was changed.

He drank opaline.

The man had known the obscure night of the soul, and lay even now in the valley of humiliation; and the tiger menace of the things to be was red in the skies. But for a little while he had forgotten.

Green changed to white, emerald to an opal: nothing was changed.

****

17.

THE RING OF FAUSTUS
by Eugene Lee-Hamilton

There is a tale of Faustus, - that one day
  Lucretia the Venetian, then his love,
  Had, while he slept, the rashness to remove,
His magic ring, when fair as a god he lay;

And that a sudden horrible decay
  O'erspread his face; a hundred wrinkles wove
  Their network on his cheek; while she above
His slumber crouched, and watched him shrivel away.

There is upon Life's hand a magic ring, -
  The ring of Faith-in-Good, Life's gold of gold;
Remove it not, lest all Life's charm take wing:

Remove it not, lest straightway you behold
  Life's cheek fall in, and every earthly thing
Grow all at once unutterably old.

****

18.

THE LAST GENERATION
by James Elroy Flecker

INTRODUCTION

I had been awake for I know not how many hours
that summer dawn while the sun came over the hills and
coloured the beautiful roses in my mother's garden. As I
lay drowsily gazing through the window, I thought I had
never known a morning so sultry, and yet so pleasant.
Outside not a leaf stirred; yet the air was fresh, and the
madrigal notes of the birds came to me with a peculiar
intensity and clearness. I listened intently to the curious
sound of trilling, which drew nearer and nearer, until it
seemed to merge into a whirring noise that filled the
room and crowded at my ears. At first I could see nothing,
and lay in deadly fear of the unknown; but soon I though
I saw rims and sparks of spectral fire floating through
the pane. Then I heard some one say: "I am the Wind."
But the voice was so like that of an old friend whom one
sees again after many years that my terror departed, and
I asked simply why the Wind had come.

"I have come to you," he replied, "because you are
the first man I have discovered who is after my own
heart. You whom others call dreamy and capricious,
volatile and headstrong, you whom some accuse of
weakness, others of unscrupulous abuse of power, you I
know to be a true son of Æolus, a fit inhabitant for those
caves of boisterous song."

"Are you the North Wind or the East Wind?" said
I. "Or do you blow from the Atlantic? Yet if those be your

feathers that shine upon the pane like yellow and purple threads, and if it be through your influence that the garden is so hot to-day, I should say you were the lazy South Wind, blowing from the countries that I love."

"I blow from no quarter of the Earth," replied the voice. "I am not in the compass. I am a little unknown Wind, and I cross not Space but Time. If you will come with me I will take you not over countries but over centuries, not directly, but waywardly, and you may travel where you will. You shall see Napoleon, Caesar, Pericles, if you command. You may be anywhere in the world at any period. I will show you some of my friends, the poets...."

"And may I drink red wine with Praxiteles, or with Catullus beside his lake?"

"Certainly, if you know enough Latin and Greek, and can pronounce them intelligently."

"And may I live with Thais or Rhodope, or some wild Assyrian queen?"

"Unless they are otherwise employed, certainly."

"Ah, Wind of Time," I continued with a sigh, "we men of this age are rotten with book-lore, and with a yearning for the past. And wherever I asked to go among those ancient days, I should soon get dissatisfied, and weary your bright wings. I will be no pillar of salt, a sterile portent in a sterile desert. Carry me forward, Wind of Time. What is there going to be?"

The Wind put his hand over my eyes.

I

AT BIRMINGHAM TOWN HALL

"This is our first stopping place," said a voice from the points of flame.

I opened my eyes expecting to see one of those extravagent scenes that imaginative novelists love to depict. I was prepared to find the upper air busy with aeroplanes and the earth beneath given over to unbridled debauch. Instead, I discovered myself seated on a tall electric standard, watching a crowd assembled before what I took to be Birmingham Town Hall. I was disappointed in this so tame a sight, until it flashed across me that I had never seen an English crowd preserve such an orderly and quiet demeanour; and a more careful inspection assured me that although no man wore a uniform, every man carried a rifle. They were obviously waiting for some one to come and address them from the balcony of the Town Hall, which was festooned with red flags. As the curtains were pulled aside I caught a momentary glimpse of an old person whose face I shall never forget, but apparently it was not for him that the breathless crowd was waiting. The man who finally appeared on the balcony was an individual not more than thirty years old, with a black beard and green eyes. At the sound of acclamation which greeted him he burst out into a loud laugh; then with a sudden seriousness he held up his hand and began to address his followers:

"I have but few words for you, my army, a few bitter words. Need I encourage men to fight who have staked their existence to gain mastery? We cannot draw back; never will the cries of the slaughtered thousands we yearned to rescue from a more protracted, more cruel misery than war, make us forget the myriads who still await the supreme mercy of our revenge.

"For centuries and for centuries we endured the March of that Civilization which now, by the weapons of her own making, we have set forth to destroy. We, men of Birmingham, dwellers in this hideous town unvisited by sun or moon, long endured to be told that we were in the van of progress, leading Humanity year by year along her glorious path. And, looking around them, the wise men saw the progress of civilization, and what was it? What did it mean? Less country, fewer savages, deeper miseries, more millionaires, and more museums. So today we march on London.

"Let us commemorate, my friends, at this last hour, a great, if all unwitting benefactor, the protomartyr of our cause. You remember that lank follower of the Newest Art, who lectured to us once within these very walls? He it was who first expounded to us the beauty of Birmingham, the artistic majesty of tall chimneys, the sombre glory of furnaces, the deep mystery of smoke, the sad picturesqueness of scrap-heaps and of slag. Then we began to hate our lives in earnest; then we arose and struck. Even now I shudder when I think of that lecturer's fate, and with a feeling of respect I commemorate his words to-day.

"On, then! You need not doubt of my victory, nor of my power. Some of you will die, but you know that death is rest. You do not need to fear the sombre fireworks of a mediaeval Hell, nor yet the dreary dissipations of a Methodist Heaven. Come, friends, and march on London!"

They heard him in deep silence; there was a gentle stir of preparation; they faded far below me.

THE PROCLAMATION

At a point ten years farther along that dusky road the Wind set me down in a prodigious room. I had never before seen so large and splendid a construction, so gracefully embellished, so justly proportioned. The shape was elliptical, and it seemed as if the architect had drawn his inspiration from the Coliseum at Rome. This Hall, however, was much larger, and had the additional distinction of a roof, which, supported by a granite column, was only rendered visible from beneath by means of great bosses of clear gold. Galleries ran round the walls, and there was even a corkscrew balustrade winding up round the central pillar. Every part of the building was crowded with people. There seemed to be no window in the place, so that I could not tell whether or no it was night. The whole assembly was illuminated by a thousand electric discs, and the ventilation was almost perfectly planned on a system to me entirely strange. There was a raised throne at one end of the building, on which sat a King decently dressed in black. I recognised the green-eyed man, and learnt that his name was Harris, Joshua Harris. The entire body of the Hall was filled by soldiers in mud-coloured tunics and waterproof boots. These were the men that had conquered the world.

As soon as the populace were well assembled the King made a sign to his Herald, who blew so sudden and terrific a blast with his trumpet that the multitude stopped their chattering with a start. The Herald proceeded to bawl a proclamation through his megaphone. I heard him distinctly, but should never have been able to reproduce his exact words, had not the Wind very kindly handed to me one of the printed copies for free distribution which it had wafted from a chair. The proclamation ran thus:

"*I, Joshua Harris, by right of conquest and in virtue of my intelligence, King of Britain, Emperor of the two Americas, and Lord High Suzerain of the World, to the Princes, Presidents, and Peoples of the said World, - Greeting. Ye know that in days past an old man now dead showed me how man's dolorous and fruitless sojourn on this globe might cease by his own act and wisdom; how pain and death and the black Power that made us might be frustrated of their accustomed prey. Then I swore an oath to fulfil that old man's scheme, and I gathered my followers, who were the miserable men, and the hungry men, and we have conquered all there is to conquer by our cannon and by our skill. Already last year I gave public notice, in the proclamation of Vienna, in the proclamation of Cairo, in the proclamation of Pekin, and in the proclamation of Rio Janeiro, that all bearing of children must cease, and that all women should be permanently sterilized according to the prescription of Doctor Smith. Therefore to-day, since there is no remote African plain, no island far away in the deep South Seas where our forces are not supreme and our agents not vigilant, I make my final proclamation to you, my army, and to you, Princes, Presidents, and Peoples of this World, that from this hour forth there be no child born of any woman, or, if born, that it be slain with its father and its mother* (a fainting woman had here to be carried out), *and to you, my terrestrial forces, I entrust the execution of my commands.*

"*Joy then be with you, my people, for the granaries are full of corn and wine that I have laid up, sufficient for many years to come; joy be with you, since you are the last and noblest generation of mankind, and since Doctor*

Smith by his invention, and I by my wise pre-vision, have enabled you to live not only without payment and without work (loud cheers from the galleries), *but also with luxury and splendour, and with all the delights, and none of the dangers, of universal love."*

I expected this proclamation to be followed by an outburst of applause; but instead, the whole multitude sat calm and motionless. Looking round I was struck by the hideous appearance of mankind. It was especially revolting to look at the ears of the soldiers in front, who had their backs turned to me. These stuck out from the bullet-like heads, and made the men look like two-handled teapots on stands. Yet here and there appeared in the galleries some woman's countenance beautified by the sorrows of our race, or some tall youth whose eyes expressed the darkest determination. The silence seemed to gather in folds. I was studying drowsily the Asiatic dresses and the nude people from Melanesia, when I heard a noise which I thought was that of the Wind. But I saw it was the King, who had begun to laugh. It was a very strange noise indeed, and very strange laughter.

III

THE MUTUAL EXTERMINATION CLUB

"You would perhaps like to stay here some time," said the Wind, "and look around. You will then understand the significance of this generation more clearly, and you may observe some interesting incidents."

I was standing with one or two other people outside a pseudo-Chinese erection, which I at first took to be a cricket pavilion, and then saw to be the headquarters of a rifle club. I apprehended from the placards that I was in Germany, and inquired in the language of the country, which I understand very well, what was the object of this rifle practice, and whether there was any thought of war.

The man to whom I addressed myself, an adipose person with iron-rimmed spectacles and a kindly, intelligent face, seemed surprised at my question.

"You must be a stranger," he said. "This is our very notable *Vertildungsverein*."

I understood: it was a Club for Mutual Extermination.

I then noticed that there were no ordinary targets, and that the cadets were pointing their rifles at a bearded man who stood with a covered pipe in his mouth, leaning against a tree some two hundred yards away.

After the report the bearded man held up both hands.

"That is to signify that he has been completely missed," said the fat gentleman. "One hand, wounded; two hands, missed. And that is reasonable (*vernunftig*), because if he were dead he could not raise either."

I approved the admirable logic of the rule, and supposed that the man would now be allowed to go free.

"Oh, yes, according to the rules," he answered, "he certainly is allowed to go free; but I do not think his sense of honour would permit him to do so."

"Is he then of a very noble family?" I inquired.

"Not at all; he is a scientist. We have a great many scientists in our club. They are all so disappointed at the way in which human progress has been impeded, and at the impossibility of a continuous evolution of knowledge-accumulation, that they find no more attraction in life. And he is dead this time," he continued, shading his eyes to look, as soon as a second report had flashed.

"By the way," I asked, "I suppose you only

exterminate - er- members of the club?"

The fellow smiled with a little disdain. "Oh, it would be illegal for us to exterminate outsiders. But of course if you would like to join...."

"Why, that's never a woman going over to the tree!" I cried.

"Oh yes, we have quite a number of intellectual women and upper-class ladies of advanced ideas in the club. But I do not think that lady is an intellectual she is more probably a passion-wreck."

She was indeed a very handsome woman in the prime of life, dressed with a little too much ostentation and coquetry in a sleeveless, transparent white blouse and a skirt to match.

My informant turned round to a skinny young student with hog's-bristle hair, and made some vulgar jest about its "being a pity to waste such a good piece of flesh." He was a super-man, and imagined, falsely I believe, that an air of bluff cynicism, a Teutonic attempt at heartiness, was the true outward sign of inward superiority. The young man fired, and the women raised the arm that was not shattered by the bullet. He fired again, and she fell on her knees, this time with a scream.

"I think you had better have a shot," said the sharp-shooter to my man. "I'm rather bad at this."

Indeed his hand was shaking violently.

My interlocutor bowed, and went over to take the rifle. The skinny student took his place by my side, and began talking to me as well. "He's an infallible shot that Muller there," he said, nodding at my former companion...." Didn't I tell you?"

To my great relief the passion-wrecked lady fell dead. I was getting wildly excited, rent between horror and curiosity.

"You see that man in the plumed hat?" said the

student. "He is coming round to say on whom the lot has fallen. Ah, he is coming this way, and making a sign at me. Good-day, sir," he said, taking off his hat with a deep and jerky bow. "I am afraid we must continue our conversation another time."

IV

THE EPISODE OF THE BABY

As soon as I turned away, rather horrified, from the merry proceedings of the Mutual Extermination Club, I seemed to be in England, or perhaps in America. At all events I was walking along a dusty highway in the midst of an inquisitive crowd. In front of me half-a-dozen members of the International Police Force (their tunics and boots gave me to understand their quality) were dragging along a woman who held a baby in her arms. A horror-struck and interested multitude surged behind, and rested only when the woman was taken into a large and disgusting edifice with iron gates. Aided by my distinguished appearance and carriage, I succeeded after some difficulty in persuading the Chief Gaoler to let me visit the cell where the mother was lodged, previous to undergoing an execution which would doubtless be as unpleasant as prolonged. I found a robust, apple-cheeked woman, very clean and neat, despite her forlorn condition and the rough handling the guards had used to her. She confessed to me with tears that she had been in her day a provincial courtesan, and that she had been overcome by desire to have a child, "just to see what it was like." She had therefore employed all imaginable shifts to avoid being injected with Smithia, and had fled with an old admirer to a lonely cave, where she had brought forth her child. "And a pretty boy too," she added, wringing her hands, "and only fourteen months old."

She was so heart-broken that I did not like to ask her any more questions till she had recovered, for fear her answers should be unintelligible. Finally, as I desired to learn matters that were of common knowledge to the rest of the world, and was not anxious to arouse suspicion, I represented myself as a cultured foreigner who had just been released from a *manicomio*, and was therefore naturally in a state of profound ignorance on all that appertained to Modern History. I felt indeed that I would never have a better chance of gathering information than from conversation with this solitary woman. It would be her pleasure, not her duty, to instruct me.

So I began by asking how the diminishing numbers of the military could keep a sufficient watch, and how it was that every one submitted so meekly to the proclamation. She answered that the police recruited themselves yearly from the more active and noble-minded of the people, that custom had a lot to do with the submissive attitude of mankind, and that apart from that, there was a great resolve abroad to carry out the project of King Harris to fulfilment. She went on to inform me that Smithia was tasteless, and would act even when drunk at meals, and not merely as an injection, that it acted on both sexes, and that it was otherwise innocuous. By now most of the well-springs, reservoirs, and cisterns had been contaminated by the fluid, of which large quantities had been prepared at a very cheap price. After gleaning sundry other details, I thanked her heartily and left the cell.

Outside in the courtyard I discovered a large concourse of people examining the baby, who was naturally enough an object of extreme wonder to the

271

whole country-side. The women called it a duck, and used other pet names that were not then in fashion, but most of the men thought it was an ugly little brat at best. The child was seated on a cushion, and despite his mother's absence was crowing vigorously and kicking with puny force. There was some debate as to how it should be killed. Some were for boiling and eating it; others were for hitting it on the head with a club. However, the official who held the cushion brought the conference to a close by inadvertently dropping the child on to the flags, and thereby breaking its neck.

V

THE FLORENTINE LEAGUE

I feel certain on reflection that the scene of the last episode must have been America, for I remember returning to Europe on a French boat which landed me at Havre, and immediately taking the train to Paris. As I passed through Normandy, I saw hardly a soul stirring in the villages, and the small houses were all in a most dilapidated condition. There was no more need for farms, and villagers in their loneliness were flocking to the towns. Even the outer suburbs of Paris were mere masses of flaked and decaying plaster. An unpleasant crash into the buffers of Saint Lazare reminded me that the engine was being driven by an amateur; indeed, we had met the Dieppe train at Rouen, sent a pilot engine ahead to clear the way, and then raced it to Paris on the upline amid enthusiastic cheers. We won, but were badly shaken.

We left the train beside the platform, trusting to the Church Missionary Society man to put it away in the engine-shed. These excellent philanthropists were unwearying in their efforts to prevent needless loss of life, and such work as was still done in the world was performed almost entirely by them and by members of kindred British Protestant societies. They wore a blue badge to distinguish themselves, and were ordered about by every one. At the call of "Anglais, Anglais!" some side-whiskered man would immediately run up to obey the summons, and you could send him to get food from the Store for you, and he would be only too pleased. They would also cook hot dinners.

I walked through the Boulevard Montmartre, and at every step I took I became more profoundly miserable. One had called Paris the pleasant city, the fairest city in the world, in the days before the Proclamation; for one found it vibrating with beauty and life. And now assuredly it was supremely a city of pleasure, for there was no work to be done at all. So no artist ever took any trouble now, since there was neither payment nor fame attainable; and wonderful caricatures of philanthropists scribbled on the pavement or elsewhere, or clever ribald songs shrieking out of gramophones were the only reminder of that past and beautiful Paris that I had known. There was a fatuous and brutal expression on most of the faces, and the people seemed to be too lazy to do anything except drink and fondle. Even the lunatics attracted but little attention. There was a flying-machine man who was determined, as he expressed it, "that it should not be said of the human race that it never flew." Even the "Anglais" were tired of helping him with his machine, which he was quietly building on the Place de l'Opéra - a mass of intricate wires, bamboos, and paper boxes; and the inventor himself frequently got lost as he climbed cheerily among the rigging.

Weary of all this, I slept, alone, in one of the public beds, and early next morning I clambered up the sacred slope of the Butte to see the sunrise. The great silence of early morning was over the town, a deathly and unnatural stillness. As I stood leaning over the parapet, thinking miserably, a young man came up the hill slowly yet gracefully, so that it was a pleasure to look at him. His face was sad and noble, and as I had never thought to see nobility again, I hoped he would be a friend to me. However, he turned himself almost roughly, and said:

"Why have you come here?"

"To look at the fallen city I loved long ago," I replied, with careless sorrow.

"Have you then also read of the old times in books?" he said, looking round at me with large bright eyes.

"Yes, I have read many books," said I, trying to evade the subject. "But will you forgive me if I ask an impertinent question?"

"Nothing coming from you, sir, could be impertinent."

"I wanted to ask how old you are, because you seem so young. You seem to be only seventeen."

"You could tell me nothing more delightful," the young man replied, with a gentle, yet strong and deep intonation. "I am indeed one of the youngest men alive - I am twenty-two years old. And I am looking for the last time on the city of Paris."

"Do not say that," I cried. "All this may be horrible, but it cannot be as dull as Death. Surely there must be some place in the world where we could live among beauty; some other folk besides ourselves who are still poets. Why should one die until life becomes hopelessly ugly and deformed?"

"I am not going to kill myself, as you seem to think," said the young man. "I am going, and I pray and implore you to come with me, to a place after your heart and mine, that some friends have prepared. It is a garden, and we are a League. I have already been there three months, and I have put on these horrible clothes for one day only, in obedience to a rule of our League, that every one should go out once a year to look at the world around. We are thinking of abolishing this rule."

"How pleasant and beautiful it sounds!"

"It is, and will you come with me there right now?"

"Shall I be admitted?"

"My word will admit you at once. Come this way with me. I have a motor at the bottom of the hill."

During the journey I gathered much information about the League, which was called the Florentine League. It had been formed out of the youngest "years" of the race, and its members had been chosen for their taste and elegance. For although few parents of the day had thought it worth while to teach their children anything more recondite than their letters and tables, yet some of the boys and girls had developed a great desire for knowledge, and an exceeding great delight in Poetry, Art, Music, and all beautiful sights and sounds.

"We live," he said, "apart from the world, like that merry company of gentlefolk who, when the plague was raging at Florence, left the city, and retiring to a villa in the hills, told each other those enchanting tales. We enjoy all that Life, Nature, and Art can give us, and love has not deserted the garden, but still draws his golden bow. It is no crippled and faded Eros of the City that dwells among us, but the golden-thighed God himself. For we do all things with refinement, and not like those outside, seeing to it that in all our acts we keep our souls and bodies both delicate and pure."

We came to the door of a long wall, and knocked. White-robed attendants appeared in answer to our summons, and I was stripped, bathed, and anointed by their deft hands. All the while a sound of singing and subdued laughter made me eager to be in the garden. I was then clothed in a very simple white silk garment with a gold clasp; the open door let sunshine in upon the tiles, and my friend, also clothed in silk, awaited me. We walked out into the garden, which was especially noticeable for those flowers which have always been called old-fashioned - I mean hollyhocks, sweet william, snap-dragons, and Canterbury bells, which were laid out in regular beds. Everywhere young men and women were together: some were walking about idly in the shade; some played at fives; some were reading to each other in the arbours. I was shown a Grecian temple in which was a library, and dwelling-places near it. I afterwards asked a girl called Fiore di Fiamma what books the Florentines preferred to read, and she told me that they loved the Poets best, not so much the serious and strenuous as those whose vague and fleeting fancies wrap the soul in an enchanting sorrow.

I asked: "Do you write songs, Fiore di Fiamma?"

"Yes, I have written a few, and music for them."

"Do sing me one, and I will play the guitar."

So she sang me one of the most mournful songs I had ever heard, a song which had given up all hope of fame, written for the moment's laughter or for the moment's tears.

"Wind," I said that night, "stay with me many years in the garden."

But it was not the Wind I kissed.

VI

OUTSIDE

I passed many years in that sad, enchanted place, dreaming at times of my mother's roses, and of friends that I had known before, and watching our company grow older and fewer. There was a rule that no one should stay there after their thirty-seventh birthday, and some old comrades passed weeping from us to join the World Outside. But most of them chose to take poison and to die quietly in the Garden; we used to burn their bodies, singing, and set out their urns on the grass. In time I became the Prince of the Garden: no one knew my age, and I grew no older; yet my Flame-Flower knew when I intended to die. Thus we lived on undisturbed, save for some horrible shout that rose from time to time from beyond the walls; but we were not afraid, as we had cannon mounted at our gates. At last there were twelve of us left in the precinct of delight, and we decided to die all together on the eve of the Queen's birthday. So we made a great feast and held good cheer, and had the poison prepared and cast lots. The first lot fell to Fiore di Fiamma, and the last lot to me; whereat all applauded. I watched my Queen, who had never seemed to me as noble as then, in her mature and majestic beauty. She kissed me, and drank, and the others drank, became very pale, and fell to earth. Then I, rising with a last paean of exultation, raised the cup to my lips.

But that moment the trees and flowers bent beneath a furious storm, and the cup was wrenched out of my hand by a terrific blast and sent hurtling to the ground. I saw the rainbow-coloured feathers flashing and for a second I saw the face of the Wind himself. I trembled, and, sinking into my chair, buried my face in my hands. A wave of despair and loneliness broke over me. I felt like a drowning man.

"Take me back, Lord of the Wind!" I cried. "What am I doing among these dead aesthetes? Take me back to the country where I was born, to the house where I am at home, to the things I used to handle, to the friends with whom I talked, before man went mad. I am sick of this generation that cannot strive or fight, these people of one idea, this doleful, ageing world. Take me away!"

But the Wind replied in angry tones, not gently as of old:

"Is it thus you treat me, you whom I singled out from men? You have forgotten me for fifteen years; you have wandered up and down a garden, oblivious of all things that I had taught you, incurious, idle, listless, effeminate. Now I have saved you from dying a mock death, like a jester in a tragedy; and in time I will take you back, for that I promised; but first you shall be punished as you deserve." So saying, the Wind raised me aloft and set me beyond the wall.

I dare not describe - I fear to remember the unutterable loathing of the three years I spent outside. The unhappy remnant of a middle-aged mankind was gradually exchanging lust for gluttony. Crowds squatted by day and by night round the Houses of Dainty Foods that had been stocked by Harris the King; there was no youthful face to be found among them, and scarcely one that was not repulsively deformed with the signs of lust, cunning, and debauch. At evening there were incessant fires of crumbling buildings, and fat women made horrible attempts at revelry. There seemed to be no power of thought in these creatures. The civilization of ages had fallen from them like a worthless rag from off their backs. Europeans were as bestial as Hottentots, and the noblest thing they ever did was to fight; for sometimes a fierce desire of battle seized them, and then they tore each other passionately with teeth and nails.

I cannot understand it even now. Surely there should have been some Puritans somewhere, or some Philosophers waiting to die with dignity and honour. Was it that there was no work to do? Or that there were no children to love? Or that there was nothing young in the World? Or that all beautiful souls perished in the garden?

I think it must have been the terrible thought of approaching extinction that obsessed these distracted men. And perhaps they were not totally depraved. There was a rough fellowship among them, a desire to herd together; and for all that they fought so much, they fought in groups. They never troubled to look after the sick and wounded, but what could they do?

One day I began to feel that I too was one of them - I, who had held aloof in secret ways so long, joined the gruesome company in their nightly dance, and sat down to eat and drink their interminable meal. Suddenly a huge, wild, naked man appeared in front of the firelight, a prophet, as it appeared, who prophesied not death but life. He flung out his lean arms and shouted at us: "In vain have you schemed and lingered and died, O Last Generation of the Damned. For the cities shall be built again, and the mills shall grind anew, and the church bells shall ring, and the Earth be re-peopled with new miseries in God's own time."

I could not bear to hear this fellow speak. Here was one of the old sort of men, the men that talked evil, and murmured about God. "Friends," I said, turning to the Feasters, "we will have no skeletons like that at our feast." So saying I seized a piece of flaming wood from the fire, and rushed at the man. He struggled fiercely, but he had no weapon, and I beat him about the head till he fell, and death rattled in his throat - rattled with what seemed to me a most familiar sound. I stood aghast; then wiped the blood from the man's eyes and looked into them.

"Who are you?" I exclaimed. "I have seen you before; I seem to know the sound of your voice and the colour of your eyes. Can you speak a word and tell us your story, most unhappy prophet, before you die?"

"Men of the Last Generation," said the dying man, raising himself on his elbow - "Men of the Last Generation, I am Joshua Harris, your King."

As brainless frogs who have no thought or sense in them, yet shrink when they are touched, and swim when the accustomed water laves their eager limbs, so did these poor creatures feel a nerve stirring within them, and unconsciously obey the voice which had commanded them of old. As though the mere sound of his tremulous words conveyed an irresistible mandate, the whole group came shuffling nearer. All the while they preserved a silence that made me afraid, so reminiscent was it of that deadly hush that had followed the Proclamation, of the quiet army starting for London, and especially of that mysterious and sultry morning so many years ago when the roses hung their enamelled heads and leaves were as still as leaves of tin or copper. They sat down in circles round the fire, maintaining an orderly disposition, like a stray battalion of some defeated army which is weary of fruitless journeys in foreign lands, but still remembers discipline and answers to command. Meanwhile, the dying man was gathering with a noiseless yet visible effort every shred of strength from his massive limbs, and preparing to give them his last message. As he looked round on that frightful crowd great tears, that his own pain and impending doom could never have drawn from him, filled his strange eyes.

"Forgive me - forgive me," he said at last, clearly enough for all to hear. "If any of you still know what mercy is, or the meaning of forgiveness, say a kind word to me. Loving you, relying on humanity and myself, despising the march of Time and the power of Heaven, I became a false redeemer, and took upon my back the burden of all sin. But how was I to know, my people, I who am only a man, whither my plans for your redemption would lead? Have none of you a word to say?

"Is there no one here who remembers our fighting days? Where are the great lieutenants who stood at my side and cheered me with counsel? Where are Robertson, Baldwin, and Andrew Spencer? Are there none of the old set left?"

He brushed the tears and blood from his eyes and gazed into the crowd. Pointing joyously to an old man who sat not far away he called out: "I know you, Andrew, from that great scar on your forehead. Come here, Andrew, and that quickly."

The old man seemed neither to hear nor understand him, but sat like all the rest, blinking and unresponsive.

"Andrew," he cried, "you must know me! Think of Brum and South Melton Street. Be an Englishman, Andrew - come and shake hands!"

The man looked at him with staring, timid eyes; then shuddered all over, scrambled up from the ground, and ran away.

"It does not matter," murmured the King of the World. "There are no men left. I have lived in the desert, and I saw there that which I would I had seen long ago - visions that came too late to warn me. For a time my Plan has conquered; but that greater Plan shall be victorious in the end."

I was trying to staunch the wounds I had inflicted,

281

Titles in the Decadence from Dedalus Series include:

Senso (and other stories) - Camillo Boito £6.99
The Child of Pleasure - Gabriele D'Annunzio £7.99
The Triumph of Death - Gabriele D'Annunzio £7.99
The Victim (L'Innocente) - Gabriele D'Annunzio £7.99
Angels of Perversity - Remy de Gourmont £6.99
La-Bas - J.K.Huysmans £7.99
The Green Face - Gustav Meyrink £7.99
The Diary of a Chambermaid - Octave Mirbeau £7.99
Torture Garden - Octave Mirbeau £7.99
Monsieur Venus - Rachilde £6.99
The Dedalus Book of Decadence (Moral Ruins) -
editor Brian Stableford £7.99
**The Second Dedalus Book of Decadence: the
Black Feast** - editor Brian Stableford £8.99

Forthcoming titles include:

Les Diaboliques (new edition) - Barbey D'Aurevilly £6.99
Monsieur de Phocas - Jean Lorrain £8.99
Le Calvaire - Octave Mirbeau £7.99
La Marquise de Sade - Rachilde £8.99
The Dedalus Book of Russian Decadence - editor
Natalia Rubenstein £8.99

All these titles can be obtained directly from your local
bookshop or newsagent, or directly from Dedalus by
writing to: **Cash Sales, Dedalus Ltd, Langford
Lodge, St. Judith's Lane, Sawtry, PE17 5XE.**
Please enclose a cheque to the value of the books
ordered, 75p pp for the first book, 50p for the second
and subsequent books up to a maximum £3.25.